OF WOMAN BORN

A BOND OF FATE TRILOGY

Part Three
Of Woman Born

GILDA O'NEILL

WILLIAM HEINEMANN : LONDON

Published by William Heinemann in 2005

1 3 5 7 9 10 8 6 4 2

First published in the United Kingdom in 2005 by William Heinemann

The Random House Group Limited
20 Vauxhall Bridge Road, London, SW1V 2SA

Random House Australia (Pty) Limited
20 Alfred Street, Milsons Point, Sydney,
New South Wales 2061, Australia

Random House New Zealand Limited
18 Poland Road, Glenfield,
Auckland 10, New Zealand

Random House South Africa (Pty) Limited
Endulini, 5a Jubilee Road, Parktown 2193, South Africa

The Random House UK Group Limited Reg. No. 954009

www.randomhouse.co.uk

A CIP catalogue record for this book
is available from the British Library

Papers used by Random House
are natural, recyclable products made from wood grown in
sustainable forests. The manufacturing processes conform to
the environmental regulations of the country of origin

ISBN 0 434 00828 1

Typeset by SX Composing DTP
Printed and bound in Great Britain by
Mackays of Chatham plc, Chatham, Kent

For Susan Sandon

Prologue

The young doctor yawned wearily. He didn't know how much longer he could take the punishment of these ridiculous hours – or the continual lies of his bosses that they would reduce them. He didn't even know how much longer he could pretend to his family that their many sacrifices to pay for his years of education, their scrimping and scraping to get him through medical school, had not all been a waste of time and money.

But how could he tell them that he wanted nothing more than to do a job – any job – that meant he could work sensible hours, like any normal person, and spend some time with Christo, the man he loved? Rather than being so exhausted that he was either downing another handful of pills to see him through another night of duty and exhaustion, or was at home having yet more rows with Christo, because he was never there when he needed him, or, if he was, all he was fit for was sleep.

And then this had happened, and he'd known he had no choice – he had had to do something. He could have called for help, of course, but everyone in the hospital was as stretched and knackered as he was. So what was the point in getting some other poor sod involved?

He'd only stuck his head out of the front doors for a few minutes, wanting to stand on the steps with a cigarette, taking a little bit of time for himself in the fresh air – if the air in this part of east London could ever be described as fresh – to get a break, however short, away from the stench of sickness and the aggression of the drunks and junkies in A & E.

As he'd taken the first long drag, feeling the hit of the nicotine, he'd seen the accident happen, right there in front of him. He knew he shouldn't have gone anywhere near her – insurance companies didn't exactly approve of the medical profession giving help to people other than within the strictly controlled and regulated premises of the hospital with the full back-up of the administration machine; and as for moving an RTA casualty, in any other circumstances, he might as well have declared himself bankrupted by the lawsuits there and then.

But there would be no one suing him on this girl's behalf. He'd seen too many like her to be worried about that.

With her flat chest, and skinny hips, she had looked more like a boy, lying there in the road, but there was no doubt about it – she was a girl. Her dress, which was now no more than a few shreds of ripped cloth, exposed a tiny, cheap nylon G-string and the unmistakably female outline of the mons pubis below the grubby, yellowing lace.

What age was she – seventeen, maybe eighteen years old?

If that.

As he'd knelt beside her on the greasy tarmac that was almost melting in the heat, he'd been aware of a ragged crowd gathering around him, the human detritus of night-time Whitechapel, curious as to the nature of this unexpected entertainment.

Back and forth they'd stared – first at the young man in the white coat who was tending the victim, and then at the bus driver.

The driver had squatted on the edge of the kerb, his hands dangling between his legs, his head down, sobbing for everyone to believe him that he hadn't seen her. That she had just run out in front of him.

The young doctor had taken the girl's hand in his.

Still warm, but no pulse.

But what had been the point in trying to revive her – with the tyre tracks across her legs and the tracks of another kind on the insides of her arms, and the blood matted in her peroxide-blonde hair from where her head had smashed up and down on the road like a bouncing ball?

She might have been another runaway – escaping from some hideous abuse in a home that didn't deserve the name – but more likely, from the look of her, she was one of the increasing numbers of Eastern

European girls – and occasionally boys – being brought over to work in the sex trade.

He'd seen more than his fill of those lately.

But wherever she'd come from, she'd wound up here, dead in the street, probably running away from some angry kerb-crawling punter who reckoned he'd not got his full ten or twenty quid's worth – or however much the girls charged.

And whatever she'd done, and whatever her reasons for doing it, it must have been unbelievably bad for her to have thrown herself under a bus.

Surely every kid, whoever she was, deserved better than that.

Chapter 1

She shook her thick dark hair back over her shoulders, swiped her tongue across her teeth to remove any stray smudges left by her cheap, slimy lipstick, and smoothed the red miniskirt down over her bare thighs. She'd made the skirt herself from the satin she'd unpicked from the back of a patchwork quilt – one of the few things she had left – and even though it was a little frayed, and the big, clumsy stitches she'd used were only just about holding it together, she was still very proud of it.

But, proud or not, it didn't offer much protection against the bitter chill of the late-January wind as it blew in from across the harbour, and despite her fake-fur jacket, her flesh was mottled with cold and she was shivering.

Could she really carry this off? Take this step into the unknown as if she knew what she was doing? Convince them?

She had to. What other choice did she have?

She set her chin, found a smile, and walked into the club – a picture of youthful beauty and confidence.

*

She could see, by the feeble illumination leaking from the scattering of ill-matched lamps dotted about the place, that the new money everyone was so excited about obviously hadn't reached here yet.

Perhaps they were planning to do it up, as they'd done with the bars at the other end of town, the places where the oilmen went. Of course they were; that's why they'd pinned up the advertisements every-where.

A fleshy-faced, middle-aged man, swamped by his heavy fur-collared, astrakhan overcoat, was leaning on the bar. He looked her up and down, and then beckoned her over to him with a tilt of his head.

'Hello, my name is Nahida,' she said, careful not to stumble over the English words she had practised again and again, praying she had remembered the proper way to pronounce them from the lessons she had had at school – in the days before the school had closed down when most of the children had fled with their parents. 'I am here for advertisement.'

She snapped open her shiny, plastic handbag and took out the crumpled paper that she had taken down from the noticeboard in the shop in the hope that no other girls had seen it – that she would be the only one here.

As she held it out to him her fingers were trembling.

'I am dancer. Good dancer.'

She kept her gaze fixed on his, praying her

boldness would stop him from seeing through her lie – and that he wouldn't be angry with her for taking the notice down.

The man flapped the paper away – an unwanted involvement – and took hold of her face. He turned her head this way and that, and then ran his fingers down the sides of her throat, tightening his grip just enough to make her widen her eyes. Then he let her go and pushed her away from him. For a terrifying moment, she thought she was being dismissed, was being denied the chance that had to be better than existing on the last of the salted fish and the vegetables that her grandfather had harvested before he'd died in the autumn. But then she relaxed as she realised the man only wanted to get a better look at her.

She stood, without comment from either of them, as his eyes slowly appraised every part of her body. Then, breaking the spell, he jerked his thumb towards the stairway in the back corner of the dingy bar room.

Nahida gabbled her thanks to the man in a mixture of the Azeri of her childhood – which he didn't understand – and Russian – which he chose to ignore.

Barely able to suppress the urge to whoop with joy, she climbed the stairs, knowing that her future awaited her behind the closed door she could see on the landing above her.

*

As she stepped through the doorway, she had to shade her eyes from the glare of the bright fluorescent lights strung wonkily across the low-ceilinged attic room. It took her a moment to focus, and even less than that for the disappointment to flood over her.

How could she have been so stupid as to think that no one else would have seen the advertisement?

She was looking at what she guessed to be about forty, very excited, but self-assured, young women. They were all luridly made up and provocatively dressed; some of them were perhaps as old as twenty, but most of them, she thought, were much nearer her own age, and, like her, had used lipstick and eyeliner to try to camouflage their youth.

Before she could find the courage to decide whether to flee or to speak to one of the girls – *and oh she had so much she wanted to ask about this amazing opportunity that looked as if it was going to be snatched away from her before she'd even been given the chance to prove she could do it* – Nahida was distracted by a much older, dowdily clothed woman who had appeared from behind a heavily soiled curtain on the other side of the room.

The woman hooked back the faded brocade drape, allowing Nahida a glimpse of the tiny galley kitchen in which the woman had been standing. The floor, shelves and wooden draining board were crammed with boxes, bottles and greasy cooking pots all piled high in tottering heaps.

The woman did a quick headcount, and then, from among the debris, she picked up a tray of drinks and, without a word, thrust it at the girl nearest her, silently indicating with a stir of her nicotine-stained finger that she should pass it round. She then stepped forward into the main room and clapped her hands until she had everyone's attention.

'Right, you are all here now. And you will celebrate your success at interview.'

She spoke in heavily accented Azeri, her thin lips revealing starkly white false teeth, with luridly pink gums.

'You will drink to this. And I will bring more.'

The woman shuffled back towards the kitchen, her slippers, with their downtrodden backs, threatening to trip her over.

She paused on the curtained threshold and, without turning to face them, she spoke again. It was a voice that demanded obedience.

'Remember: smile, you must always smile.'

It sounded like an order, but it was one that found a ready reply in Nahida. She didn't think she would ever stop smiling again.

Chapter 2

Lisa O'Donnell slipped her arms into the pure white, cashmere coat that Richard Middleton was holding up for her.

'Lovely to see you as always, Richard, and while it was good to look at all those bits of paper, you know I'm going to ask the bottom-line question before I go.'

'I wouldn't expect anything less of you, Lisa.'

She smiled archly. 'Glad to hear it. So, I'm still doing okay, am I?'

'As usual, I'd say rather more than okay. In fact, if I had a few more portfolios like yours to handle, I would not only have a very easy job, but I would be on my way to becoming a very rich and very happy man. And my wife could indulge herself in shoe shopping at an even more eye-boggling level.'

Lisa drew her fair, shiny hair over her shoulder.

'You're hardly on the breadline,' she said, looking around the vast, very traditional City office.

She turned back to face him, steadily meeting his gaze. 'You make enough, don't you?'

'I'm not sure if that's possible,' he said, ducking round her and grasping the handle of the panelled oak door that led through to the reception area.

He stood there, without opening the door, staring down at the carpet. 'Are any of us ever truly content with what we have?'

'Do you know, Richard, I think you may have a point there.'

He nodded absently. 'A little more security never comes amiss.'

'I didn't mean that,' she said, easing on black leather gloves that were scarcely thicker than another layer of skin. 'In my case, it's not more money I want, it's – I don't know – fulfilment maybe. No, more than that, I want some excitement.'

'Really? I thought you were off men.'

'Don't be so cheeky, Richard,' she said, tapping him on the arm in a way that could have been playful, but could also have been a warning for him not to take a single step further in that direction.

'I'm not being *cheeky*, as you put it. I'm being serious. I know you've had your fingers burned, but there are plenty of decent men out there, Lisa, and if you settled down with the right person, I'm sure that –'

'Enough, Richard. My God, you sound like my mother.'

'You know we both only want what's best for you.'

'I'm a big girl now.'

Her tone warned him to stay quiet; Lisa O'Donnell

had more than enough of her father in her to make it clear that she would brook no argument.

'I've been thinking about it for a while now. And I've decided I need to do something. In a word, I'm bored.'

Richard tensed up. 'May I ask what sort of thing?'

'I don't know. Something to make it worthwhile getting up in the morning. Something a bit more challenging than going to the gym. Maybe set up something like Mum did.'

'Lisa, you won't do anything rash, without speaking to me first, will you?'

She put her hand over his and opened the door.

'Richard, don't start lecturing me, okay? Coming from a family like mine, I do know how to take care of myself.'

With that, she put her hands on his shoulders, leaned forward and kissed him on the cheek.

'Now stop fussing.'

Before Richard could say anything, someone piped up from behind them in a perky Essex-man twang: 'Hello, Richard. Who's this then? She a friend of Mrs Middleton's?'

Lisa turned round and Richard craned his neck over her shoulder to see a man sitting in the reception area on one of the studded-leather, wing-backed chairs. He was holding a copy of a country sports magazine, grinning suggestively at them over the open pages.

12

Lisa wasn't impressed; she had seen plenty of his sort – confident, good-looking and bloody full of themselves. It wasn't hard not to resist the urge to smile politely.

'I prefer it when people speak to me directly,' she said, standing there, watching as he openly checked out her clothes, judging her – taking in her tall, fit body, and approving.

'Fine by me. How about if I take you for a drink later on and I promise I'll speak to you *directly* all night? Then again, maybe you should take me for a drink seeing as you can afford to dress like that. No, I know what, I'll take you slumming in the East End. Show you some proper boozers.'

Without shifting her gaze from the stranger, Lisa said to Richard: 'Aren't you going to introduce us?'

'Of course.' Richard stepped forward. 'Lisa, may I introduce Jason Carter?'

She couldn't be certain, but as he spoke, Lisa was sure she noticed a certain stiffness in Richard's manner. If there was, it was typical, and she was getting a bit fed up with it – having to prove that she was a grown woman who was more than capable of handling her own destiny.

'Hello, Mr Carter. I'm Lisa, Lisa Taylor.'

She saw Richard relax a little as she used the alternative surname he had set up for her all those years ago.

'Glad to meet you, Lisa. Well, you gonna meet me

for that drink later then? We can make a night of it.'
That grin again. 'Could even really treat you, and
finish off with a bowl of jellied eels from a nice little
seafood stall I know in Aldgate.'

Richard jumped in. 'Jason I really don't think that
Ms Taylor would want –'

Lisa didn't appreciate Richard speaking on her
behalf.

'Okay,' she interrupted him, 'I'll have a drink with
you, Jason, but I don't have the time this evening to
go slumming, as you so charmingly put it.'

She also didn't like being told where she was
going. And much as she'd probably have enjoyed a
trip to the East End with this flash sod, she wasn't
going to let him start dictating where and when she
went.

'Do you know the Tent Bar?'

'Sure.'

'Good. I'll be there in an hour.'

She turned to Richard. 'See you soon.'

He didn't return her smile.

Jason watched appreciatively as Lisa walked over
to the lifts.

'You've kept quiet about her, Richard.'

'I've no idea what you're talking about.'

'No? Then why the protective bit?'

'She's a client.'

'So what's the problem with me taking her for a
drink then?'

14

'I'd rather you didn't, that's all.'

'You dirty old devil, Richard.' Jason chuckled. 'You bloody fancy her, don't you? Now what would Mrs Middleton have to say?'

'I'm not joking; I want you to stay well away from her. I won't have her mixed up with the likes of you.'

Jason's face suddenly clouded. *'You won't have her mixed up with the likes of me?* Don't be stupid, Richard, cos let's face it, mate, you're in no position to tell me what to do, now are you?'

Chapter 3

David Kessler scooped up a handful of sugar-white sand and let it trickle slowly through his fingers. He was stretched out on a soft, padded sunlounger, with his ankles crossed and his eyes closed behind his sunglasses against the intensity of the Jamaican sun. Outwardly relaxed, he was, in fact, concentrating intently on the conversation he was having with the concerned-looking man squatting beside him.

Apart from the two uniformed guards dozing in the shade of a patch of palm trees beside the perimeter fence, they were the only people at that end of the resort – most of the other guests preferring to be further along the bay by the water sports stations and the open-all-hours beach bars.

'You do know how put out we were over what happened last time, don't you, Vito? How very put out.'

David Kessler spoke just loudly enough for the other man to hear him, knowing his flat, Estuary accent sounded anonymously classless – almost impossible to place – to the Italian in the hammock beside him. But the menace in his tone was more than clear for anyone to understand. David Kessler was not a happy man.

'I assure you, it won't happen again.'

'Too fucking right it won't. And that's the main reason we agreed to come all this way to meet you, you snivelling little git. We don't want you sorting out any more of the import deals for us. Me and Paul are gonna be making other arrangements from now on. So once you've introduced us to your contacts here and in Miami, that's it – you're finished.'

'David, please. You don't understand. There are new people involved, from Eastern Europe, and these are not people you can just go to. You have to build a relationship with them. They have only agreed to do this deal through me because they know me, because they trust me as a fixer – the man who fixes deals for them with many people. That's how they do business.'

David sat up suddenly and Vito flinched – Vito had already had a 'slap' from him when he'd gone to the airport to pick up him and his brother.

'Well, they're gonna be doing business another way from now on.'

'David, I can only offer my apologies and my assurances that I am so sorry for the misunderstanding about the last lot of girls. And that is why I insist that I pay for your stay here, and why I hope you will be pleased with this new proposal.'

David fumed inwardly. As if he'd let this Italian ponce pick up the bill. No one acted bigger than David Kessler. No one. But he couldn't help but be intrigued.

'What proposal?'

'This time you pick the girls yourself.'

'What? You got a photograph album in your britch or something? Or a video maybe? Like *find yourself a Thai fucking bride?* Do I look like a fucking mug? No thanks, Vito.'

David took off his sunglasses and glared at the foreigner, glad to see him squirm; he wasn't being stitched up again.

'For the sort of money we've paid you over the years, you should have hand-picked them tarts fucking personally, not have left it to some idiot who thinks he can pass us off with any old shit. And as for expecting me to fucking do it, you must be having a fucking laugh.'

'My selecting them would certainly have been one way, David. But sadly, if you want a smooth passage for the other part of our current deal – and, you have to believe me, it's the only way these people will let it go ahead – then I have to leave for Miami in the next few days. With the increased airport security over there, things are even trickier, and more expensive, than before.'

Vito held up a hand in surrender, realising what he'd just said. 'Of course there will be no additional cost to you. But, unfortunately, if I do this service – as I hope you will allow me – then it means it will not be possible for me to give you my personal attention in picking the girls.' He sighed, making it clear how unhappy he was about the situation. 'Believe me, if you want the Miami deal, David, I really do have to be there. But I think you will see that this doesn't matter. I can do better for you with the girls.'

Vito got to his feet and took an envelope from the back pocket of his immaculately pressed linen shorts.

'Here is an address, and flight details for you and your brother – you will have to fly via the American mainland, but I promise it will definitely be worth it. Because when you reach the place in that envelope, you will meet someone who will take you to a place where you can choose your own consignment. And it is a place where they have girls from areas that have hardly been touched yet – beautiful, grateful, fresh young girls. Not knowing, worldly girls who cause trouble or who look tired before they even begin. And, after you have chosen, all you need do is pay Misha – the man who is in charge there, who is another fixer who works for these people – one-quarter of the price and the other three-quarters to me. This is not a great deal of money for you, and I know you will not try to avoid this payment, because I have told Misha he can trust you. Also, if you do this, then Misha will understand what you are looking for, and will know your requirements for future purchases, which he will then be able to select himself – as your agent.'

Vito handed him the envelope. 'Please, think about it.'

David tapped the envelope on the palm of his hand. 'Get me a rum and Coke.'

Vito nodded politely and began walking off towards the busy end of the bay, his perfectly pedicured feet barely disturbing the warm, shallow water lapping the edge of the beach.

Then he stopped and called over his shoulder: 'Will I be joining you for a drink?'

David said nothing. He just sat there. He waited a full thirty seconds before ripping open the envelope and scanning the contents.

He looked up; Vito was still waiting for his reply.

'Yeah, you can join me for a drink. There's some things I wanna ask you.'

Chapter 4

An hour later, David was hammering his fist on the door of his brother's suite.

'Come on, Paul,' he shouted at the wood. 'Your jet lag can't be that bad. You've been asleep all bloody afternoon. I need to talk to you. Now.'

After a few moments, the door opened. Paul stood there. He was stark naked, clearly at ease with his well-toned body. At thirty-four years old, he was eleven months younger than his brother David, but being the same five eleven, and with the same cropped, light brown hair and dark brown eyes, they could have passed for twins – in looks at least.

'I've not exactly been asleep, Dave.'

Paul stepped back to let his brother see into the room. Draped diagonally across the huge bed was a smiling woman, her black skin beautiful against the tangle of white sheets.

'Just been enjoying the facilities they keep going on about.' He grinned broadly. 'I wasn't sure before we got here, you know. I thought it'd be better meeting up with the Italian in a villa or something – somewhere more secluded, where you could read him his fortune in private. But I think I've changed me

21

mind. These resorts are a bit of all right. The real business, in fact. Tell you what, Dave, why not join us?'

'Tempted as I am, Paul,' he said, without taking his eyes off the woman, who was now stretching languorously. 'But I'm sorry to say: we're leaving, mate.'

Paul groaned loudly. 'Aw come on, Dave. I know you're a bloody workaholic, but we only got here yesterday. Give us a break.'

David pointed to the louvred doors on the other side of the room. 'Let's go out on the terrace.'

'But, Dave –'

'Outside, Paul.'

He might have been his brother, the person closest to him in the whole world, but even Paul wouldn't make the mistake of angering David Kessler.

'He wants us to go *where*?' Paul asked, tying the belt of his cotton robe.

'It's somewhere in Bosnia.'

David took his cigarettes from the pocket of his shorts, and handed one to his brother.

'Fucking hell, Dave. You sure about this? Dad's gonna go spare. The whole point of us coming here was to give the Italian a good hiding and tell him to sling his hook, and for us go direct to the Miami lot.'

'Why should I give a fuck about what the old man thinks? He still thinks it's the *good old days*, feuding

22

with them Irish cunts, the O'Donnells, fighting over little bits of east London.'

'But, Dave . . .'

He sparked his lighter and lit his and Paul's cigarettes.

'Look, Paul, Vito's learnt his lesson, all right; had a little reminder that no one messes with the Kessler brothers. But I'm not gonna waste me time fannying around worrying about all that, there's too much to do. Any details – we'll discuss them later. I'll go and settle the hotel bill and send a fax through to the office to transfer some dough over here, cos I don't suppose this bloke we're gonna have the meet with will be the sort to take credit cards.'

Paul frowned at the address on the note Vito had given his brother. 'No, I don't suppose he is.'

'In the meantime I want you to phone the yard, and tell Bernie to get a truck ready and moving – today if possible.'

Paul sighed, resigned to knowing he had no choice; once David had made up his mind over something, you didn't argue with him – but if *he* decided to change his mind, you didn't argue with him then either.

'Okay to make the call from the room, Dave?'

'Sure. Just say we're going to need the motor to arrive by Friday. At the latest. Tell him he's going to Italy; one of the towns we've done kosher runs to before. We can give him the full SP tomorrow, when

23

he's on the road.' David scanned the beach in front of them, taking in the oiled bodies offering themselves up to the sun. 'When we're somewhere a long way away from this place. I was having a drink with Vito just now, and according to him, you wouldn't believe who some of these people are. Or why they're here.'

Paul didn't comment on the irony of his brother's remark, instead he took a long draw on his cigarette, exhaled and narrowed his eyes against the smoke.

'And why exactly do we have to go to see this bloke in this town I've never even heard of?' he said eventually. 'Why isn't Vito sorting it out for us after that last balls-up of his?'

This time it was David who was grinning.

'First of all, Vito's gonna be busy sorting out the other bit of our deal. It's a big run, and he knows I won't be happy if there's a screw-up, so he's going over to Miami to oil the wheels personally.'

'But I thought we –'

David spoke right over him. '*And* as for where we're going . . . Well, let's just say it's like that farm where Mum used to take us as kids. You know, where we used to go to get the strawberries.'

'Now you really have lost me, Dave. What the fuck have strawberries got to do with anything?'

'You remember, Paul: it was that place where you *picked your own*.'

'What?'

'We, Paul, are going shopping for birds, mate.'

Chapter 5

It wasn't only the rocking and lurching that was making Nahida feel ill, it was the vile stench that was clogging her nose, eyes and throat. She could pick out the smell of rust; and urine; of fuel oil; vomit and sweat. But, most of all, there was the stink of fear – worse than anything else.

She tried to work out how long she had been trapped in this terrible place. A day? Two? Maybe more. But the drugs they'd given her were still clouding and messing with her thoughts. She knew they must have drugged her, with the drinks the woman had given them in the room above the club – how else would they have got them inside this place?

And then there was the humidity; it had been bitterly cold at first, but now it was worse than it had been at her grandfather's home in the height of summer when the insects came in off the water. When they had buzzed and whirred all night and had bitten your flesh and you slapped your arms and legs until they were as red as freshly boiled beets. That was the price of being by the water.

Water.

She remembered now. They had given her a whole bottle, when they had shoved her in here. Where was it? She needed it.

Needed it now.

Panic gripped her as she groped around the small part of the space that had become hers, searching in the stifling darkness for the precious plastic bottle.

Now it was relief that engulfed her as she found it wedged by her head.

With shaking fingers she unscrewed the top and sucked at the tepid liquid, rationing herself to two meagre mouthfuls.

But the relief was momentary. She felt herself drowning in impotent despair at the realisation of just how quickly she had been reduced to this – a frantic creature desperate to meet nothing more than her basic animal needs.

She started, as the girl next to her cried out. The one who spoke no English at all, not even the few phrases the advertisement had said all applicants needed to speak to get the dancing jobs – the work they had been promised, the promise that had led them up to that room above the club.

Another wave of nausea rose inside her as they crashed over yet another swell.

Having lived all her young life in the lowlands, never having so much as travelled to the mountains before, Nahida had decided, in one of her more lucid moments, that it had to be water that was causing the sickening heaving; that they were in the bowels of a ship – maybe far out to sea somewhere.

For a short moment she wondered if they were being taken to another country. What would it be like? But the thought of the people who could treat them like this soon brought back the gut-wrenching fear of what was going to become of them, dispelling all traces of curiosity about their destination as surely as the first of the winter winds stripped the trees of the last of their leaves.

The ship bucked again and, as her head spun, she had drowsy, chaotic visions of herself as a little girl, remembering how her grandfather had taken her out fishing on his boat when they had visited his house on the shores of the Caspian. On rough days like this she had sat with him on the porch, perched on his lap with his arms holding her safe, and they had watched the faraway swell rise to the height of the rail on a mule cart.

She wanted to feel those arms around her again, but that was all long ago, long before the soldiers had come and had taken her grandfather away with all the other men, and the mines had been planted, and the war had destroyed everything. Destroyed everything more devastatingly than even the floods had done after they had built the dam and the villagers had had to flee from their homes.

Nahida missed her grandfather more than anything else about her old life, and not only because he was the last link she'd had with the happy memories of her childhood, but because, she was sure, he had saved her life when he had hidden her at the abandoned farm where she had last seen her mother.

The three of them had made a sort of camp at the farm, using whatever they could find – making sure that the things didn't belong to anyone, but had been left there or thrown away.

And it hadn't been so bad – better than some of the places they had stayed when the troubles had come and they had had to leave all their own things behind. But still her mother had left her. She had said that Nahida had to stay at the farm with her grandfather, while she went to find a new place for them all to live – a good place – and then, she promised, she would send for them to join her, and Nahida would have new shoes, and pretty dresses and ribbons for her hair. Just like she'd had before the bad days had come.

Every night Nahida had lain awake, listening for the sound of her mother calling her name, shouting to Nahida, her voice full of joy, that she'd come back for her and that everything was going to be all right. But she never heard her voice again.

It had been three long months since her mother had left them at the broken-down farmhouse, when Nahida's grandfather told her he had to talk to her. He sat her down on the big tree stump he used as a block when he chopped the wood, and told her that she

28

mustn't be frightened, but the soldiers were getting closer. He had talked to her gently, telling her how she could take care of herself, and that she was his special, brave girl. And then he had made her hide up in the rafters of the roof and said that she could only come down when he told her it was safe.

But that wasn't what happened.

She had watched through a gap in the tiles as the soldiers had trotted into the farmyard in a ragged line. Her grandfather had stood outside the rickety front door, his only weapon a short-handled axe. The soldiers had laughed at him, and one of them had poked his rifle in her grandfather's back, herding him along, kicking and rearing like a reluctant bullock, until he was out of sight.

She waited in the roof. The sun disappeared and night fell. Nahida must have drifted off to sleep, because she was wakened by the sound of a cock crowing and a thin, dusty ray of sunlight was slanting through a hole in the roof.

She knew then that her grandfather had not come back, and she prayed until she wept that her mother would send for her very soon.

But she didn't. Nor did she come back to the broken-down farm to collect her. She never heard from her mother again.

Nahida was a fool; she should have learnt back then that people do not keep their promises.

But at least she had the comfort of knowing that

now she had no one left there was no one who could be hurt if she didn't do as she was told.

She felt the tears burning her eyes and the terror turning and knotting her gut.

Chapter 6

Jason scoped the bar. There she was sitting in the corner, but definitely not hiding away; she looked more like someone who had bagged the trophy spot and wasn't about to be shifted. He admired that sort of style. It was a hard room to play. One of the big old banking halls – all marble and cornicing – that had been turned into an overpriced watering hole for City boys with too much money splashing around in their expense accounts and no limit on their company credit cards. Not the easiest sort of place for a woman by herself to look confident in, but she was pulling it off in spades.

He signalled to a waitress, and pulled up a chair, positioning it so that he could sit opposite Lisa – close but not intrusive.

'I knew you wouldn't be able to resist me.'

Cheeky so-and-so. She let a beat go by.

'How could I not be impressed by a man who offered to buy me a whole bowl of jellied eels?'

'That's what all the girls say. Now, how about a drink?'

He winked at the waitress. 'Get us some fizz,

babe,' he said, handing over his card. 'And make it a big bottle.'

Lisa smiled up at the young woman. 'Make that an ordinary-sized bottle, will you?'

Jason didn't say a word – she was determined to be nobody's fool, he'd give her points for that.

'So, you say you've been studying.'

She nodded. 'In Edinburgh. An MA. Combined French and Business Studies.'

'I'm impressed – clever as well as good-looking. But you don't sound Scottish. Mind you, you can never tell with posh birds. You all sound the same to me, wherever you come from.'

'Actually, I'm a Londoner through and through, and I'm hardly posh.'

He shrugged. 'If you say so, love. But I'm from Essex and you seem well posh to me.'

He held up the now empty bottle and waved it at the waitress. 'Another one, darling,' he mouthed.

Lisa raised an eyebrow. 'My mother warned me about men like you, Jason. You're what she would call a *bit of a wide boy*.'

'Snob is she, your mum?'

She considered for a moment. 'Not exactly. Not in the way you mean anyway.'

He looked at her simple, exquisitely cut dress. 'How did you earn your living then, while you were studying? Or did you get an allowance from Daddy?

Beneficiary of a nice little trust fund, is the way I'd bet.'

'Actually, my father's dead and I'm completely independent. I inherited some property, and a stud farm over in Ireland. My aunt – well, my father's half-sister – lives there and runs it for me. She had an accident when she was young. It scarred her face, and she doesn't like mixing with people. So it suits us both.'

Jason didn't show any sign that it was obvious he was listening to a story that had been rehearsed and repeated many times over – you couldn't kid a kidder.

'You give out a lot of information at a first meeting.'

She felt herself colouring – her blushing was something she hated about herself, one of the few things she had no control over.

'Nothing to hide, I suppose.' She sipped at her drink. 'How about you?'

'I'm lucky, me. I went into the City soon as I left school and worked my way up. Sixteen I was. Trading by the time I was nineteen. It was obvious to them that I had a real flair for it. Risk-taking. Holding my nerve. And I was soon doing business with the big boys – like your mate Richard Middleton.'

'That's why you were at his office this afternoon?'

'Exactly. And you were there . . . ?'

'He handles my financial affairs.'

Jason nodded approvingly. 'They must be some

33

affairs, Richard doesn't exactly deal with Post Office Savings accounts.'

'You're obviously not doing too badly either.'

'I suppose. But I've only got where I am because I got started in the eighties, when you could do that. I'd never have got anywhere if I was starting out now. The City's changed too much.'

'So you wouldn't hold out much hope for me then – if I wanted a job there?'

He laughed disbelievingly. 'You get a job? Why would you wanna do that?'

'I wouldn't. But I am thinking of setting something up. Something of my own.'

'Bloody hell, Lisa. Why put in all that effort? If I was in your position, I'd just hang out enjoying myself, have a laugh until I fancied settling down. Why go to all that fucking trouble and aggravation? Excuse my French.'

Slowly, she put her drink down on the table in front of her and frowned.

'Do you know, Jason,' she said, 'despite all my years of studying I never realised "fuck" was French.'

He was still laughing when the waitress came back with the second bottle of champagne.

Chapter 7

She didn't know how, but she must have fallen asleep. Her ear and the side of her face were hurting from where she'd been pressed up against what she presumed was a ridge on the floor – or was it the wall? How could she tell? What she did know was that she couldn't put it off, it was time again for her to crawl over to the foul-smelling makeshift lavatory in the far corner.

As she steeled herself to scramble over the sobbing and silent bodies – and over other things she didn't want to even think about – Nahida wasn't sure which was worse, the noises some of them made or the silence of the ones who were too petrified to even cry.

She had just braced herself mentally – and physically, against the metal to lever herself to her feet – to continue the disgusting journey, when, completely unexpectedly, the movement stopped.

The girls were all suddenly alert, or as alert as they could be after spending God Himself alone knew how long in such vile conditions.

They listened, with a varying mix of fear and anticipation, to the sound of boots scraping on gravel – *gravel, it couldn't have been a boat* – and then to the unmistakable sound of a key undoing a padlock. Then another one. And another. Then the creaking of metal as a door was dragged open.

They were being released.

But into what?

As they stumbled out into the darkness, the man who let them out poked and herded them forward as if they were goats, swearing in Russian about the stink rising off them.

She could see now that they'd been held inside a metal container on the back of an articulated truck – the man must have been the driver. The writing on the side was in Russian.

Flakes of snow swirled around them, but she was too dazed to care about the cold, and even her pressing need to urinate had been forgotten. Like the other girls, she made no attempt to run away, she just stood there, waiting in the darkness, listening to the sound of dejected weeping.

Then there was a sound of men talking, growing louder as they came nearer to the truck. Fear made her keep her chin down, but she dared to move her eyes to look in their direction. She saw lights shining behind them: a street of low, mainly makeshift-looking buildings; then she saw that there were three men – big, well wrapped up against the snow – and a much smaller woman in a black fur coat and knee-length leather boots. The woman had her arms folded and was laughing, throwing back her head and showing white, expensively cared-for teeth.

The four of them stopped by the man who had let them out of the container. They spoke for a few moments, turned and looked at the girls, did a quick headcount and then one of the men handed the driver a roll of money.

He put it in his pocket without counting it and set about closing up the container and driving off. Nahida felt a very strong urge to run after him, to beg him to take her with him. At least no one could hurt them while they were in the container. What would happen to them now he was leaving?

She didn't have to wait long to find out.

'All of you,' snarled one of the men in broken Azeri, grabbing a girl who was crying by the arm, and dragging her along beside him so that she had to break into a run. 'Get moving. Now. Follow. And keep your mouths shut.'

Without a single word, but with much shivering and quiet weeping, the girls did as they were told.

He only made them walk a few hundred metres, but it was far enough to allow the snow to seep right through their cheap shoes, and to make their leg muscles scream after their days of inactivity.

He signalled with a lift of his gloved hand for them to stop outside a drab, rectangular, single-storey building. The woman with the fur coat unlocked the door, went inside and flicked on the overhead fluorescent lights.

It was one big room.

Along one side was a run of four open, white-tiled, utilitarian showers, and adjacent to that a long trestle table covered with piles of clothes and shoes. The other two sides of the room were lined with bunk beds.

The woman looked the girls up and down. Not bothering to hide her disgust, she pointed to a cane hamper stacked with towels. Then, with her nose wrinkled and her lip curled, she snapped something at the man who had led them there.

He nodded, and turned to the girls, translating the woman's words. 'Make yourselves clean. Leave your clothes over there and then take new ones. You will have some food then sleep. Fold your new clothes carefully; you will be needing them tomorrow.'

A couple of them began crying loudly, but a girl standing close to Nahida stepped away from the others and began stripping off her wet, stinking clothes.

As she stepped out of her underpants, she turned and looked levelly at the fur-coated woman. 'Can we have soap?'

After eating two full plates of greasy stewed meat and potatoes, Nahida had fallen asleep surprisingly easily, but she was suddenly awakened from dreams of her mother by the sounds of someone screaming and of men laughing. It was still dark outside, but there was a lamp shining at the far end of the room.

It took a moment for her eyes to adjust and for her to make out what was happening: a man was forcing himself on to one of the girls who was pinned down on the floor by another man who was kneeling behind her, holding her arms tight behind her head. Three other men were standing watching and smoking, laughing as the girl sobbed for them to leave her alone.

Nahida didn't stop to think; she threw back the covers and was about to climb down from her bunk to go and help her, but an urgent hissing from the bunk below made her hesitate.

'Don't!'

It was Ana, the girl who had asked for the soap. 'Pretend you're asleep. They want you to see what they can do to you, how they can hurt you, so you'll be afraid of them, and so they can control you. Don't let them do that, or they will have won.'

Chapter 8

The day dawned bright and crisp: a perfect early-February morning that promised spring would be just around the corner. David and Paul Kessler were sitting in the back of a black stretch Mercedes; it had tinted windows and a glass privacy screen between them and the driver – top of the range, meant to impress. They were being taken from the place near the airport where they had stayed the night before, to a hotel where they had been told they would find Vito's contact – Misha, the man who, if David gave the okay, would become the Kesslers' agent.

'You know, Paul, Dad's always going on about how they had to cope with them Irish bastards in the sixties and seventies. Well, I reckon the O'Donnells would crap themselves if they'd ever come across this lot. We're talking serious stuff here. This mob don't run manors, they run fucking countries. And people? They mean nothing except how much dough they can get for them. They can even get fresh body parts for your poor sick relatives, if that's what you're after.'

'Leave off, Dave.' Paul shivered, and not only because the lightweight jacket he'd bought for the Caribbean trip was not exactly suited to the sub-zero temperatures. 'I've heard all that old toffee before. It's one of them urban myths. Like in that film we saw. A load of bollocks.'

'Well, that's where you're wrong, little brother. And it's one of the reasons I decided to give Vito another chance. Who knows, we might want to expand our business interests, start up some new ventures. See, a new kidney is just one of the goodies that Vito said they'd be more than happy to supply – at a price. Like some weird fucking menu they've got. I'm telling you Paul, this lot *do not* care about anything. And why should they? They've seen everything, things we couldn't even imagine. They've seen their grandmothers starved and their mothers and sisters raped and murdered. They've been tooled up with automatic weapons since they were kids – they've had to be. So what could frighten them? They're fucking fearless. Absolutely no sentiment about anyone or anything. Just money – that's all they're interested in.'

'I must say, Dave, you make doing business with them seem very attractive.'

'Don't get fucking sarcastic with me, Paul. These people are like us. Players.'

Paul rubbed his chin, trying to figure out how to put his fears into words without sending his brother off into orbit.

'Look, all I'm saying is, shouldn't we think this through a bit more? We're just walking right up to them like open bloody targets. We do a trade with them, and what do they do? They snuff us out.' He half turned in his seat, facing his brother full on. 'If what you say is true, what would it matter to them if they got rid of us? In fact, Dave, I'd like to know why we're even here, let alone dealing with them direct.'

'I told you, Paul, it's this lot who're running these things now. Why would we piss about dealing with the little people?' He ruffled his brother's hair. 'Don't worry, we'll be fine. We're business people, about to give them money for girls and for the coke run that Vito's overseeing with them in Miami. And if the coke's the quality Vito says it's gonna be, we'll be doing plenty more deals with them and all. Specially once we open the casino. So why would they want to get rid of us? They're not stupid. We're like a fucking hole-in-the-wall cash machine for 'em.'

'If you say so.'

'I'm telling you. They might be horrible bastards, but they're clever. You might not believe this, but Vito said some of the Russian big boys are even paying for people to go through business schools. He knows of one bloke being paid to do a PhD in Asian Studies.' He shook his head in wonder. 'Asian fucking Studies – so they can understand what's happening in the world. But most of all, they favour the computer boys. They use them to transfer money to different accounts – it's like money laundering with electronics. Clever bastards. See, it's considered normal to transfer fifty million dollars by email, but you have that little lot in your hand luggage and someone's going to ask why – even if you're fucking Swiss. Especially with all this new security everywhere.'

'Fifty million by email?'

'You know, electronically. I'm telling you. And they don't even bother nicking money from other people's accounts any more. Why should they? These people have got billions. Because they've pretty much got all the businesses they'd ever want all sown up. Drugs. Arms. People. You name it – it's theirs. Including kidneys and livers.'

David laughed to himself.

'Vito was telling me this story. Before we turned up in Jamaica there was this young Russian couple in the suite next to his. Every morning, Vito would come out on the terrace to have his breakfast and find all these wet clothes draped out over the bushes that divided his place from theirs. He reckoned the bird wasn't much more than a kid and she obviously wasn't used to staying at places like that, so she'd been doing her own washing. All this really expensive, designer gear, and she was washing it out in the bath. And they used to get pissed every night, and fight like cat and dog – smash the place right up. None of the maids would go in there unless they were escorted in by security. But no one said a word. They had so much cash no one cared. That hotel is very discreet, and they're used to dealing with people like that. That's why Vito uses it.'

'You his best mate now, are you?'

'What?'

'Vito's. You've been talking about him for nearly two hours now.'

'Don't start getting flash with me, Paul. He's a servant, that's all, a servant who gives us an in.'

'Ne'mind that for now, Dave.'

Paul squinted out of the window. 'Where the fuck is this?'

David lowered his window and took in the crater-ridden roadway, its gutters piled up with heaps of filthy slushy snow. It was lined on either side by a ragged collection of what looked like big wooden sheds.

'Some of them'll be the coffee houses he was telling me about.'

Paul turned to his brother. 'What, knocking shops, d'you mean?'

'Yeah, and the others'll be the places where they sell all the contraband. See? Look at all them jeans stacked up in that doorway. And over there, look, cases and cases of Scotch.'

Ducking his head to see out of David's window, Paul let out a long, slow whistle.

'Fuck me,' he breathed, pointing along the street to one of the bigger, more permanent-looking buildings.

Hanging from a rusty iron bracket was the hotel

sign they'd been told to look out for. With its cracked, filthy windows and chipped and peeling paint, it looked far from welcoming.

'I can't wait to see what he's got lined up for us in that poxy hole.'

Chapter 9

Paul, now more nervous than ever, spoke slowly to the driver – emphasising that he should wait for them, that he shouldn't even think about moving, whatever anyone said – only then did he follow David inside.

'Not quite Negril, eh, Dave?' he said, taking in the shabby lobby, with its worn carpets and grimy chandelier that boasted more cobwebs than light bulbs.

'What are you, Judith Chalmers's uncle? We ain't here to do a fucking holiday report, Paul. But if this all goes as well as I hope, you can spend a whole month back in Jamaica if you feel like it. And have that tasty little bird for room service – breakfast, dinner and tea.'

He walked over to what he presumed was the reception desk – more of a table than a counter – where an elderly woman, swaddled in layers of scarves and cardigans, sat knitting.

'Misha.' He said it loudly, as if she were deaf. 'We're here to meet Misha.'

The woman said nothing, but just stabbed her needles in the direction of a set of once grand, panelled double doors.

'Bloody hell, Dave.'

Paul and David stood in the doorway of the faded ballroom, taking in the bustling scene that resembled nothing more than a cattle market. But instead of there being livestock in corrals for sale, there were girls – at least two hundred of them – standing on wooden crates, dressed only in their underwear, their outer clothes that they had chosen the night before folded in neat piles on the floor beside them; most of them had their heads bowed. And, instead of farmers poking plump bovine haunches with sticks, there were men examining and judging the young female flesh, hair and teeth, with their eyes and hands.

A tall, gaunt man in an electric-blue, shiny mohair suit, his silver-grey hair slicked back flat to his head, appeared at their side. Behind him stood an even taller man in a tight denim jacket and pale, stone-washed jeans, who looked as if could have eaten the skinny man – plus all his family – for breakfast, and still have had room for a full fry-up.

The grey-haired man spoke to them.

'From your tropical attire, gentlemen, I presume you are the businessmen from the UK who Vito told me to expect.'

His English had a formal, old-fashioned tone to it, with just a hint of an American accent.

'And you'd be Misha.' David held out his hand. 'Now, how about a price list?'

47

Taking in the whole of the extraordinary room with a sweep of his arm, Misha's manner was matter-of-fact.

'You will appreciate that we have a range of merchandise for sale here, gentlemen. The cheapest, those who would work on the street, begin at six hundred dollars. Then we go on to sauna quality. After that, we have material suited to more tradi-tional, let us say more upmarket, brothels and for lap-dancing clubs. And, finally, there are those suitable for film work. Depending on your choice, they can go up to two, some even three thousand plus. As you must realise, this is very competitive pricing, so they clearly have good resale values, if that is what you intend to do with them. But that would be your business to negotiate with your own customers. If you require any help, please, let me know. And, of course, if you have any special requests, we can discuss those privately. The prices in such cases would reflect, let us say, the novelty of what is required. Now, please, make your selection, gentlemen, and then I will prepare your bill.'

With that he walked away, goon tight on his heels, leaving David and Paul to it.

They were nearly a third of the way round the room, when Paul leaned in close to his brother. 'I can't get over how good-looking these girls are,' he said.

'What you whispering for, they're only –'

David didn't finish, he touched Paul's elbow, bringing him to a halt in front of Nahida.

She was standing on a crate next to Ana – the girl who had been bold enough to ask for soap and who had protected her the night before, when she had been foolish enough to think she should help the screaming girl. And even though she could hardly believe this was happening to her, she couldn't deny that men were coming up and touching her in places where no one had ever touched her – her grandfather would have beaten them to their knees. And then they were arguing with the man they called Misha because she was too expensive. It was impossible, but it was true.

She was for sale.

And now two more men were standing in front of her.

'This is the sort we want, Paul. Young. She'll do for a start.'

David went to touch Nahida, but pulled back his hand. 'Don't know where she's been, eh?'

He then jerked a thumb at Ana. 'And her.'

Eighteen other girls, along with Nahida and Ana, were eventually picked out by the two men. Most of them were from the original group that Nahida had travelled with on the terrible journey from the club where they had been drugged, but a few of them she hadn't seen before. And the girl who had been attacked by the men seemed to have disappeared altogether.

Something in Nahida made her glad she didn't have to face that girl, that she didn't have to confront her own shame at pretending to be asleep.

Once they had been selected, they were told to get dressed and then they had been led outside to a truck. And now – Nahida could hardly believe this was now happening, the thought alone made her shake – they were being told to get inside another container.

This one also had writing on the side – not Russian this time, and most of which Nahida didn't understand, but which she could recognise as English. If she hadn't been in shock – at the men's brutality the night before and the humiliation of what had happened to them this morning – this container would have seemed almost luxurious, especially when compared to the one they had been forced to travel in before.

This time there were only twenty of them in a similar amount of space that nearly forty of them had been crammed into; and there was a layer of blankets on the floor; a lamp hanging from a hook; and they had been given some bread and cheese and two bottles of water each. Best of all, there was a big bucket with a tight-fitting lid that had been fixed to the wall so that their waste didn't spill over on to the floor, and they didn't have to sit in their own filth.

And the men who had picked them – *bought them*

– the ones she had heard the others call Kessler, hadn't touched them in the way that the other men had. Those men had handled them as if they were picking over rotten vegetables in the market, deciding which ones to discard. And the Kesslers had asked the man who spoke Azeri to tell them that if they kept quiet and did everything they were told then everything would all be all right. Only if they misbehaved would they be in trouble.

And Nahida had to believe them.

She had nothing else left to believe.

Chapter 10

Lisa O'Donnell looked at her mobile again. No voice message. No text. No missed calls. Nothing.

Come on.

She was aware she was spoilt, and had never been the most patient of people, but having to sit and wait alone in a restaurant was as close as she wanted to get to living in agony.

'Lisa!'

At last.

She looked up to see an elegantly dressed woman in her early sixties – who could easily have passed for being in her late forties – and for being Belgravia born and bred if it hadn't been for her throaty cockney accent.

'Hello, darling, sorry I'm late.'

Sandy smiled graciously as a waiter helped her settle at the table, acknowledging him with a bob of her head.

'Bloody warden only wanted to argue the odds about me parking outside till I pointed out me resident's permit. Cheeky sod. Suppose he reckoned only bloody duchesses are allowed to park round here. Little creep.'

She snatched up the glass from the table, knowing it to be the vodka and tonic that Lisa would have ordered ready for when she arrived, and gulped down almost a third of it in a single swallow.

'Know what I'm gonna do? I'm gonna order a bottle of wine, drink the lot, and leave the car where it is. Get a cab home and come back for the car tomorrow. That'll show him who can park here and who can't. Bloody cheek.'

Lisa smiled. She wouldn't have given the parking attendant much of a chance if Sandy had decided to really turn on him.

'Can I say hello now?' she asked, half rising to her feet, and kissing her on both cheeks.

Sandy took out her cigarettes. 'So spit it out, babe, what's all this about then?'

'Do I need an excuse to meet you for lunch?'

'Come on, Lisa, this is me you're talking to. I can always tell when something's up. I could hear it in your voice when you phoned me this morning.'

'Really?'

'Really. So tell me, what's so important?' She reached out and took Lisa's hand, squeezing it gently. 'You gonna tell me you've met the right bloke at last? And that you're settling down and getting married?'

'Not exactly.'

Deep breath.

'Listen, Mum, I've been feeling really restless lately. And I think it'd help if we had a talk. Nan's been dead over a year now, and I think it's about time I knew the full story. All of it.'

There was a long pause.

'What story?'

'For Christ's sake, I'm nearly twenty-nine years old.'

'Yeah, and you've had twenty-nine years of being sheltered and looked after.'

'I know I have, but it's not as if Nan's still around to get all hysterical and protective any more. At least do me the favour of treating me like an adult.'

'Lisa, you know I've always just wanted to forget all that, to give you a good life away from all that scum.'

'That scum you're talking about are still my family. I'm entitled to know. It's like I'm adopted and no one will help me find my birth parents. All I've got is the stuff I found in old newspapers, and everyone knows how they twist stories, make everything sensational. Please, Mum, I did everything you and Nan wanted, I didn't see Aunt Pat and Uncle Pete or their daughter – I don't even know her bloody name. And as for names, I wasn't even allowed to use mine.'

A waiter, pad and pencil poised, approached the table.

Sandy handed him her now empty glass. 'A double vodka and tonic and a bottle of Sancerre. We'll let you know if we want any food.'

*

54

Lisa had sat and listened for over an hour as her mother had unwound the story, and now they were sitting in silence, both staring down at the table.

'You wanted to know,' said Sandy, her gruff voice barely audible.

'I suppose they only did what they thought was right.'

'Right? Did you not hear what I said? The O'Donnells and the Kesslers spent two generations murdering one another.'

'They were different times.'

'Don't come it with me, Lisa. Gabriel – your grandfather – and Brendan would be exactly the same if they were around today. The businesses they ran might have gone in different directions, but they'd still be cruel, selfish, heartless bastards who made trouble for anyone they came in contact with.'

'You said you loved Dad.'

'Oh, I loved Brendan all right, and so did almost every other woman who met him.'

Lisa swallowed hard. 'He gave you a good life.'

Sandy shook her head. 'You sound like you're trying to defend him.'

'He was my father.'

Sandy sighed and picked up the menu. 'Let's order something to eat before they chuck us out.'

If only her beautiful daughter knew the half of what her scumbag family had got up to. But how could she load that on to her? The stories still haunted

Sandy's dreams and would go on to haunt Lisa's too if she ever heard them.

Dogs eating the remains of a body; a firebomb in a car that had blown up and killed a woman pregnant with twins; a young girl being shot dead by her own brother-in-law; Lisa's father being murdered by his own brother . . .

And so it went on.

How could Sandy ever do anything other than protect her from all that?

No, whatever happened, she wouldn't let the past touch her baby.

Chapter 11

David Kessler shook his head – in a delighted rather than a puzzled or negative gesture – as he punched in the number on his mobile.

It was answered immediately.

'Who's this?' The voice was pure East End – and openly suspicious.

'Dad, it's me, David.'

Daniel Kessler, still struggling not to wear reading glasses despite being in his sixties, put down his fork and squinted at his phone. 'This ain't the number you told me you'd be using.'

'That phone didn't work here for some reason. I had to get hold of another one.'

'You and Paul all right?'

Kessler pushed his plate of pie and mash away from him across the marble table, raising his hand to silence the man sitting opposite him. 'Sorted out the import arrangements with our friend, have you?'

'Yeah, that's all in hand, Dad.'

'So where are you now then?'

'On our way back to the airport, going through a place I won't even try to pronounce.'

Kessler rolled his eyes at the man opposite. His son the genius.

'What's not to pronounce in Jamaica – Kingston or Montego Bay?'

'We're not in Jamaica any more, Dad. Look, even this signal's not going to last, there's mountains all round us. So, just listen for a minute. Like I said, our Italian friend has sorted out the pharmaceutical side, and me and Paul have got the merchandise for the clubs. Twenty of them. And not one of them looks over seventeen years of age.'

'David, son, please tell me you haven't bought another load of worn-out, scraggy-arsed, half-barmy junkies off that Eyetie? Think of the shit he rowed off on us last time.'

'Don't start that again, Dad, you know that was a one-off.'

'And once was more than bloody enough.'

'I know.'

'I should never have let you two go and do business alone. You're just like your Uncle Sammy, the pair of you. He had the same idea back in the sixties. Indians he wanted to bring in. Indians if you don't mind. On fucking boats across the Channel. It was a stupid idea thinking about getting involved in what he didn't know then, and it's fucking stupid now.'

'All right, all right. Don't let's go over all that again. You know we sold half of that first lot on and put the rest in the saunas. And you know I more than broke even on that deal.'

And you knew what we were doing all along, and that's why you were more than happy to transfer all that dough over when I phoned you four days ago, you old hypocrite, he thought, but he didn't dare say.

'But this time it's different, Dad. I didn't want to worry you with the details, but this time it's our container we're using, and one of our trucks. With one of our blokes supervising things all the way. Bernie, you know him, really reliable sort of feller.'

Kessler snorted. 'Still sounds risky to me, boy. When's delivery?'

'They left here a couple of hours ago. But it's all right, Bernie's offloading them at night. So by next Tuesday, Wednesday at the latest.'

'What, are they walking? How comes it's gonna take so long? If it's the same as before, they –'

'No, listen to me, Dad. This time we're routing them through France.'

'Through France? Why the fuck are you doing that?'

David went cross-eyed at Paul and pointed to the phone.

'Because, Dad, they're being dropped near the theme park, that's why. The one me and Paul took the kids to last Christmas.'

'Which kids were they then, David?'

Daniel Kessler's never even temper was about to boil over into anger.

'You'll have to remind me, cos what with all the girls you and your brother have knocked up over the years, I tend to get a bit confused.'

'Dad, this is not the time to start going over all that nonsense again.'

No response.

'Okay – at least you're listening – that's when I came up with the idea.'

'What, to send them on fucking holiday? Make sure you treat 'em all to candyfloss and buy 'em some party hats and a balloon each, won't you, son.'

David shook his head wearily at his brother.

'Please, just listen, Dad. Now they've got these new scanners for the trucks, it's going through British customs that's the problem. They pick up people, no trouble. So, like I say, we offload them in France, tidy them up and calm them down. And before you know it, we've transformed them into a happy group of girls. And when they get on the train –'

'Tell me you didn't just say get on the train?'

'Yes I did. And no one's going to know they're not just another hen party coming back home to England for one of them to get married to her nice little feller from some poxy concrete housing estate. I've figured it all out. One of them's even going to be wearing a bride's headdress, have L-plates stuck on her back, the lot. And we'll make sure they're all half pissed, just like the birds me and Paul saw down there back in December. Perfect. No real checks to speak of at the station, UK passports just get waved through. Better even than routing them in through Ireland. And – you'll like this, Dad – you know how Grandad always used to say: Never have an empty truck? Always have a payload and a returnload? Well, once the birds are offloaded, the container's gonna be replaced with one stuffed full of fags. Three million of them, we've worked out we can fit in – all crated up and tucked away under a batch of cabbages. Cabbages, if you don't mind. And I'm telling you, a load of snout'll be a bit harder to detect than a truckload of whining women.'

David winked at his brother.

'And when you work it out, Dad, that comes to well over six hundred and fifty k's worth we'll be shifting. Add that to the dough we're gonna make from what our Italian friend's sorted out for us, in Miami, and I think it'll make us all very happy indeed. So, Dad, who's a clever boy now then?'

David didn't wait for his father to answer.

'I'll be in touch in a day or so about you getting Mick the Passport over to France to meet us. And I want a couple of the older girls from one of the clubs to come over with him. The two who cover Diamond Dan's'd be ideal. Cos after all this effort me and Paul have put in, we don't want any of the merchandise thinking it can just clear off.'

Phone call over, Daniel Kessler picked up his spoon and fork and dragged his plate of pie and mash back across the table. He scooped up a big heap of pie and coated it in liquor.

'You know,' he said to the burly, broken-nosed man sitting across from him, 'there's no laughs in this game no more. I know we've all gotta earn a living, but we might as well be buying and selling bloody stocks and shares the way they go about things nowadays.'

He shoved the food in his mouth, screwed up his face in disgust and threw down his fork, making it ping on the marble table top.

'Fuck it, now me poxy dinner's gone cold. I'm telling you, them boys are gonna be the fucking end of me.'

Chapter 12

This time, when the truck came to a halt, no one came to let them out; there was no noise, no gravel-scrunching feet approaching – nothing. So they just sat there, waiting.

Nahida felt as if they were sitting there for hours, but it was impossible to judge how quickly or slowly time was passing. Still, however long they were there, she was all too aware that it was more than long enough for her to have all sorts of terrifying possibilities running through her mind about where they were, and, worse, why they had been brought here in the first place.

She tried to tell herself that it wasn't so bad sitting there in the container, and not nearly as frightening as being in the back of the other truck had been. Only one of the girls was crying loud enough for the others to hear, and they were all in far better shape than they had been after the previous journey had ended.

And surely them being in better conditions was a good sign – a reassurance almost that these people were going to look after them and take them on to the dancing jobs they had applied for.

And it wasn't only the conditions inside this

container with the English writing on the side that were better – the driver had even shown them some consideration. He had stopped half a dozen times so that the girls could get out and stretch their legs for a few minutes. He had allowed them out one at a time – watching them closely as they each walked about on the stony terrain in the freezing cold wind – making it clear to them that the others would suffer terrible consequences if anyone tried to run away.

He had explained this to them through a combination of sign language and a few mumbled, almost embarrassed words. He hadn't seemed to Nahida like such a bad man, but probably just someone like them – a person who had found himself in bad circumstances, while trying to earn some money, trying to make a decent life for himself, and maybe his family.

Nahida wondered if he had a daughter of his own, a child that he would like to think someone would look after if she ever needed help.

Some of the girls had whispered to each other about how they too appreciated the way he was treating them – as if they were people and not animals – and speculated that, as they were being driven by such a decent man, they must be going to a really great place. One even thought that they must be going to the United States like a friend of hers had. But other girls said that was stupid and why would they have been drugged and made to parade themselves like tarts working down at the harbour?

Ana had been most scathing of all, saying that he was just doing as he was told: keeping them fit, making sure he didn't deliver a load of *damaged goods*.

But even though Nahida didn't say so – she badly needed Ana to remain her friend – she wanted to believe the girl who thought he was a good man and that they might be going to America. But really, so long as the place they were being taken was okay, she didn't care why the man had let them out – she was only glad that he had done nothing like the man called Misha had done to them.

Misha.

Nahida hated that man.

All the girls had been afraid of him – even Ana – and they despised him for humiliating them when he had made them stand on those wooden crates in only their underthings, and had poked at them and slapped them, treating them as if they were nothing more than fish on a slab in the marketplace. But Nahida had seen an even worse side of him, recognising him as one of the men who had stood there watching – smoking and laughing – as the screaming, terrified girl had begged for mercy while a man had held her down while another one forced himself on her.

Even Ana had to admit that this driver was a much better man than him. But if he hadn't treated them well, it wouldn't really have mattered. He needn't even have worried about warning the girls not to run off. They were now either totally exhausted and numb, or, the smart ones like Ana, savvy enough to have weighed up the odds, and long since realised that they had nowhere to go. And even if they did have somewhere – how would they get there?

And so the journey had passed.

Nahida, frantic to keep Ana close to her, had tried keeping her attention by asking her questions about her family and where she had come from, but Ana had not wanted to talk about herself and had snapped at her to be quiet and to stop making her ears ache with her non-stop chattering. Nahida had just begun to really panic, fretting that she had spoilt everything with this new friend of hers – and that the gossamer-fine thread of hope and strength that she offered would break and be gone for ever – when, without warning, the container was opened, and they were finally let out into the fresh air, all of them together this time.

They found themselves in a dark country lane, in a place they didn't know, and which didn't even have so much as a familiar smell about it. But they were all still relieved to be there, outside in the open with fresh air cooling their skin.

Nahida looked about her, trying to see something more of this unfamiliar landscape – were they in a different country? Was this America, like the other girl had said?

She lifted her face to the night sky, not caring that

a thin drizzle was coming down, enjoying the sensation of the rain on her cheeks.

Even though they didn't have coats to keep them dry, this just didn't seem as bad as before. This place felt good, benign.

Nahida's spirits rose. Maybe everything would be all right after all. They would be given jobs as dancers and earn money and have a good life, just as the advertisement had promised.

This place even felt warmer.

The driver spoke to them and gestured, and the girls all did as they were told, with a bit of whispering and a few tears but no outright complaints, and lined up with their backs to the container, waiting – again – to see what was going to happen next.

Nahida made sure that she was standing close to her friend, Ana, the brave girl who made her feel a little braver too.

Chapter 13

Only a few minutes had passed – during which time the driver kept checking his watch – when four dark blue people carriers appeared in the lane and parked in a line behind the truck.

The first two were driven by the men in the light summer clothes, the ones who had picked them out from all the others in the big ballroom – Kessler, that's what Nahida had heard Misha call them. The two remaining vehicles were driven by women. They looked as if they were in their thirties, about the same age as Nahida's mother, but there was nothing else about them that was anything like her.

They were wearing clothes – leather trousers and thick, warm sweaters – that would have cost so much money it would have been enough to buy food and new gas bottles for a whole year. And their long, shiny hair was beautiful, like nothing Nahida had ever seen before, streaked with different shades of blonde from wheat to deep gold; and their make-up made them look as if their skin was shining, like the angels in the icons in the village church where she had gone as a child.

Suddenly, all the girls stiffened, and leaned back

closer to the truck. David Kessler was pacing along the row – a monarch inspecting his subjects.

'Five of you,' he said, stabbing his thumb over his finger. 'Five of you in each motor. Get a move on.'

Nahida could have wept with relief when one of the two beautiful, shiny women ushered her towards the vehicle Ana had been directed to.

They had been driving for over two hours, when they turned into a huge, floodlit car park; Nahida knew it was more than two hours, because she had braved lifting her gaze to glimpse at the green numbers of the clock set in the dashboard. And it now read almost seven.

They pulled up beside a dull, two-tone beige Fiat motor home that had been parked well away from any other vehicles on the big tarmac expanse.

There was a brief discussion between the Kessler brothers, and then the quieter of the two accompanied the girls, one at a time, into the Fiat.

Ana, up front as usual, was taken in first. She was in there, according to Nahida's silent count of the seconds, for about ten minutes. Nahida couldn't be sure, of course, but that didn't seem long enough for them to have done anything bad to her.

As Ana was led back down the steps to join the others, Nahida stepped forward, boldly volunteering herself to be next, to get it over with – whatever it was. And she knew it couldn't be that bad, because

Ana had smiled at her, a brief reassuring movement of her lips.

Nahida was sure of it.

'You're one of them that understands a bit of English, aren't you?' said Paul, stepping aside to let her in.

She nodded vaguely at him, her attention almost entirely focused on the interior of the vehicle. It was like a perfect little house. She could have lived in it with her mother and grandfather and still have had space to be alone and private. She would save her money and maybe one day she would have enough to buy one of these and then she could go and find her mother.

She would have to learn to drive, of course.

'Good. Well, this here is Mick the Passport.'

Paul Kessler pointed to a shaven-headed, middle-aged man whose massive bulk was squeezed into a tightly zipped bomber jacket. He was sitting at a little fold-down table, with a lamp angled down over three short stacks of maroon-covered passports set out in front of him like a towering, high-rise version of chase the lady.

'Name?' the man called Mick snapped without bothering to make eye contact with her.

'Nahida –'

He interrupted her with a snort of laughter.

'You can forget that, darling.'

He flicked through the passports, fanning them out

as if he were studying a hand of cards. He then picked one out and opened it.

Lifting his big football head, he pointed at her with his chubby sausage of a finger. 'Natalie, that's who you are now: Natalie Wilson.'

He stood up, looming over her.

'Stay still for a mo,' he said, producing a camera from the bench seat, and snapped her, making her blink. 'Right, that'll do.'

He sat down again and clipped a pair of bulging magnifying lenses over a pair of ordinary-looking spectacles, and then began working away with surprising delicacy at removing the existing passport photograph with a fine surgical blade, the tip of his raspberry-pink tongue nipped between his lips.

'Now let's see,' he said, easing back the edge of the laminate covering. 'Age?'

No response.

'*How old are you really?*' he asked, annunciating the words loudly and carefully as if she were deaf rather than foreign. 'Just out of curiosity, like.'

'Eighteen years,' she said hurriedly, nibbling her lip with excitement. She was being giving a passport! This must be good.

'Yeah, course you are, Natalie. And I'm twenty-one next birthday. But what's the odds? We've gotta make you legal, n't we, love?'

Paul, smiled, nodding his approval.

'You know, Mick, I really like to see that in a man.

The real pride you've got in your work. You don't see that much any more: craftsmen doing a job like that.'

'And you won't be seeing it at all soon, not the way things are going. I'm telling you, this game's gonna be a thing of the past before long.'

'No. Surely there's always gonna be a market for your sort of gift.'

'I'm telling you, Paul. This trade is being swamped by cheap Romanian imports.' Mick sighed loudly, a man regretting the ways of the modern world. 'You wait and see. These Eastern Europeans'll be taking over the whole fucking shooting match before long. You name it, they'll have it. Cos they're cheap, there's plenty of 'em, and they don't give a fuck about whose doorstep they shit on.'

Nahida stood there with her head bowed – not understanding every word, but understanding enough. She was determined not to cry.

Chapter 14

Lisa tossed her passport on to the bedside table and heaved her suitcase on to her bed. She unlocked it and tipped out a pile of clothes that wouldn't have disgraced a changing room in Bond Street – the bedroom itself would have had the editors of broadsheet style sections salivating at the prospect of featuring it in their latest editions.

She stared down at the clothes. Sod it. She'd sort them out later. She'd enjoyed her few days relaxing at the spa, but she hadn't been so revitalised by the experience that she felt like doing her unpacking.

Lisa was halfway up the stairs to the upper floor of the duplex, making her way to the kitchen area to see if there was any wine in the fridge – of course she knew there would be – when she caught sight of the photograph that James had taken of her in the park. There she was in timeless black and white: head thrown back in laughter, clinging to the branch of the tree he'd dared her to climb. He'd said he wanted a good shot, she'd said he just wanted to look up her skirt, and he'd said he loved her . . .

The bastard.

What was it her nan had always drummed into her?

How do you make God laugh? Tell Him your plans!

Well, her plans had been to marry James, have the kids and the black Lab and even learn to cook for them all. It would have been perfect if a wife hadn't suddenly materialised.

Christ, she hated him for doing that to her. Even nearly three years on it still stung like hell.

It wouldn't be long before she'd be knocking on thirty and yet what had she done with her life? She'd had her heart broken, had picked up an education, had spent an awful lot of money on completely unnecessary things, and had had meaningless sex with men she couldn't – or rather wouldn't – commit to, not only because of what that pig had done to her, but because she wasn't who – or what – they thought she was.

Would she ever be brave enough to tell a man the truth? Expose herself to being rejected because of what her family had once been? Would she ever really chance that, after the upbringing she'd had, with all the constant warnings about not letting people know her 'business'?

It had left her lonely at times – no, more than lonely, isolated and fearful about her future – and always cautious about how she behaved, what she might give away. The false name, the practised stories, the withdrawal as soon as things got difficult. In fact, up until now, the riskiest thing she had ever done was finally moving out of her mother's house.

She wiped a finger across the photograph of that happier time – or what she had then thought was a happier time – and climbed to the top of the stairway to where it opened out on to the big open-plan living and kitchen space that took up the whole of the top floor.

She went over to the wall of floor-to-ceiling windows and looked out along the bend of the river towards the night view of the place known to its newcomer residents as Docklands. It was a view that could still make her catch her breath with its beauty.

She was just trying to decide whether she could be bothered to open a bottle of wine or if she'd rather just fall into bed, when the phone rang.

'Lisa, it's me, Jason.'

For some reason, she felt herself smiling at the sound of his voice.

'I'm just ringing to ask you why you haven't called me. Usually when I give a girl me number, she's on the blower the next day. What's up with you? Spent all your money on new clothes and can't afford the phone bill? Or maybe you think I'm too rough for the likes of you?'

Uncharacteristically, Lisa chuckled almost girlishly.

'That's what I like to hear, Lis. Now, are you coming out with me on a proper date or what? Cos I'm not the type of bloke who puts up with girls messing me about.'

'As you asked so nicely, how could I possibly refuse?'

'Good, dinner tomorrow then. I'll call you in the morning when I've booked somewhere.'

As Lisa put down the phone, she was still smiling.

Jason wasn't.

He took a breath and went back inside the bar.

'I promise I'm gonna get this sorted,' Jason said to a tall gangling man leaning against the wall in the corner of the dimly lit bar. 'I know I'm into you for a lot, mate, and you've been more'n kind letting me run up such a big tab, but I've come up with a guaranteed way of paying you back every single penny. And I'm putting the first bit of the deal in place tomorrow dinner time. I've got a solid-gold plan, mate.'

The man, known as Hoxton Marcus, was wearing a black suit – tight, drainpipe trousers and a high-collared jacket cut tight into his waist and flaring out down over his thighs, and black, tooled cowboy boots – the overall effect being that of an eighteenth-century dandy.

He sighed wearily. 'I am becoming very slightly impatient with you and your promises, Jason. Like most of my clients, you earn a great deal of money and yet you always spend even more. Are you really so foolish to think I'm prepared to continue subsidising your stupidity?'

'For Christ's sake, Marcus, I bring you in enough trade, don't I? You must be supplying charlie to half the fucking Premiership by now. And them introductions are all mine. All down to fucking me.'

'Don't use language like that in my presence, Jason. Try a little restraint for once.'

'Marcus –'

'I'm not listening any longer, Jason, I want proof of your intentions.'

With that he levered himself away from the wall and began to made his way towards the door.

He paused and turned round.

'I'm going to make *you* a promise this time, Jason – I promise you won't like it if I grow *really* impatient. You have until the end of the month.'

Chapter 15

Each of the girls had now been given a new, fake identity – with Nahida and Ana doing their best, in a cobbled-together mix of Azeri and Russian, to help those with less English than they had to understand what was going on. They were now standing along-side the fleet of people carriers, while one of the Kesslers addressed them.

It was David. He smiled, mouth only – after all, he wasn't planning on being their fucking friend – but he did need them grateful and compliant, especially for the next bit of the trip. No matter how confident he'd acted when he was speaking to his father, David wasn't entirely convinced that this plan of his was going to go quite as smoothly as he'd hoped, or even whether it would work at all.

'All right, girls, let's get this straight right away,' he said. 'You're in luck it's me and my brother who're going to be looking after you, cos that means you'll be getting somewhere decent to live and a few quid in your pocket.' He held up his hand and rubbed his thumb and finger together. 'You know, a few quid – money. And, if you behave yourselves, it'll be a good life working for us, one you'll have to show you appreciate by not causing any trouble. Because, believe me, if you'd stayed in that place where they took you to in Bosnia – with that horrible lot in their so-called *coffee bars* – you'd have no money, be given no protection . . .'

He paused.

'You know, *protection*? Condoms?'

He considered grabbing his crotch by way of illustration, but immediately thought better of it. 'And they'd give you regular good hidings thrown in for free – that's what they're like.'

Satisfied that he'd fulfilled the role of kosher employer and had got them all on board, David lit a cigarette. His hand was shaking very slightly – whether from excitement or tension, it would have been a hard one to call, even for him.

'Now, get in them motors, and we'll get you done up good enough for a night out on the town.'

He turned to the two Englishwomen.

'Make sure you get them pissed just enough to get them on the train, girls. Nothing over the top. We don't want any scenes.'

None of the girls – not even Ana, who probably spoke the most English – had any real idea what David had been talking about, or even what the majority of his individual words meant.

It wasn't long before they were even more confused.

With the help of the two Englishwomen they were

now clambering around in the back of the people carriers trying on clothes that had been laid out in four big nylon suitcases.

The girls' eyes widened and they chattered excitedly to one another as they pulled out yet another pair of jeans, and then a pink, calf-length suedette skirt; a spangly T-shirt covered with armour-like sequins across the chest; off-the-shoulder tops; crocheted ponchos, and a whole heap of embroidered denim jackets. Even the girl who had cried for almost the whole journey stopped sniffling for a while when one of the Englishwomen produced a plastic carrier bag half full of make-up and brushes and colourful bands and clips to put in their hair.

Nahida couldn't believe her good fortune; she had never seen, let alone worn, such clothes. And the lipsticks! She held one out for Ana to smell.

Ana took it from her – 'Hold you mouth like this' – and carefully painted Nahida's lips.

Nahida closed her eyes. It was like tasting the scent of ripe autumn fruits mixed with the perfume of fresh summer flowers. It was wonderful.

With all the girls in their people carrier finally dressed in the clothes of their choice, with their hair done and their faces made up, they were just beginning to dare to whisper to one another that everything really was going to be okay after all, and that the dancing jobs were surely theirs, when Mick, the big man in the bomber jacket, slid open the side door.

80

'Here you are, girls,' he said, popping the cork of a cheap bottle of cava and pouring it into plastic disposable beakers. 'A little drink for you. One for the road.'

Nahida should have known such good luck could not last.

She really didn't want a drink, little or otherwise, not after what had happened the last time, when they had drugged her and tricked her into that foul container, but when she shook her head, she saw from the expression on the big man's face that she wasn't being given a choice.

He pressed a cup into her hand.

'Come on, love,' said one of the Englishwomen, who was now standing behind Mick and grinning broadly as if she had just thought of something hysterically funny. 'You've got to have a drink. To celebrate. So we can wish you well for the future. Cos I've just decided – you're going to be the bloody bride!'

Chapter 16

With bellies empty of food – save for the bread and cheese that had been finished off the day before – and with their heads now befuddled by alcohol, the girls trudged sleepily, resignedly, towards the station. There were led along by the two Englishwomen, one standing on either side of Nahida, who, for no reason she could fathom, was decked out in a shoulder-length bride's veil, and had a card with a red letter L hanging down her back.

Maybe she was supposed to marry one of the men.

But which one?

She only prayed it wasn't the big man with the passports.

Again she had to fight back the threat of tears, but she was determined she wasn't going to give in – not now she'd come this far.

At the rear of the group were David and Paul Kessler – still in their sharp tropical suits – and Mick the Passport looking massive and menacing in his black jeans and bomber jacket.

They passed a smaller gaggle of stumbling young women – although these were giggling as they staggered along – who were heading in the same direction, only with less decision in their step as they didn't have anyone to urge them on and keep them moving forward.

'Oi!' one of them shouted, as Mick passed by, her accent pure south London. 'You! I'm talking to you. Why have that lot got minders then? They famous or something, are they?'

Mick the Passport stopped and turned to speak to her.

He had to bend almost double to whisper in her ear.

The girl did her best to listen to him, but she was distracted by having to adjust the flashing red devil's horns hairband that was threatening to slip down over her eyes.

She frowned, trying to grasp what he was saying.

A moment passed, as his words penetrated through her drink-slowed brain, and then she elbowed her friend whose arm she was hanging on to, and stared more closely at his charges.

'Here, you've gotta listen to this,' she slurred. 'This big geezer here, he only reckons that that dark-haired bird with the veil's gonna marry that bloke what plays for Chelsea.'

She sneered nastily. 'That's a well fucking lie, that is, innit? That dark-haired bird's never gonna marry him.'

Her friend's response to such a ridiculous proposition was to sway from side to side and stare glassily into the middle distance.

'You believe what you like,' shrugged Mick, 'but I never told you nothing, right? Cos we don't want no one calling the papers, thinking they can earn a few bob out of it, now do we?'

'No.' The drunken girl wasn't having any of it. 'You're having us on. Look at the state of her clothes. Look at the state of all of them. I ain't stupid, them footballers are all millionaires. Everyone knows that. They'd have all designer gear and that.'

'Darling, if you looked like her, you could get away with wearing a bin bag, and they'd still be gagging for you. But you don't though, do you? And that's why she's getting married to him and you're not.'

'Thanks very much, you ugly, fat fucker.'

'My absolute pleasure, love, but now I think you two had better forget standing here abusing me and get a move on, cos the rest of your mates are waiting for you. And if you're not careful, you'll miss your last train home. Then what'll you do?'

'I don't care if we do miss our train. We can go back tomorrow and spend the rest of tonight in that country and western bar. It's well good in there.'

She leaned unsteadily against Mick's massive chest.

'Fancy doing a bit of line dancing with me, do you, darling?'

She breathed up into his face, making him rear back from the fumes of three solid nights of booze and junk food all nicely whipped together by three solid days of stomach-lurching trips on white-knuckle rides and roller coasters.

'Go on, don't be boring. Me and me mates'd love to meet some footballers, and I know you've got the in with 'em. So how about introducing us? Me and her'd make it more than worth your while.'

She made a tottering grab for his balls, but Mick was too quick for her, stepping sideways like a matador.

'Whoa, there, Nelly, no thanks. I've got a job to do.'

'Fuck you then, you slimy, fat old poof.'

'Shame, cos I can't say I ain't disappointed,' he grinned. 'I never could resist having a shag with a bird what's a proper lady.'

Chapter 17

Lisa looked out of the windows that made up two whole walls of the corner office.

'I'm impressed, Jason. This is all very . . .'

'Swanky? Posh? Impressive?'

'They're just some of the words I might have used – that's some view for an office.'

'Not what you expected eh?' He sounded more offended than proud. 'Not what you were thinking I'd have?'

'I didn't mean –'

'Hang on, I ask you for lunch, suggest you come and meet me at my office – because I happen to be proud of what I've achieved – and then you as good as insult me. What, you didn't think a bloke like me could be important enough to have all this?'

She felt badly enough about her behaviour for her cheeks to flush – however slightly.

'That was rude of me. And I apologise. I'm very impressed that you've achieved all this – and in your own right. I've never really had to struggle for anything I've wanted in my life.'

'Lucky girl.'

God, she was making a mess of this. 'Not entirely,'

she jumped in, trying to make amends. 'The rose-covered cottage, the husband, kids and the Labrador haven't happened yet. But give it time, eh? Someone's bound to be able to see past my big mouth.'

'Let's just forget it and start again, shall we?'

'I'd like that.'

'Good.' He smiled, a warm, proper smile that lit up his eyes. 'Now I'll get my coat and we can go to lunch. And, I have to say, I'm intrigued to find out why a good-looking girl like you is still single.'

She was touched that he was making it so easy for her. If someone had behaved like that towards her she'd have slapped them.

'You didn't have to go to this extravagance, Jason.'

They were standing by the entrance of a restaurant in the most exclusive hotel in the whole riverside development. A restaurant that Lisa knew usually had to be booked well in advance.

'Expenses,' he said with a lift of his eyebrows.

Jason's eyebrows lifted even higher when the maître d'hôtel greeted Lisa with a slight, but deferential bob of his head, and a smiling 'Good to see you, Ms O'Donnell. No Mrs O'Donnell today?'

'Not today,' she said, following him into the room, without there having been so much as a mention of a reservation being needed.

87

She looked over her shoulder at Jason, turned down her mouth and shrugged. 'It's sort of my local.'

He shrugged back. 'Right.'

'What was all that about him calling you O'Donnell?' he asked, leaning back so the waiter could flick his napkin across his lap.

Shit! She hadn't even noticed.

'It's my mother's name,' she said lightly. 'Second marriage. It's too complicated having to explain that I'm actually called Taylor every time someone makes the mistake, so I just let it go.'

She found a smile. 'No harm done.'

They were well into their meal, including the second bottle of wine that Jason had assured her it would be fine for them to have – even though it was lunchtime and he was expected back in the office in less than thirty minutes – when his mobile rang out loudly, a jangling, downloaded rendition of the theme tune from *The Dukes of Hazzard.*

He was about to answer it, but seeing the appalled look on Lisa's face as every eye in the restaurant turned towards them, he changed his mind.

He stood up. 'Sorry about this, Lisa. Work. You know. I'll just nip outside and take it.'

If Lisa had studied Jason's reflection in the mirrored wall as he strode out of the room staring at the caller ident, she might have been surprised to have seen the look of naked fury on his face and that he was gripping the phone so tightly his knuckles had gone white.

'What is it now, Shaylee?' he demanded, pacing up and down as if he were a caged animal waiting for its keeper to come along with a haunch of raw beef. 'How many times have I got to tell you not to call me when I'm at work?'

'When can I call you then, eh, Jason? Tell me that, will you?'

Her voice was harsh, the whine he had come to expect buried beneath her anger.

'I mustn't call you at work, I mustn't call you at home. It's not fair.'

'Look, Shaylee, I've not got time for this now, I'm with a client. So just cough it up, will you?'

'I wanted to remind you it's Alfie's school concert tonight.'

That's why she was so mad with him – this was about the kid.

'I'm busy.'

'But, Jay, this is important, it's –'

'I said *no*, Shaylee.'

'You do know you'll be the only dad who's not gonna be there.'

'D'you reckon? I didn't think any of the kids at that dump of a school had dads. Well, not ones who

89

weren't inside or who hadn't pissed off and left 'em.'

'If it's so bad, Jay, why don't you get us somewhere decent to live, with decent schools?'

'Because I don't give a fuck, Shaylee, that's why, and if you don't like it – tough.'

With that he stabbed the call-over button and headed towards the lavatories, patting his top pocket, reassuring himself that the cocaine was exactly where it should be.

'Like I said, I'm sorry about that, Lisa.'

He smiled apologetically as he sat back down at the table, a humble little laugh in his voice, and eyebrows pressed down low.

'If you wanna go out with me again, you'll have to get used to all this: pressure of work, being in demand. It's what happens when you're good at your job. Although I have to say, I know it must kill some of the old school in the firm that they have to put up with a right herbert like me.'

Go out with him again? Lisa would usually have baulked at such presumption, but there was something about him; he was so different from her other dates. Definitely the rough-diamond type – a cliché maybe, but a very apt one, as far as Jason Carter was concerned. Bright, able, self-made – probably not a million miles from the sort of man her father had been . . .

He looked directly into her eyes, trying to read what was going on in her mind. Intrigued? Ready for another date?

Not easy to say.

'Look, let's not worry about that for now, Lisa, let's have another drink and I'll see if I can tempt you to have one of them chocolate things they do here. I have to say I have not met a woman able to resist them yet.'

Still she said nothing. Whatever the phone call had been about it had left him really buzzy, animated and full of energy; he obviously enjoyed every moment of being in demand. Perhaps she'd be like that one day, someone driven, with a purpose, a person who took real pleasure in doing a job well done.

'Well?' he asked. 'Chocolate?'

'I don't know, Jason.' Her voice was flat. 'Tell me, what is it about you?'

He frowned, wasn't sure where this was going. 'Give me a clue.'

'Well, how do you do it – keep coming up with all these offers I just can't possibly refuse?'

As she walked back along the riverside towards her flat, Lisa smiled to herself as she remembered the chaste but still very pleasurable brush of lips they'd exchanged when they'd said goodbye.

She took her phone from her bag and keyed in the number of Richard Middleton's direct line.

'Richard, hi, it's me, Lisa. I'm just calling to thank you.'

'Really? What have I done? I must say you sound very animated.'

'You introduced me to Jason Carter.'

No reply.

'Richard, are you still there?'

'Yes, yes I am.'

She could hear him breathing.

'I've just had lunch with him and I had a wonderful time. He spoilt me rotten, and I'm seeing him again. Soon.'

She yawned, pressing the back of her hand to her mouth. She checked her wristwatch – a quarter past three. She couldn't remember drinking quite so much wine at lunchtime in ages – nor could she remember when she'd felt quite so happy either.

She was only half listening as Richard dropped his bombshell.

'Lisa, I know I've asked you to do some things in the past that you haven't much liked, but this time I'm not asking you – I'm insisting. I don't want you to see him again.'

She stopped dead in her tracks, only just avoiding a Lycra-clad cyclist who swore at her over his shoulder as he swerved away.

She gripped the railing and stared unseeingly down into the grey, swirling waters of the Thames.

'I never would have believed that a man who

always said that he only ever wanted what was best for me wouldn't be delighted to see me actually being happy. Something I wasn't sure would ever happen to me again after that rat broke my heart.'

She tutted loudly and smacked the railing with her gloved hand.

'Richard, this wouldn't have anything to do with Jason's background, would it? The fact that he didn't have your sort of privileged upbringing?'

'Lisa –'

'In fact, you should be more worried about him than me. I mean, do you really want people you do business with having anything to do with a family like mine? Shouldn't you be warning him to run a mile from me before it's too late, before I taint him?'

'Lisa, please, it's –'

She could hear him digging around for a reason.

'It's nothing to do with any of that.'

'What is it to do with then?'

'Look, I just can't bear the thought of you being hurt again. Please, please don't see him again.'

Lisa frowned as she pressed the call-over button.

She immediately dialled Sandy.

'Hello, Mum. I know this sounds daft – especially as he's married and everything – but you don't think that Richard could possibly fancy me, do you?'

Chapter 18

Nahida was awoken by the sound of car horns blaring and loud, angry shouting coming from the street below. She sat up, rubbing her eyes, confused, not immediately sure where she was. Then she remembered, they had been brought here after their journey on the beautiful train with its special boxes of food – ham in bread so soft and white it was like the soft under-feathers of a goose – with Nahida wearing the bride's veil clipped to her hair and the strange red letter hanging down her back.

What did that mean? Why had they put those things on her?

And there were so many other questions, so many things she had desperately wanted to ask, but the Kesslers and Mick, the other man, and the two Englishwomen had made it clear that they were to keep their mouths shut.

But when the Englishwomen had brought six of them here to this strange, dusty room and had locked them in, they had all begun to speak at once.

Was this the place where they would be staying?

Would they soon be working?

Would the jobs be well paid?

Ana had been more interested in when they were going to get their next meal.

But exhaustion had soon caught up with them and, one by one, they had fallen into deep dream-filled sleep.

But now, with the continuing noise from down below, Nahida was wide awake.

She could only wonder how the five other girls were still asleep.

Slipping out of bed, she pulled the sheet around her, careful not to disturb them. Weaving her way across the low-ceilinged space through the cramped maze of single beds and old boxes – the room was the upstairs storage area of one of a surprising number of shoe shops on the Kingsland Road that were no longer trading – she went over to the window and lifted the thick curtain.

The bleak, wintery afternoon light that filtered in through the grubby glass surprised her; she had thought it was still night-time.

'What is it?' asked Ana, who was now shivering by her side, completely naked, not having seen the need to shield her modesty despite the fact that she was standing at the window in full view of the passengers on the top deck of any passing buses.

'Those men,' Nahida said. 'They are arguing. Their cars have crashed.'

'Look at his hair,' giggled Ana, pointing down at the squat, black man with waist-skimming dreadlocks, who was being spreadeagled over the bonnet of his battered, metallic lime-green BMW, by the white, business-suited owner of a shiny dark blue Peugeot.

'How has he made it into ropes like that? I wonder what it feels like to touch it.'

'Should we help him?' asked Nahida.

'No,' said Ana, suddenly serious, pulling the curtain back over the window and plunging the room back into night. 'Never become involved in such things.'

'But –'

'No!'

The door opened, startling them both into silence, and the two Englishwomen who had travelled on the train with them the night before, and who had then brought them to the room and locked them in, stood there, framed in the light from the landing window behind them.

'Come on, girls,' said one of them, clapping the palms of her hands together, with her fingers splayed back as if she were scared that her long brightly painted nails might break. 'Time to get up.'

She twisted her way across the room between the beds, careful not to brush against them. 'Nearly three o'clock.'

She threw back the curtain, grinning at the look of confusion on Nahida's and Ana's faces, and the look of incomprehension on the faces of the other four, who were clutching the bedclothes to their chins – a grubby woollen defence against who knew what.

'Yup, you heard right – almost three. You'll get used to the funny hours soon enough. Work all night, kip all day.'

'Now,' said the other one, 'I'm going to show you the kitchenette and where the stuff is for you to get yourselves some breakfast. Then you can get yourselves into the bathroom and get ready for your big moment. And you want to hurry up and all; the other fourteen are there already, and if we're going to sort this out before opening time you'll have to get a move on.'

She looked from Nahida to Ana, jerking her head in the direction of the four girls still in their beds. 'Explain what I said to them dummies, will you?'

Then she turned to the other Englishwoman. 'Jesus, we don't get paid enough to spend our time sodding about like this.'

'It's that David,' said the other one. 'He thinks he can charm us into doing anything he bloody well likes.'

Her companion laughed loudly. 'And he's bloody well right.'

The two women escorted the six girls along the busy main road past a parade of ethnic restaurants and grocers' shops, grimy windowed shoe wholesalers, video stores and incongruously up-to-the-minute bars and clubs. Then they turned down a narrow side street and walked a few more yards then stopped outside a plainly painted pub with blacked-out windows and a small, brushed stainless-steel sign on the door that read: *Diamond Dan's Gentlemen's Club.*

Ana sighed knowingly.

'Of course, that type of dancing; what else?'

Before Nahida could ask Ana what she meant, the door swung open and they were being pushed inside by the two Englishwomen.

Chapter 19

Daniel Kessler was sitting at the bar of Diamond Dan's with his sons, David and Paul. He wasn't in the best of moods, having been called away from a marathon card game that had been running from the previous evening. This was even though it was Kessler in the first place who had insisted that they should call him as soon as the girls were ready for inspection – so, as he had made clear, he could see exactly what his money had been spent on.

'You know what?' Kessler said to his sons, as he sipped at a steaming mug of the instant coffee that the boys were continually trying to wean him away from, hoping to replace it with what they considered were hot drinks that made a better impression – espresso or latte, anything Italian-sounding. 'If you ask me, everything's gone fucking mad.'

He dragged the back of his hand across his mouth, wiping his lips with a loud *aah* sound, looking about him at his surroundings as if seeing them for the first time.

'I used to think your grandfather – may God rest his soul – was out of touch with the modern world, but when you boys first started talking about setting up this lap-dancing lark, you made me feel like a dinosaur. I couldn't believe what I was hearing. Back in the old days, you couldn't even have a tit wobbling or you'd get closed down. And now what's happened? Stark naked tarts rubbing 'em in your face. And where are they? Soho? No, all over the bloody place, as good as respectable. City types popping in after work like it's nothing. It amazes me how we get away with it.'

David smiled. 'Not knocking it, are you, Dad?'

'No, course not. But all this change . . . it can be depressing. It's like the betting shops – those I could understand – but spread betting? They might as well be talking about Chinese fucking puck-a-poo for all it means to me. You don't know how glad I am not to have to worry about all this.'

David couldn't prevent his smile from breaking into a grin.

'And that, Dad, is why we don't bother you with all the boring details. We know you've got no interest in all that. We just get on with it. So long as we carry on turning a good profit, eh?'

David winked at his brother, a man pleased with a job well done, and Paul winked in return; but their pleasure didn't last long.

'I might be getting on a bit.' Kessler's tone was still conversational. 'But I ain't ready to turn me toes up just fucking yet. And I ain't stupid either. That's one thing I've never been.' He stabbed a finger at

David. 'But I think you need reminding of the fact sometimes, son. And you wanna remember an' all that it's me who's in charge of this fucking business. Me. Every fucking bit of it.'

He slammed his mug down on the bar.

'Now, where're these birds?'

Paul jumped in before David had a chance to start. 'I'll fetch them in.'

Daniel Kessler gave the twenty girls that the Englishwomen had lined up along the back wall a cursory glance.

'That one and that one,' he said, pointing to the two standing nearest to him – Ana, as ever at the front, and Nahida sticking close by her side. 'Them two just about pass. They stay. The rest are crap. Send 'em down to Forest Gate.'

With that he stood up, buttoned his overcoat and walked towards the door.

Pausing with his hand on the lock, he turned to face his sons.

'You two think you're so fucking clever, but you wouldn't have lasted five minutes back in my world. You don't know what being hard means. So do me and yourself a favour, and don't treat me like a cunt, eh, David?'

As his father let the door slam behind him, David Kessler was ramming a glass under the vodka optic.

'The way that old bastard talked to me, Paul. And

in front of everyone. Like I've got no idea. Like I'm a fucking kid or something. And that's after he's admitted to us himself that he's a fucking dinosaur.'

David swallowed the vodka, screwing up his eyes against the burn of the alcohol in his throat and immediately poured another.

'Now what are we supposed to do? Eighteen of them girls he wants shunted off to Forest Gate. *Eighteen*. What's wrong with the man? He knows we can put any old slappers in down there, and no one gives a shit. They'll shag anything.'

'Calm down, Dave. Just do as he says for now, and we'll change it back later, when we're ready. Like you said, what does he ever notice except the profits? He's got no interest in who – or even what for that matter – dances round them poles.'

'I know all that, but he's started giving me the right hump. He has nothing to do with making the businesses succeed, but he can't stop interfering with everything we do.'

'Exactly, so, just to be on the safe side, in case he decides to come back in the next few days, we'll do as he says. For now.'

'Why?'

'Cos he's getting old, and he don't like it. Let's just cut him a bit of slack, eh? It won't hurt.'

David lit a cigarette.

'What, you're a fucking counsellor now, are you, Paul?'

'Dave –'

'Just get them out of my sight, will you? Before I start working out what this is going to cost us and get myself really annoyed.'

Paul went over to the two Englishwomen, who had been acting as if they couldn't see or hear a thing.

But Ana had been watching openly, and now, with a faintly smug look on her face, she continued to watch as the other eighteen girls were shepherded roughly through a door behind the bar by the two women.

Nahida just listened with her chin lowered as the Englishwomen spoke, trying to make sense of their words.

'I'd have sent the whole lot of them down to the saunas in Forest Gate if it was up to me.' She jabbed her thumb over her shoulder towards Nahida and Anna. 'I don't see what's so special about them two back there. Soapy-looking mares if you ask me.'

The other woman laughed behind her hand. 'Not jealous, are you? Not worried David Kessler'll start getting tempted by the fresh young meat?'

'Don't be so stupid. And what's David got to do with anything?'

'You're jealous, that's what.'

'What, of illegal scum like them?'

'Illegal scum or not, that's the way of the world today, love – they want 'em cheap, disposable and very, very young. And you'd better get used to it.'

Nahida grabbed Ana's hand. 'Did you hear what she said?'

Ana squeezed her fingers. 'Ignore them. Think – this means we will have the room to ourselves now.'

'Less of your noise, you two,' one of the women shouted at them from the doorway – the last of the girls having disappeared from sight. 'You've got to save your energy for your dancing lesson.'

Nahida's chin was now almost touching her chest.

'Today is my birthday, Ana,' she said quietly. 'I am sixteen years old. Maybe not so young any more.'

Chapter 20

Jason held open the door and Lisa walked through into the bar.

She looked around the room. It was decorated in what style magazines would have described as BoHo – Bohemian Hoxton – chic. There were battered leather sofas; low, rickety tables; bare, unvarnished, splintery floorboards; and dim lighting, with the occasional bright spot illuminating amateurish-looking paintings for sale at decidedly professional prices. The staff and crowd of customers might have been aged anything from sixteen to sixty, but all were dressed and coiffed as *über*-trendy twenty-somethings. The music was loud and, to Lisa's ears, discordant, sounding momentarily melodic then veering off into strange chords and rhythms she didn't understand – or particularly like very much.

Jason flashed her one of his most charming smiles. 'You sit yourself down here, Lisa, and I'll go and get us some drinks. Vodka tonic.'

Lisa bridled slightly – he had made it sound more like a statement than a question – but there was something about this man, she wasn't sure what, that made her let him get away with it.

'That'd be lovely.'

'Good. I'll bring it over, then I'll be two minutes – tops – I've just got to have a quick chat with someone.'

He did exactly that; he brought Lisa her drink and then went over to the far end of the bar to speak to someone – a tall man with dark hair curling down on to his shoulders: Hoxton Marcus in his trademark black suit and cowboy boots.

And, true to his word, Jason had gone over to him, had huddled close and, with his back firmly to the crowd, had discussed whatever business they had with one another – the brief conversation leaving Marcus looking not very happy – and was back at the table all before Lisa had taken the second swallow of her drink.

'Right, that's settled. Now, do you want to drink up and get going? You don't look very comfortable.'

As he spoke to her, Jason flashed a look at the man, who was now busily talking to someone on his mobile.

Lisa picked up her bag. 'It's not really my sort of place.'

Jason's attention was still half on the man at the bar, but Lisa didn't seem to notice. She was reaching for her drink with one hand and holding up her other, palm outwards, stopping him from speaking – not that he was about to.

'I know I sound rude after you've brought me here,

but Hoxton . . . This used to be such a real place, now look at it. How about going somewhere more like this part of the world should be? A pub – a proper boozer?' She knocked back the last of her drink and turned to him. 'I'm sorry, I can't hack this, Jason. It's so phoney.'

The man at the bar was now striding towards them, his long, flaring jacket flapping behind him. Jason gripped the arms of his chair.

Even in the gloomy light Lisa could see that the colour had drained from his face.

'God, Jason, don't be like that. We'll stay for another if you like.'

'All right, Marcus?' said Jason as the man came closer to their table. 'Be seeing you soon, mate.'

'Too right you will,' the man said, his voice a deep, almost aristocratic drawl.

He paused and looked very briefly at Lisa.

'Not exactly what I'd call proof of your intention,' he said, and walked on past them, without so much as a glance at Jason.

'What was that about?' said Lisa, staring after the man as if she would happily have thrown her vodka at him – if she hadn't already drunk it.

Jason shook his head. 'Too much booze.'

Lisa watched as the man opened the door, her lips pressed firmly together.

'As I was saying.' She stood up. 'What'll you have? Same again?'

Jason turned and watched as Marcus left the bar, closing his eyes in a brief moment of relief. Then, with elbows planted on his knees, glass held out in front of him in both hands, he dropped his chin and let out a long, slow breath.

He looked around the room. 'You're right. This place is a dump.'

He jerked his head towards a group who had draped themselves across a sofa on the other side of the bar.

'Look at the state of them.'

Despite the warmth of the room, the group were all dressed in multiple layers of ill-matching clothes and itchy-looking woollen headgear that would have been more suited to the high Andes than a bar in N1.

'So, how about my suggestion?'

'Sorry?'

'Concentrate, Jason. Going to a pub – remember? Then I'll treat you to a Vietnamese meal. I know a great place only five minutes' walk away from here. On the Kingsland Road.'

'You know that area – Little Vietnam?' Jason was frowning as if he was trying to figure out something. 'I wouldn't have thought the East End was your sort of place.'

'I do live in Docklands,' she said defensively.

'Yeah, but come on.' Now he couldn't hide his amusement. 'That's a little bit different. Not exactly the mean streets of Hackney, now is it?'

'I went to the restaurant ages ago. A boyfriend took me,' she said, still standing in front of him. 'I liked it a lot, and I thought you might too.'

There she goes again, thought Jason, watching her button her topcoat over her understated, perfectly fitting designer suit. The quick, pat answer to any difficult question. What was it with her?

'So what do you think?' she asked, shaking her hair back over her shoulders. 'May I buy you dinner?'

'I never could say no to a pretty girl.'

'Good, because I wasn't about to take no for an answer.'

Chapter 21

'Stand still and keep your eyes open wide or I'll hurt you.'

Ana had Nahida pinned against the wall of the tiny shower and lavatory cubicle that led off from their bedroom over the shop in Kingsland Road.

Nahida's head was tilted back so far that she had to gulp in order to swallow as Ana swiped the mascara on to her lashes.

'I am going to make you look even more beautiful. And all the men will be chasing after you; they won't be able to say no to you.'

'I am uncomfortable; can we sit in the bedroom?'

'No, the light is better in here.'

'Can't we leave it? I don't like so much on my face. It feels too thick. Like paste.'

'How can you earn good money if you don't look right? You heard what the Englishwomen said – you have to look the part, like an actress in a play. You have to have much make-up. And your hair made big.'

Nahida screwed up her face, pulling away from her. 'I don't know if I want to earn money like this.'

Ana's hand stopped in mid-air, mascara brush held aloft.

'Are you a crazy girl? We have that whole room through there just for the two of us. It's dry and it's warm, and we've made it clean. We have plenty of food, running water – *hot and cold* – this bathroom, and the kitchen to cook in. And we have each other. We are friends, Nahida. What more do you want?'

'I don't like the dancing.'

Ana puffed out her cheeks and let out a little sigh of air. Gently, she stroked Nahida's hair.

'This dancing is nothing. I have done many far more difficult things, and have not even been given enough food to fill my belly in exchange.'

She clicked the lid back on the mascara, and busied herself searching through the bag of cosmetics that the Englishwomen had given them. 'When I am here I have a good life. Not like at home. We even manage to keep some of the tips we earn.'

She took out a lipstick and began stroking it across Nahida's tightly closed mouth, her own lips moving in sympathy as she applied the colour.

'I know it is not proper money like the local girls, but they are legal.'

Nahida grasped Ana's wrist, making her drop the lipstick on the blue vinyl-covered floor.

'I like to have the money too, Ana. Of course I do. And the food, and the warm room.' The fatigue in her voice made her sound far older than her years. 'But I don't like the dancing. I hate it.'

'You are being foolish, like a child. We are lucky

111

to be here, Nahida. Think of the girls back home. And think of the girls they sent to the saunas.'

Nahida turned her head so that her kind new friend couldn't see her face.

'The saunas . . . I pretended I understood what they are. But I don't.'

Ana leaned back against the washbasin and folded her arms.

'Truly? You don't understand?'

Nahida nodded. 'Truly.'

For a brief moment, Ana still wasn't sure if Nahida was serious, but the look on her face, as her lips quivered and her eyes brimmed with tears, told her that Nahida was telling the truth.

'Don't be sad, Nahida,' she said, taking her hand. 'I will explain to you. The saunas are places that pretend to be one thing, but are really something else. A cover. Men go to them for sex. They are cheap places. Not so nice. And the girls who work there, they are not so good. I have known some girls who have had their front teeth knocked out, so they can please men better.'

Nahida pulled her hand away.

'I still don't understand, but I know I would never let men do that to me.' Nahida's voice finally cracked as she began to cry. 'Not for money. Not ever.'

'So you haven't . . .' Ana hesitated, this was crazy. 'You haven't *danced* in the private upstairs rooms yet?'

Nahida swiped away her tears with the knuckles of her tightly clenched fist.

'Look at me, Nahida. Look at me. Have you ever been with a man?'

'No. Never. And I . . .'

Her words dissolved into sobs as she buried her face in her hands.

'Nahida, it's okay, I'll help you. We only have to do what these people want for a few months, and then we'll have saved enough money to leave here and do what we want. We can travel to places. Buy nice clothes. A car. You can learn to drive – think of that, Nahida.'

Nahida shook her head.

Ana turned away from her, twisting her body in the tiny space, until she was facing the mirror over the sink. She looked at her reflection, flicking at her hair and checking the mask of foundation layered over her skin.

'I don't know why you're making so much fuss. It's not so bad. I have done it with men for money since I was twelve years old.'

Nahida's head jerked up; she stared open-mouthed at Ana's reflection.

Ana shrugged. 'What? What's wrong?'

'But you were a child.'

'No,' Ana laughed mirthlessly. 'I was a child when I was forced to do it for nothing by the soldiers. After

113

that I began to do it for money; then I wasn't a child any more.'

'Ana.'

There was a long moment before she answered.

'Yes?'

'I'm not sure what they want to do to me. Or what I have to do to them. I saw those men hurting that girl. Heard her screaming. Is that what they want?'

Ana manoeuvred herself back round so that she was facing Nahida.

'Do you know anything about being with a man? Not being forced, but by choice?'

She leaned forward, so that their faces were nearly touching, her eyes fixed on Nahida's as if she were trying to see into her mind.

'And about your body – do you know how it works? How not to get diseases? Or get stuck with a baby?'

Nahida had to look away.

'My mother left when I was very young. When my time came, I thought I was bleeding to death. I went to my grandfather; he told me to keep myself clean. Nothing more. But then there was a girl. She was from a travelling family. They set up camp for a few weeks, on the old farm we had squatted. They were in the orchard, a run-down, neglected place – far worse than the farmhouse. One day, she saw blood on the tops of my legs, when I was climbing to collect the withered apples, all that were left, to put in our stew

– it made the meat from the sausage go further. She laughed at me when I didn't understand what the blood meant. She told me I had become a woman and should find a husband before I was too old and nobody would want me and my grandfather would have to slit my throat because I would be worth nothing.'

Nahida swallowed, doing her best to control her voice to stop it from cracking again.

'But I told her: I didn't want a husband. I wanted my mother.'

A tear trickled slowly and silently down her heavily made-up cheek, but when Ana wrapped her arms around Nahida's still childlike shoulders, the crying became a sob – not only for her mother, but for her grandfather, her home, and for the life she knew she would never know again.

Chapter 22

Jason and Lisa were walking through a little side street that threaded through from Hoxton Square to Kingsland Road, in which the only halfway remarkable building in the whole of the otherwise run-down, boarded-up terrace was a traditional corner pub. What was notable about it was the fact that it looked as if someone had given it a makeover that was deliberately intended to make it look inconspicuous rather than attractive to passing trade.

Its plain door – painted the same uninviting, dull battleship grey as the rest of the Victorian tiled building – was shut, as were all the blacked-out windows. On the door, a small, brushed stainless-steel sign read: *Diamond Dan's Gentlemen's Club*.

Neither Lisa nor Jason appeared to take much notice as they passed by, but they both stopped in their tracks and spun round to see what was happening when a roar of male anger burst out of the now wide-open door.

They watched as two massive bouncers hauled a City-suited drunk, kicking and cursing out on to the pavement.

'If you don't let me go, you cunts,' he bellowed in the sort of bland, featureless Home Counties accent that belied the fact that its possessor might know such words, 'I'll be back here with my friends to teach you some fucking manners.'

'Don't be stupid,' said one of the bouncers, grinning at his equally amused companion. 'Cos I bet our mates are all bigger than your mates.'

Wrong approach. The drunk threw back his head and butted the now no-longer grinning bouncer full in the face.

The blood spurted like water gushing from a compressed hose.

The bouncer had just drawn back his fist, ready to see, by way of reply, how much blood he could smash out of his assailant's nose, when a tall, attractive woman, dressed in a simple black trouser suit, stepped out of the club and said in a light, pleasant voice: 'Everything okay here, chaps?'

Lisa watched, fascinated, as the woman not only talked them into stopping the fight – as easily and as calmly as if they were no more than kids scrapping in the playground rather than testosterone-fuelled, adult men – but also, in no time at all, she had completely defused the situation. She had called a cab on her mobile, the injured bouncer had been sent inside to get his nose patched up, and the drunk had been dispatched into the night, with a mumbled agreement that if he wanted to visit again,

117

he would conduct himself in a manner more appropriate to a classy establishment such as Diamond Dan's.

The woman was now supervising a middle-aged cleaner who was swilling the blood off the pavement with a mop and bucket.

'I can't believe that, Jason.'

'Yeah, I know. Bloody yob. I don't know what gets into some blokes. Soon as they get their beer goggles on, they have to have a fight.'

'No, not that, I'm talking about that woman, the way she dealt with it. She was so impressive.'

Jason laughed. 'Never seen a door bitch in action before?'

Lisa, still staring at the woman in open admiration, shook her head. 'No. I've heard that they have them in clubs, but I've never actually seen one.'

'That's because there's not enough of them to go round. It seemed a bit strange when they first started coming on the scene, but the club owners soon realised they could use them to search girls for drugs and weapons and stuff without being accused of trying to feel them up. And, like you just saw, blokes don't like showing themselves up by arguing with them, so things quieten down rather than kick off. Sometimes you need a bit of extra muscle, but, all in all, the clubs love having women working the doors. And when they do a good job, they earn a lot of money.'

Lisa nibbled her lip, a delighted smile now lighting up her face as she felt something kick in – the feeling that this was somehow the real world.

'I'd lay money on the fact that she's not bored.'

'I reckon you're right there, Lisa.'

'Do you know, Jason, I'm envious. There's something I'd love to do.'

'*You?* Be a door bitch? I've heard it all now.'

'No, not do the actual job. But I could set up an agency to manage them – supply the clubs with all the women they need. In fact, I bet I'd be brilliant at it. My mother did something similar once. And she always said how much she loved the challenge of running her own business.'

Jason looked at her sideways; she was now staring at the club's once again firmly closed door as if it were a Christmas tree full of presents – all meant just for her.

'Are you telling me your mum ran door bitches?'

'No. It was a different sort of agency.'

'Oh yeah? What sort?'

'Never mind that now.'

She turned to face him, knowing that what she was about to suggest would, in her mother's eyes, be only just short of criminal – the very thing she had fought all her life to protect her from.

'Jason, I'd love to speak to that woman. Come in with me?'

'You do know it's a . . .' He hid his amusement and

gave himself some time by coughing into his fist.
'Gentlemen's club?'

'Yes, but I don't suppose there are many gentle-men in there.'

He looked at her for a long moment, his mind beginning to race with ideas as it occurred to him – with all the sudden force of the drunk's forehead smashing the doorman's nose – the size of the opportunity that was just being handed to him on a dainty, designer-dressed plate: *contacts on club doors . . .*

Oh yes!

Not only would this bird be the one to bring the gear in for him, she'd be the bloody outlet as well.

He kicks, he scores!

He was a fucking genius!

'Okay,' he said.

Chapter 23

Jason rang the bell and spoke quietly into the intercom, his mind working overtime; okay, meeting Lisa could turn out even better than he'd ever hoped for, but he had to play it right.

She had money, and she didn't need this. But he did.

The outer door swung open and they were faced with another far less anonymous inner one. It was chrome-framed glass, etched with a cartoonish parody of a naked woman: impossibly tiny waist, pneumatic breasts and buttocks, standing on a single, pointy tiptoe, the other leg raised high at the knee, and with her head thrown back in an expression of ecstasy. On each of the side walls of the tiny inner vestibule was a vivid, matching splash of colour: flashing candy-pink neon signs showing a winking, moustachioed man in top hat and tails, with a cane in one hand, and raising and lowering his hat with the other.

Lisa could feel the excitement rising in her. This was a world that belonged to men like her father, her uncles and her grandfather, a world she had been 'protected' from, and that – she couldn't deny it – had fascinated her since she had heard those first hints about the real nature of their businesses and all the wealth the family had accumulated over the years.

As Jason opened the inner door, a wall of music hit them, not so much loud as pulsating, the throbbing beat coming up through the floor.

Lisa stood there taking in her first glimpse of the interior of Diamond Dan's Gentlemen's Club.

The room had low, subtle lighting on the walls, and was dotted around with tables and chairs, but Lisa's gaze kept being drawn back, is if by some invisible force, to the centre of the room. It was dominated by a spotlit podium pierced by three gold-coloured metal poles that ran from floor to ceiling. Three young, good-looking women, in tiny, bottom-skimming dresses and spectacularly high heels, were up on the platform, dancing seductively, writhing to the music, apparently only moments away from bringing themselves to orgasm against the poles.

'Fancy having a drink at the bar?'

Lisa turned and stared at him as if he'd just pinched her.

'Sorry. Yes. Thank you. I was miles away.'

She had actually been thinking back to those times – usually after her mother had had one or two drinks, when she'd been 'celebrating' some family anniversary or other – when Sandy had first begun to tell her daughter stories about the O'Donnells, and the ways in which they had made their money. Rather than telling her about her family history, the stories had been more of a series of not so veiled warnings about why she should never have anything to do with that way of life.

As she followed Jason over to the bar, a new song began booming out from the sound system, and young women in little more than a few scraps of lace and garters that served as billfolds for fans of banknotes, began gyrating in front of the men who were sitting at the tables. Most of the customers were in groups egging one another on, but a few were alone. All of them looked smartly dressed, and most of them looked reasonably capable of getting a girlfriend without having to pay for the privilege – if perhaps not one quite as glamorous as those dancing inches from their faces. In fact, if Lisa was brutally honest, she thought that they would probably have had very little chance with most of the girls in there if there hadn't been a commercial transaction involved.

She looked about her, trying to spot the woman who had dealt with the drunk on the pavement outside, but she couldn't see her. What she did see was a row of booths on the far side of the room. In one of them, clearly visible through the gauzy curtain, a naked woman was straddling a man's lap. He was licking at her nipples as she brushed her breasts back and forth across his open mouth.

Lisa jumped as a very pretty, dark-haired girl, who looked to be about sixteen or seventeen years old, edged past her and Jason. She was leading a middle-aged man towards a spiral staircase at the far end of the bar.

As the girl mounted the first couple of steps, the man's fingers squirrelled their way into her G-string. There was a moment's hesitation, before the girl turned and smiled down at him over her shoulder.

'So how do these places operate?' Lisa asked, climbing on to one of the high stools at the bar.

'How would I know?'

'Come on, Jason.'

'You got me bang to rights, guv,' he said, holding up his hands and smiling. There was more to Lisa than met the eye. He'd have to watch himself. 'Well, for a start, the girls do really well out of it. They pay a few quid for the privilege of working here, and then they cop a tenner for the top to come off, and thirty for a full strip. Every single dance. And there's no touching.'

'Oh no? So what's going on over there?'

'That's up to them; they're adults, and that's a private booth.'

'You come here often, do you?' she said, unable to stop herself from flicking further glances at the three girls still twining themselves sinuously around the poles on the central stage – if they were having such a hypnotic effect on her they must be driving the men crazy.

'It's a good place to bring clients.'

124

'That's what we like to hear,' someone said from behind them.

Lisa and Jason twisted round on their stools to see two men standing there. They were clearly brothers, possibly even twins.

'Hello, Jay,' said one of them.

'Hello, Dave,' said Jason, shaking the man's hand and nodding to the other one. 'All right, Paul? Don't often see you two in here this early in the evening.'

'We were nearby and thought we'd nip in and make sure everything was okay. We got a call from Debs to say there'd been some trouble. She said she'd sorted it out, but we just wanted to check for ourselves; there's no way we want anyone acting stupid and getting the place closed down.'

David looked approvingly at Lisa. 'Now who's this?'

'Sorry, I'm forgetting me manners – this is Lisa.'

She held out her hand. 'Lisa Taylor.'

Before David or Paul could speak, Jason, looking steadily at Lisa, weighing up how far he could go and how quickly, said: 'She was just admiring Debs's work, and mentioned how she could find you all the door bitches you need – if you'd give her the exclusive contract, that is. Keep all your places nice and clean – no trouble.'

'Were you now?' said David. 'Well, we'd better introduce ourselves if there's a chance we'll be doing business. I'm David Kessler and this is my brother Paul.'

Lisa blinked. Jesus Christ. *Kessler*. Surely they couldn't be *the* Kesslers? If they were then she'd been entirely wrong earlier – as far as her mother would be concerned, coming in this place would actually be criminal.

David Kessler smiled at her. 'We can never get enough reliable girls to work the doors. How many have you got on your books?'

'I'm just . . .' She hesitated, feeling a fool. 'Starting up.'

'I see.'

David lifted his chin and scratched the side of his neck, staring at Jason – where did he find these birds?

He turned back to Lisa. 'You'll have to come back and see me if you do ever get a team together.'

With that he nodded briskly and began walking away.

Jason slipped off his stool. 'Lisa, I've just got to have a quick word.'

Lisa watched as Jason caught up with David Kessler and his brother just before they disappeared through a door at the back of the club.

'Dave, I think you might have got the wrong impression of Lisa. She's a smart girl, and she'll get you all the staff you need if you give her the chance.'

David frowned. 'Why is it so important to you?'

He grinned. 'I'm trying to get into her knickers, of course, and I want to show her I've got some clout.'

'All right, but why would I let an amateur run my doors?'

'I'm telling you, Dave, she's well clever, and the girls definitely wouldn't be amateurs. I guarantee it.'

'This is stupid.'

'As stupid as me bringing you in all the business that I do? All them footballers with more money than sense? All the City boys I've brought over here who wouldn't have found this place even with a map and a fucking compass? The ones that I was gonna persuade to take out membership for your new casino? The ones who could just as easily go to some other clubs that I just might find myself recommending to them? I don't think it'd hurt you to at least have a proper meeting with her. Do you?'

'You've got some front, Jay, I'll give you that.'

Jason hoisted himself back on to the stool next to Lisa.

'Well, I reckon you owe me now, girl. I have just got David Kessler to agree to have a meeting with you about you doing business with him. Sometime next month, I suggested. Give you a bit of time to go into it, sort out the wrinkles, so you can give a good account of yourself. I'll help you if you like.'

'Really?' She just about managed to suppress her excitement. 'Why would you do all that for me?'

'Completely selfish motives, I'm afraid,' he beamed, without a moment's hesitation. 'Because then you can get me into all the clubs for free. I'm not as daft as I look, you know. What do you think?'

'That I really do owe you. Thanks.'

She was going for it. He could have kissed her.

In fact, he could have kissed her anyway – she was well fit.

Chapter 24

It was nearly four o'clock on the sort of wet and windy late-March afternoon when the clocks hadn't been put forward yet, and only a thin grey light, the colour of the underside of a pigeon's wing, was able to filter through the tightly sealed lid of clouds that had dominated the sky since dawn.

Nahida and Ana were walking the now familiar route to work – Nahida with her head down, Ana with her chin in the air, proudly showing off her newly home-bleached blonde hair – their arms linked, tottering on the vertiginous heels that had come to seem almost normal to them.

'I can feel you are upset again, Nahida, but you must try harder, please, for both of us. We have to work to earn money, and we have to earn money to get away from here. That is what you want, isn't it, Nahida, to get away from here?'

'You have said all this before, Ana. Many times. And I have told you that I am upset not only for myself, but I am worried for you too. You are so thin, and you look so tired.'

Ana squeezed Nahida's arm and said lightly: 'Of course I look thin and tired, I dance all night and

hardly ever see daylight. What would you expect –
that I should be as fat as a calving cow, with a face as
brown as a fisherman's?'

'I want to go home, Ana.' Nahida's voice was
small and weary.

'Home? Where is home? That broken-down farm
run over with gypsies that you talk about all the time?
A place that didn't even belong to your family? Or do
you mean the fields with the mines? You want to
walk through those again, do you? Have your feet
blown from your legs? Or perhaps you want to go to
a place where the men who are meant to protect us
roam the countryside looking for women to rape and
then beat them into silence?'

A man in soiled painter's overalls, standing
smoking in the doorway of a bookmaker's shop,
whistled at them as they passed by. He waved a
handful of banknotes.

'Want to help me spend me winnings, do you,
girls? Come on, how about you, blondie? I've always
had a soft spot for blondes.'

They continued walking, but Ana looked at him
over her shoulder and pouted sexily.

'Another time, handsome; I cannot resist big,
strong men,' she said and, without a pause, carried on
speaking to Nahida. 'A few more months' work,
Nahida, that is all we need to do. Then we can go.
Together. Just as we've planned. And things aren't so
terrible here, are they? Until maybe they bring in new

130

girls, we have the room to ourselves, and our job is not so bad. Some of the girls have a terrible time over here. I was talking with a girl who works in another place for the Kesslers –'

'What girl?'

'It doesn't matter, just a girl. But what does matter, Nahida, what you have to understand is – we are lucky. The lucky ones who have a good life here.'

'I don't feel lucky. I feel bad. Bad inside me.'

'Shh, Nahida. Stop worrying. Close your eyes, and I will guide you along the street, while I tell you a story about the place where we will live, and all the things we will buy. The beautiful soft things we will wear, like the Englishwomen at the club, and the warm house we will have, and the car you will drive for us . . .'

'Open your eyes, Nahida,' hissed Ana, as she pushed the bell by the door of Diamond Dan's.

One of the Englishwomen's voices came over the intercom. 'Yes?'

'Ana and Nahida,' said Ana into the mesh of the speaker.

'About time and all,' said the woman, buzzing them in. 'We're bloody opening in ten minutes.'

They walked in and the Englishwoman threw up her hands.

'For Christ's sake, will you look at the state of your

hair? What did you use – Domestos? And look at the gob on that miserable mare of a mate of yours.'

'What is wrong with it?' Ana put a protective hand to the stiff bleached hair that had, only a couple of hours ago, been a deep, shiny black.

'I'm not even gonna waste my time trying to tell you if you don't know, and I suppose some of the punters might even like it, if the lights are dim. And I'm definitely not gonna waste my time telling her again either. She's either stupid or half deaf or both. But I'm warning you on her behalf, Ana, because perhaps you can get some sense through that thick head of hers. This is the last time. And if you don't explain, once and for all, to that dozy, sour-faced cow that she's got to smile and look pleasant – like she wants to have herself shagged half senseless by the punters – then she's out. And that means she's gonna wind up down the saunas or, worse, standing on a street corner down in Spitalfields. In fact, it might do her a bit of good if you take her for a little stroll down Commercial Street after work tonight. Let her have a look for herself what goes on down there.'

The woman stared for a long, challenging moment into Ana's eyes.

'And don't bother coming over all innocent with me, Ana; I know you've already found your way down there, doing your little deals – and don't bother looking at me like that either, like butter wouldn't fucking melt. I know everything about the staff in this place. Everything. But little Miss Muffet here, let's see what she makes of it when she sees what she could be doing – no, what she *will* be doing if she don't buck her bloody ideas up – and when she gets to clock the sort of customers she'll have to put up with on the street. Do you understand me? I want her so frightened of what might happen to her, she's gonna be up and down them stairs like a smiling fucking yo-yo.'

Ana nodded. 'Yes. I will explain.'

'Good, and I'll know if you've taken her there or not, cos I've got eyes everywhere, remember. By this time tomorrow I want this moaning mare to realise how lucky she is. Because – and I'll make this very, very clear – I'm one of the assistant managers in this place, and I'm not having that whining little tart driving the punters away and sending the takings down. I like this job and I intend keeping it. Okay?'

'Okay.'

'Good, now get out the back and get her tidied up.'

Ana dragged a now sniffling Nahida towards the women's lavatory that served as the girls' dressing room.

'Hang on.'

It was the Englishwoman again; she was striding towards them, finger poking at Nahida, words being spat at Ana.

'And I don't want her upsetting any of the other girls in there, all right? Now get her to blow her nose and stick her tits out. She might be prettier than most of you, but I mean it this time. I'll have the Kesslers sack her from the club in a fucking heartbeat, and be clapping my hands with fucking joy when let that lot down Commercial Street get their hands on her.'

She grabbed Nahida by the arm. 'And there's no point you even thinking you can run away.'

Her face was so close, Nahida could smell the mix of cigarette smoke and toothpaste on the woman's breath.

'Because you know what'll happen to Ana if you do try anything like that, don't you? She'll suffer like nothing she's even dreamed of. It'll make whoring in Commercial Street look like going to a fucking tea party.'

Then she let Nahida go, and paced over to the bar.

'Give me a drink,' she snapped at the bikini-clad girl who was flicking a duster over the optics. 'I knew this would happen. I told David all along – bring in these bloody foreigners and they'll cause trouble for all the rest of us.'

The girl didn't blink. 'What would you like?' she asked in a throaty Polish accent.

Chapter 25

'And that, spreading out in front of us, Lisa, is the Jalon Valley.'

As the Mercedes 4x4 crested the top of a small rise in the road, the view opened up before them.

Lisa put her hands on the dashboard and leaned forward, taking it all in. 'The scenery when we were driving down through those back roads in France was pretty, Jason, but this it truly beautiful.'

She opened her window and breathed in a deep lungful of air. 'These big blue skies and all the trees in blossom, the wild flowers in the orchards . . . It's almost impossible to believe it's not even the end of March.'

When Jason had called her last week, only the day after they'd gone into Diamond Dan's, telling her he'd booked them a break in Spain to celebrate her new life as a businesswoman, she hadn't known what to think. Part of her had resented his presumption – she hadn't even had the meeting with the Kesslers, let alone decided if she was going ahead with the idea – and she really wasn't used to being bossed around. But another part of her responded in a very different way. Jason was so unlike the men she usually went out with – and that could only be a good thing.

A very good thing.

She turned to face him with a smile. 'We should have come in my convertible, and enjoyed this wonderful weather.'

'That would've been nice, Lisa, but believe me, you're going to be glad we came in this brute of mine. The house is up a dirt road, nearly halfway up the foothills of those mountains.'

He indicated the general direction with a dip of his head.

'You're gonna love it, I just know you are.'

'I can't wait.'

'Not long now, but first we're gonna stop in a little village I know. It's only a couple of minutes' drive from here and we can get a few supplies. And I can phone Guillermo – that's the bloke who's lending it to us – to make sure he's had the cleaner in to air the place for us and find out where he told her to leave the keys.'

Lisa sighed happily as she felt the sun warming her skin. 'I didn't think I'd be saying this at this time of year, but I'm beginning to wish I'd brought my bikini.'

'That's no problem. There's plenty of nice little places to go shopping. We can go down to the coast. Javea's really nice. You'll like it there. It's a fishing village, but it's still got the old town up on the hill,

136

and there's a lovely beach. And there's a parador and a right friendly yacht club in the marina where we can go for a meal. Or we can go into Alicante, or Valencia maybe, if you want to do some serious shopping.' He winked at her. 'Let's face it, Lisa, we can do whatever we fancy. We've got seven whole days to enjoy ourselves – so, you name it and we can –'

'Oh Jason, I'm sorry to interrupt, but look.'

She pointed ahead, directing his view to the gully running alongside the road that divided the tarmac from the almond and orange groves. An elderly man, dressed in varying shades of brown and grey, was stretched out with his back propped against the sloping, grassy edge of the dip, his hat tipped over his face to shield him from the sun, and his wooden crook resting across his belly. He was surrounded by a herd of plump, shiny black and brown goats and their kids, all nibbling away at the lush greenery that, in a few short months, when the real heat descended, would be nothing more than a memory.

'I can't believe this place, it's like going back in time.'

Without thinking, Lisa put her hand on Jason's thigh, her eyes still fixed on the goatherd as they drove past him.

'Thank you so much for bringing me.'

Jason looked down at her hand. 'And thank you for coming.'

*

'I've travelled a lot, Jason,' said Lisa, pulling the plastic weave chair closer to one of the aluminium tables that stood outside the tiny bar in the far corner of the village square – the only place open at half three in the afternoon. 'But I have to admit that this is – and I don't want to sound shallow here – so real. On my usual holidays I top up my tan, eat food, drink drinks, change my clothes more times a day than anyone really needs to, and chat to people I don't much like. And that's it. But this, as I said, is so real. I didn't think this sort of Spain existed any more.'

'I'm glad you approve. Now, what do you want to do? We're going to have to wait for half an hour or so until the siesta's over and the shops open up again.'

'Coffee would be great.'

As Jason disappeared into the cavernous darkness of the bar, Lisa took off her sweater and settled back to look at the sun-baked square. In the centre, doves were gorging themselves with water from the pool beneath the gently splashing fountain. A colonial-style church, with a single, squat bell tower and white peeling stucco, dominated one side of the miniature *plaza major*; cloisters with shops, tightly shuttered against the already-to-be-avoided afternoon sunshine, lined two of the other sides – with the final part of the quadrangle being edged by a little playground: swings and a slide on a rough patch of sandy soil dotted with patches of tough, aggressively spiky, low-growing grass.

138

Lisa closed her eyes, let her head fall back and smiled contentedly.

She was so glad she'd decided to come.

Chapter 26

'Right, that's the shopping stowed.' Jason clunked down the back door of the 4x4. 'Now I've just got to make that call to Guillermo to sort out where he's left the keys for us, and then we can be on our way.'

'I'm so excited,' said Lisa, climbing into the passenger seat.

Jason, with one hand still on the open passenger door, checked his watch and then took his phone out of the back pocket of his jeans and studied the screen.

'Dammit, no signal. I'll have to have a wander around till I pick one up. Sorry about this, Lisa, but I promise I won't be more than two minutes, and I won't go anywhere I can't keep an eye on you.'

Lisa grinned. 'Do you think I'll drive off and leave you here?'

'No, I just don't want any of them old Spanish blokes wandering out of the bar and thinking they can chat you up.'

'How gallant.'

'That's me,' he called over his shoulder as he walked across the square towards the church, 'born bloody gentleman.'

*

Jason returned Lisa's cheery wave, as he spoke into the phone. 'I'm guessing from what you're saying, Guillermo, that you can't talk now.'

He narrowed his eyes, thinking.

'Tell you what, I'll get up to the house, and call you in about half an hour. How'd that be?'

He listened for a moment then turned off the phone and strolled back to Lisa.

'Well?' she asked shading her eyes with her hand.

'Everything's fine. I should have known he'd have everything sorted.'

He tossed the car keys into the air and snatched them into his fist. 'Time for you to see your home for the next seven days.'

'Well, I have to say, Jason, you have truly excelled yourself. This is absolutely beautiful.'

'Magic, eh?'

'That's the only word for it.'

Lisa stood with her hands on her hips staring at the old, honey-coloured *finca* that nestled in a riot of colourful flowers, shrubs and ancient, gnarled olive trees.

'Up until only a few years ago, this place was a complete ruin, an old farmhouse with nothing but feral cats and lizards living here, and weeds growing up through the floors. Guillermo made it his mission to have the whole place restored, stone by stone – exactly how it used to be. A real labour of love, it was.

141

It had been his family's home for generations, but when his old grandad died in the Civil War his granny lost the will to carry on and the family lost everything. Some of her kids went abroad and others went to live in the big towns and cities in other parts of Spain. Guillermo always swore that when he'd made enough money he'd do up the place. And now, look at it. His only regret is that the old girl never lived to see it.'

'That is such a lovely story, Jason. Sad but romantic. He must be a very special man.'

'He's that all right. Now I've got a surprise for you. The best part, I reckon. The pool. He keeps it heated right up until June.'

'So I really am going to be needing that bikini.'

'Go round the back and have a look, while I dig the keys out from their hidey-hole in that log pile.'

Jason waited for Lisa to disappear round the corner, listening to her footsteps on the flagged pathway getting further away, then he took a set of keys from his pocket and opened the front door.

'Right, that's you then, Lisa,' said Jason putting her bags in one of the bedrooms. 'I'll take myself outside by the pool with a beer, and enjoy the last of the sunshine, while you get your shower. Then I can either take you out for dinner, or if you'd prefer I can rustle up something for us to have here.'

'You can cook?'

'Course I can. What, did you think I was one of them useless gits who can't do anything?'

'You'd better not be,' she laughed, moving towards him, 'because I was going to ask you to help me have a shower.'

As they stood under the gushing water, exploring each other's bodies for the first time, Lisa was daring to think that not only did she desire this man, but that he really might be the one who would understand if she told him who she really was.

What Jason was thinking was something a little more prosaic: that this had been a bonus he hadn't been expecting – well, not quite so soon he hadn't.

But then again, posh birds always did like to think they were up for a bit of rough.

And he certainly wasn't going to start complaining.

Jason left Lisa in the bedroom to dry her hair and went outside to stand by the pool.

'Guillermo? It's me again.' Jason had his gaze fixed on the pathway that led back to the front of the *finca*. 'Can you speak now?'

'Yes.'

'Good. I've brought the motor over; it's all prepared and ready to go, soon as you give the word.'

'That is good, but you know I need to be sure. You've never done such a big deal, and I would not like to think you would disappoint me. You do have the money here with you, don't you? Because there is no possibility of me going ahead without it.'

'I told you; I'm funding this one myself. The credit-card cloning went like a dream, and I've got a whole stash of euros just waiting for you.'

'I do hope so.'

'There is one thing, mate.'

'What thing?'

'The bird . . . the woman who's gonna be driving the motor, she knows nothing about any of this, nothing at all, all right?'

Jason pressed the call-over button and took a long swig of beer. He just hoped that Guillermo came up with some gear he could do some serious chopping and cutting on – he really did need a massive return on this one, and then it was only going to be the start of getting him out of trouble.

Christ, he wanted to get out of having to go to work every sodding day.

And he'd got himself in so far over his head with Hoxton fucking Marcus that sometimes he could hardly breathe.

He could only thank fuck that Lisa was a spoilt brat who, as far as he could tell, really did know nothing about anything.

Chapter 27

Nahida sat up yet again. Usually she just collapsed into bed and fell into unconsciousness through exhaustion, but tonight, like the past few nights, she really couldn't sleep. But it wasn't the shouting of the drunks as they tumbled out on to the pavements from the illegal after-hours drinking clubs, or even the constant wailing of sirens as police cars sped past in the street below, that were disturbing her – it was the thought of those hollow-eyed girls in Commercial Street. The ones that Ana had taken her to see after work last week.

To Nahida, some of them had looked even younger than she did, as they stood in the street in their tiny outfits, waiting to give what she had learnt from Ana were called blow jobs – *was it really only a few weeks ago that Ana had explained to her what she had called the 'facts of life'?* – oral sex for any man who cared to stop his car beside her. No matter who he was or what he was: old, ugly, diseased, filthy . . . He, not the girl, had the power to decide what happened.

But it wasn't only the men and the girls' youth that had shocked Nahida; she had been stunned that they were not all foreign girls like her and Ana – only here because someone had *made* them come. And then, when Ana had spoken to one of them – one who did look foreign – it was clear that they knew one another. But how?

That Ana might have a life that Nahida knew nothing about scared her more than anything, adding to the uncertainty of this mad world she had found herself in.

The girl's skin was dark, much darker even than Nahida's. And she was bold like Ana, chatting away to them both as if they had all been friends for years. She looked as if she might be Indian – like some of the customers who came to the club – but she said she had been born in London, had pointed over her shoulder, *close by*, she'd said. Her family still lived there but she didn't speak to them any more.

It all seemed so wrong, so strange to Nahida, and even stranger when Ana spoke to the girl about another friend of theirs.

Who were all these new friends? Why had Ana never mentioned them before?

And then Ana wanted to know if their other friend had left something for her. The girl had said yes and had slipped something into Ana's hand and Ana had looked very happy.

Then a car had pulled up beside them, and Nahida couldn't understand why a policeman, or the girl's father or her mother allowed this to happen. This was right out on the street near the girl's home – where everyone could see. Why hadn't they stopped this going on? Why did no one come to rescue her? Why didn't they take her and keep her safe from the big, angry man who was shouting at the top of his voice for her to *stop yakking and get back to work*. Even if her family had rowed with her and they no longer spoke, how bad could their disagreement be for them to let her carry on doing this?

Then Nahida started thinking about herself and Ana.

She felt terrible having such selfish thoughts, but what chance did she and Ana have if they stayed in this place, when even local girls were being forced to do such things so close to their own homes, and still nobody cared?

Nahida threw back the bedclothes. This couldn't go on. She knew what she had to do; she had to persuade Ana that they must leave – the pair of them, together – as soon as possible. Right now. Not wait until they had saved money for the clothes and the home and the car that Ana spoke about whenever Nahida had any doubts.

If they left, everything would be okay. They would protect one another. And that would be enough for now. They could worry about buying and having things later, when they were safe. Away from here.

She would explain to Ana that they must leave before it got light, and then no one would realise for hours that they had gone. And no one would be able to find them.

'Ana. Ana, are you awake?'

No reply.

Nahida sighed. Ana had been looking so tired, perhaps it was best if she didn't disturb her until after she had washed and dressed herself and made them both some breakfast. That would be okay; they could still leave before daylight.

As quietly as she could, Nahida stepped on to the bare lino, padded across the room and opened the door to the landing.

She froze.

There was a strip of light visible under the kitchen door.

Someone was in there. Maybe the Englishwoman had sent someone to punish her for looking sad. Or perhaps it was someone who was foolish enough to think they had things to steal.

There *was* food in the cupboard, and even here in England there must be people who were hungry.

She backed into the bedroom and sat down gently on the edge of Ana's bed. She would have to rouse her carefully, warn her not to shout, let her know that someone had broken into the flat.

But the bed was empty.

Nahida clapped her hand over her mouth and threw back her head with relief.

Ana.

It was Ana in the kitchen.

She went back out on to the landing and pushed open the kitchen door with a broad smile on her face.

'Ana, I am going to make us some breakfast, and then I will tell you –'

Nahida stopped in mid sentence; she couldn't make sense of what she was seeing. Ana was sitting on the floor by the sink, with her back leaning against the damp and peeling wallpaper. Her head was drooping forward but, and this was the bit that really puzzled Nahida, she had a belt – the one she wore with her tiny, low-slung satin shorts – fastened around her arm. The end of the belt was between her teeth, and she was plunging a needle into the crook of her elbow. It was the type of needle that Nahida remembered the nurse at the clinic sticking into the top of her leg, while her mother held her on her lap and told her not to cry. It was good, her mother had said, it would stop her from becoming sick.

'Ana. What are you doing?'

Nahida knelt down on the floor beside her. 'Are you sick? Shall I ask the Englishwomen to call for a doctor?'

Ana raised her head. She was smiling. 'We are all sick,' she said, her expression and her voice oddly detached. 'This helps me forget it. You should try.'

She took a deep shuddering breath as she withdrew the syringe from her flesh.

'I liked the stuff a customer gave me once, but this

is cheaper, Nahida. Better. My friend, she will get it for you. You'll like it. It makes things easy.'

With that she closed her eyes and drifted away to somewhere Nahida couldn't reach.

Slowly, Nahida stood up and backed away from her, tears rolling down her cheeks, watching her last hope disappear in front of her eyes.

She just wasn't brave enough to do this without Ana.

Chapter 28

As Lisa looked out across the water to where the clear, bright blue of the sky met the milky turquoise of the Mediterranean, she wiped her fingers on a thin paper napkin. The restaurant was little more than a rough shack on the beach, with oilcloth-covered wooden tables and communal benches, and see-through plastic awnings to protect the diners from the still sometimes sharp late-March breezes. But the fish was as fresh as only a just-landed catch hauled in at the local harbour could be, the wine was chilled and the view was stunning. Lisa couldn't have been happier sitting in the grandest of rooms, dining on food cooked by a Michelin-starred chef – especially as she was with Jason.

'You look like you enjoyed that,' he said, gesturing for the waiter to bring them another bottle of wine.

'Who wouldn't?'

Jason shrugged. 'I don't know. A lot of people. Someone with no sense of adventure; someone who wouldn't be seen dead in a place like this.'

He flashed her a smile. 'With everything you're used to, all you've been brought up to expect, I'm really impressed you're not like that.'

She cocked her head to one side and looked at him. 'That is such a nice thing to say, Jason. It's like you've bothered to get to know the real me.'

She immediately looked away from him, concentrating on wiping her already clean fingers. *The real me.* Who was she kidding?

Jason took a taste from the new bottle of wine, as the young waiter hovered anxiously at his side – he might have been the cook's son on an afternoon off from his regular, low-season job at the canning factory, but he took great pride in the family business. And not only that, he had served Jason before, and knew him well as a big tipper, especially when he had someone with him, and particularly if that someone happened to be female.

Lisa watched as Jason nodded his approval. And in his face she saw not only his easy charm, but his decency – the way he could deal with anyone and everyone, and not judge them, but treat them according to how they behaved towards him – and in that moment, she decided that she knew she would be able to tell him the truth and that he wouldn't judge her.

And she *would* tell him – when the time was right.

Lisa relaxed and smiled her thanks as the waiter filled her glass, and then she stretched her legs out under the table, almost unable to believe that after all this time looking for someone she could trust, she had just bumped into Jason in Richard's office and that was that.

She sipped at her wine. Her mother had always said that's how it would happen – *when you least expect it* – and Sandy was usually right. With the life she'd led, she'd had to learn to be.

She took a bigger gulp of her drink. Christ, Sandy would go off her head if she found out about the Kesslers. But she'd decided, she was going to do it, going to go into business, be part of that world . . .

'You okay, Lis?'

'Yes. Fine. I just can't, you know, believe we've only been here for a couple of days.' She smiled. 'Thanks again for bringing me.'

She reached across the table and stroked his cheek.

He half rose in his seat, leaned forward and kissed her softly on the mouth.

'My pleasure, believe me.'

He sat back down and took out his cigarettes. 'Mind if I smoke?'

'Of course not.'

He took a moment opening the soft, European packet – screwing up the cellophane, tapping the box on the side of his hand, sparking his lighter, inhaling and then blowing out the plume of smoke.

Ritual over, he turned his gaze back to Lisa.

'Any ideas yet for your meeting with Dave and Paul next week?'

'A few.'

She looked away from him, sheltering her eyes with her hand as she followed the progress of a

153

windsurfer sailing by so gracefully, knowing from experience how hard it was, and what strength it took, to make anything in life look so apparently effortless.

Jason swallowed down a desire to shake her – it was okay for the likes of her not having to worry about the bloody future. But how about him? He had to get her on board. And had to do it soon.

'Do you really think you'd be able to go back to spending your time doing nothing? Wasting all that education? Setting up a business would be perfect for you.'

She laughed, dropping her hand from her eyes down on to her lap. 'And that's why I'm probably going to do it.'

She turned to face him; he was looking directly and steadily at her.

He reached out and took her hand, all his will urging her to see things his way.

'I tell you what I'm going to do, Lisa, I'm going to go with you when you see the Kesslers next week. You know what they say – two heads and all that.'

And give me more than a dog's chance of getting out of the fucking mess I've got myself into, and getting that cunt Marcus off my case.

Lisa was saved from having to answer him by the sound of his phone ringing – and she was glad. She was growing very fond of Jason, but she wasn't having any man – whoever he was – treating her as if she were a kid. And the last thing she wanted was to spoil things with a row.

'I knew I should have turned this bloody thing off,' he said, staring at the screen and then looking about him as if seeking strength. 'I just don't believe this.'

He stood up. 'It's only bloody work, innit? The senior sodding partner himself. Sorry about this, Lisa, but I'll have to answer it. But I'll be as quick as I can, okay.'

He strode off, waiting until he was out of earshot before turning to give Lisa a rueful little smile of reassuring apology, and then hissing into the mouthpiece: 'Okay, Guillermo, it looks like we might have lift-off, mate. I'll let you know for certain in about five minutes, but I reckon it's not gonna take long. If I play this right, you can collect the motor first thing tomorrow morning, and then the packing job can go ahead soon as you want. So, give me that five minutes, all right? And I'll get straight back to you.'

Chapter 29

Lisa frowned when she saw the expression on Jason's face as he walked back towards their table.

'Is everything all right? You look as if you've had some bad news.'

'You could say that,' he said, dropping down on to the bench across from her. 'I just do not believe that man.'

'Who?'

'The senior partner – or should I say the bastard?'

'He's the one you don't like, the one who makes you want to leave your job.'

'A bit of an understatement, but yeah, that's him, a real charmer.'

Jason waved his mobile at her.

'He's only gone and stuck a full three-line bloody whip on me. The arsehole. I mean, you'd think they could do without me for a week or so, wouldn't you? But no, not them. Do you know, Lisa, I sometimes think they reckon they bloody own me. Like I'm their property or something.'

'What did he say?'

'He's decided I've got to get back to London, to be at some meeting on Friday. And that I'll need to *prepare*. Do his bloody job more like.'

He slammed his phone down on the table and shook his head.

'I am bloody furious about this, Lisa, and, I'm really sorry, but we're going to have to leave here – tonight.'

'But, Jason . . .' Lisa held up her glass. 'We're well into the second bottle.'

He rubbed his hands over his face. 'Aw Christ, he's got me so wound up, I'm not even thinking straight. How can we go tonight when I've had a drink? I won't be able to drive until tomorrow morning at the earliest. What a screw-up. If only we'd flown over . . .'

'Well, why don't you fly back? Surely that would mean you could stay here at least a little longer.'

'Yeah, now that's an idea. If we went by plane we could leave it till . . . what, Wednesday morning?'

'And we could have three more days together here.'

'That is one tempting idea, Lisa.' He took her hand and kissed the palm. 'You don't know how much I want to say yes and spend those extra few days – and nights – with you.'

He tapped his knuckles on his teeth, thinking. 'In fact, I will say yes. Sod it. And sod them. We'll leave the motor here and I'll book us on the first flight out on Wednesday morning.'

'I won't even let you think about leaving it here;

you can't. I know how pushed you are for time, Jason, and it would be a complete nightmare for you trying to fit in coming back over here just to drive it back to London.'

She lifted her glass in salute. 'And that's why I'm going to drive it back for you.'

He pulled his chin back into his chest – the very picture of puzzled shock at such a thought. 'You take the motor back alone? No way. There is absolutely no way I'm gonna let you do that, Lisa.'

'I won't hear any argument. I'm driving it back for you, and that's final.'

'I can't believe you'd do that for me.'

'Why ever not?'

'Because I'm not used to that sort of thing.'

'What sort of thing?'

'Kindness.'

'Jason . . .'

'All my life I've expected the shitty end of the stick from people, and now you're offering to do this – for me.'

He gulped, visibly moved by her gesture. *That'll clinch it.*

'And I'm sorry for being so coarse, using that language, but I forget myself sometimes and it just comes out. It's, you know, how I was brought up.'

'Look, there's nothing to apologise for; let's just finalise plans.'

'No, Lisa, it's not that easy – I'm really going to have to think about this.'

'Jason, there's nothing to think about.'

She let go of his hand, reached across the table for the wine and topped up his glass.

'I am a fully grown woman, and I insist on doing this. For you. And I don't take no for an answer. You'll have to get used to the fact.'

He sighed loudly. 'All right, I'm almost convinced, but say –' a helpless wave of his hand – 'just say the motor broke down, and you got stranded in the middle of nowhere? I'd never forgive myself, Lisa. Never.'

'But the car's fine.'

'It might be all right now, but I'm not letting you take any chances. No, definitely not. You mean too much to me. Thank you, Lisa, thank you more than I can say, but I couldn't ask you to do that.'

She was beginning to feel just a little annoyed. 'Can't we have the thing checked over? There must be a local garage.'

'I suppose Guillermo must know where we can get a reliable service done.'

'Exactly. And think – three more whole days together . . .'

He blinked slowly, a man clearly in torment. 'That is hard to resist.'

'Impossible, I'd say.'

'Okay, you're on. I'll get hold of Guillermo and

ask him to take it to the best local garage there is. And then, when it's got a clean bill of health – and only then – I'll agree to you driving it back home. And we can enjoy our extra time together.'

Lisa smiled, clearly delighted to have got her own way.

'But you've got to realise, Lisa, I am gonna to be making this up to you – big time.'

He put his hand on his heart.

'It's gonna be Brighton or bust the first weekend we both get free, all right. That's a guarantee from me, girl, good as having it written down on paper – a heart-sworn contract.'

'Fool!'

'I must be, leaving you here when I've seen that bikini you've just bought. But honestly, Lisa, I am gonna pay you back for this, and I know exactly how. You're insisting on helping me, and I'm going to help you.'

'I'm intrigued.' She leaned towards him, resting her chin on her fist, one eyebrow raised. 'What can you be suggesting?'

'I've decided I'm definitely going with you to meet the Kesslers. Get that contract sewn up and get you on your way.'

He held up a finger and shook his head to silence her protests, but before she could even open her mouth, Jason had picked up his phone and was on his feet.

'And now, I'm going to call Guillermo – right this minute, before I panic and change my mind. Get him to pick up the motor from the *finca* first thing in the morning and get it in the garage. Because there is no way I'm going to miss having three more days alone with you, darling.'

Lisa watched him as he walked up and down the water's edge, speaking into his phone.

She'd never let a man speak to her like this before, but then she had never known anyone like Jason before.

Perhaps it was time to admit that what she felt for him was something rather more than fondness.

Still following him with her eyes, Lisa took her own mobile out of her bag, checked for a signal and then pressed a speed-dial number.

'Mum?'

'Hello, love.'

'I just wanted to let you know that I'm in Spain.'

'How lovely. What's the weather like? It's peeing down in London.'

'Couldn't be better. I'm sitting in a little restaurant on the beach. We've just had a fantastic meal –'

'We?'

'I'm here with a friend – Jason.'

'A special friend?'

'Might be.'

'Well, you'd better tell me all about him.'

Jason began walking back towards her.

'Mum, I have to go now, but I'll be back in a few days. I'll come and see you then, okay.'

Sandy laughed. 'Good, I'll make you a proper cup of tea with decent milk instead of that long-life stuff they have over there, and you can tell me all your news.'

Chapter 30

'Will it be okay if we get out here?' asked Lisa, as the taxi bringing them back from the beach restaurant turned off the tarmac road and started to make its way along the rough, stony driveway. 'It's such a lovely afternoon, I'd love to walk back up to the house through the almond groves.'

'That's a great idea.'

Jason paid the driver and took her shopping bags out of the boot – bikini, sun hat, factor 15 – while Lisa slipped off her shoes. Then they made their way up through the sweet-smelling, blossom-heavy trees towards the *finca*.

When they were well away from the main road, but still a few hundred yards from where the orchards merged into the gardens, Lisa stopped and turned to him.

'Put the bags down, will you, Jason?'

'Are you okay?'

Christ, don't let her get sick now; she had to drive that fucking motor back to London.

'You're not feeling unwell or nothing, are you? Shellfish can do that to you sometimes, you know.

Make you feel a bit queasy. I've got some stomach pills back in the house.'

'No, stop worrying, I'm not unwell. In fact, I've not felt better in a very, very long time.'

She moved closer to him, reached out and slowly began undoing the buttons of his shirt.

They stood there under the trees, holding one another's gaze, and then he pulled her towards him, and breathed into her ear.

'Lisa, you don't know how sorry I am, having to go back without you.'

She took his face in her hands and kissed him, dragging him down on top of her as she sunk into the carpet of warm grass and wild flowers, breathing in his scent, thinking how wonderful her life was, and that – maybe – this time she really had found the man she could share her life with, the one with whom she might eventually be able to share the truth with. The truth about who and what she was, the real person – Lisa O'Donnell – not the Lisa Taylor that Richard had invented all those years ago to protect her.

Chapter 31

Nahida lay there silently in the booth with the man pumping away on top of her. He was not that old or even particularly ugly, but still he sickened her; he was using her as if she were nothing more than an object to satisfy his needs.

There were some things that Nahida knew without any doubt: she knew that she would never understand how someone could treat another human being in this way; she knew she would never get used to having sex with the customers – whoever or whatever they were – and that if the Englishwomen hadn't threatened her with the saunas and the streets she would never have done it at all; and she knew that she would never ever do what Ana had told her to do – act as if she liked doing it just to get more money or drugs from the men who did this to her.

It wasn't that she wouldn't be like Ana, it was more the fact that she couldn't be like her. Sometimes, lately, Nahida had begun to wonder if that was a good or a bad thing.

Now the man was digging his fingers into her shoulders as he nuzzled hard at her breasts, grunting and moaning as he neared satisfaction, while Nahida stared past him into the middle distance, seeing nothing but a tear-blurred kaleidoscope of colours around the light fitment and feeling nothing but loneliness and the man's weight pushing her down into the mattress – the mattress that she had been pushed down into three times already that same evening.

With a final groan the man shoved himself into her even harder and came to a shuddering climax.

Without a word to Nahida, he rolled off her, swung his legs around and sat on the edge of the bed. Then, with brisk efficiency, he set about removing his condom, stood up and dropped it on the floor with a contemptuous sneer thrown in her direction. He then sloped off to the adjacent lavatory to clean himself.

Nahida lay there, without moving, wishing time and her life away.

She heard one of the Englishwomen talking to the man.

'You don't look very happy. Was everything all right for you?'

'Depends what you mean by all right?'

'You know.' The woman's voice was flirtatious, cajoling. 'We always like to make sure that new customers have a good time and enjoy themselves.'

There was a pause and Nahida imagined the woman putting her head on one side, lowering her lashes and slowly licking her lips – just as she always did when she was talking to customers.

'Because we think that word of' – suggestive

166

pause – '*mouth* is everything in this business,' the woman went on.

'Well, if you must know, no, everything's not all right. It's not all right by a long chalk. That little prick-tease in there was dancing around downstairs, flashing off her body, rubbing her hands over her tits and her arse, but then, when I brought her up here, it was like she'd turned the fucking lights off.'

'How do you mean exactly?' The woman now sounded concerned, professional.

'To put it bluntly, darling, it was like poling a dead fish, and I want my money back. And I'm sure you'll be more than willing to oblige when I say that I'm on the job.'

The Englishwoman drew in a sharp breath. He was a bloody copper. Why hadn't anyone downstairs warned her?

'No question, sir, and maybe we can offer you a drink on the house.'

'I'll be wanting a bloody sight more than that, sweetheart.'

He zipped his fly.

'Now, I am going back downstairs, and you can arrange for me to have several drinks sent over – large ones – and then, when I'm ready, you can show me personally what this club is supposed to offer. And I mean personally. You might have a few more miles on the clock than that one in there, but at least you look like you're up for it.'

The Englishwoman said something that Nahida couldn't hear and then caught the man mumbling a grudging agreement.

The next thing she knew was that the English-woman was in the private booth, standing over her as she lay on the bed; the woman was gripping her arm so tightly that Nahida thought she might break it.

'Don't you dare start snivelling,' growled the woman, digging her nails into Nahida's bare flesh, 'because I have just about had it with you. That customer is upset, very upset. And you had better realise that so am I, because now I've got to get my kit off and fuck the bastard. And I am telling you, you miserable-looking twat, that if the Kesslers hadn't paid good money for you, and gone to the trouble of getting you over here, you and your mate'd be right out of here on your scraggy, foreign arses. But I'm warning you, you useless piece of shit, that if you don't start doing as you're told, I have got some very nasty surprises I just can't wait to pull on you. Surprises that won't just make you cry, they'll make you wish you'd never left whatever godforsaken hole you came from in the first place. Do you understand me?'

Chapter 32

Lisa sighed as she rested her head on Jason's bare chest, and watched the morning sun streaming in through the slats of the wooden louvred blinds, casting diagonal patterns across their naked bodies.

'It doesn't seem right you going home alone, Jason. Not when you could be here in bed with me.'

'Don't, it's bad enough leaving you here without torturing ourselves.'

He ran his hand over her back, drawing her even closer; he'd been surprised by just how good the sex had been, and part of him actually meant it when he said he was sorry to go, but he had to do this right, be disciplined. This was the long-term plan to get him out of the crap he was in with that fucker Marcus, and the chance to chuck in his job. This was business, not a bit of fun. He could get fun any time and any place he wanted.

'Jason.'

'Mmm?'

'You know you said that Guillermo is bringing the car back tomorrow afternoon?'

'That's right, yeah.'

'Well, can't you phone him, tell him to bring it

back earlier? Then I can drive you to the airport in the morning, and we can have another few hours together.'

'Don't think I haven't been selfish and thought about that myself, Lisa, but you have got to put that out of your mind, okay. You mustn't even think about it.'

He touched his lips to the top of her head. *Like he was going to risk getting stopped by the Spanish police in that thing.*

'The airport's not only in the wrong direction for you to get on the motorway home, but it'll mean you getting up really early, and I'm not having you driving while you're tired. I want you to take your time, because I want you to drive safely. You see, I'm not going to risk anything happening to you, Lisa, not ever, do you understand? You mean too much to me. And just think – you can enjoy the sun for another few hours. Relax by the pool, while you're waiting for Guillermo, then, like I say, you can drive home safely, not knackered from getting up at dawn. That's what I want you to do, Lisa – for me – be safe.'

'But –'

'I won't hear another word, all right. I'll be fine. I've got the cab booked and, if this last day we've got together here goes the way I've planned, you're going to need to sleep in in the morning – to get your strength back.'

He bent his head and kissed her on the mouth,

easing her body around until she was astride him.

'And,' he said, running a finger playfully down her nose and tapping it on the tip. 'I want you to spend that drive back thinking about when I take you to see the Kesslers. Use that brain of yours, think about what sort of a deal you want off them, and what you should put in a proper contract and everything. You know, the sort of things you'll have to get straight. Cos I'm really excited about this Lisa, it'll be a blinding chance for you. Blinding. And me helping it happen, well, that'll the icing on the cake for me – the perfect way for me to thank you.'

She smiled slyly. 'Whatever have you got to thank me for?'

'Do you really need to ask?' He ran his hands down her throat, her chest, and on to her breasts. 'This time together has been really special, because you're really special to me – do you know that, Lisa?'

'Am I, Jason? Am I really?'

'Let me show you.'

He slipped himself inside her and took hold of her by the hips making her throw back her head and gasp with pleasure.

As their bodies rocked and bucked, and Lisa moaned with desire and love for this man, Jason's mind whirred with plans about drugs and distribution and clubs and control of the doors – all without losing his rhythm for one single moment.

It was all going to work out; he was going to be a

player again, and he would get that bastard in Hoxton off his case once and for all.

And he really couldn't think of anything that would make him happier.

Chapter 33

Sandy stood in the doorway of her house watching her daughter lock the four-wheel drive she had just parked on the road outside.

'Hello, Mum.' Lisa ran up the steps and kissed Sandy on the cheek. 'How are you? You look well. Lovely haircut.'

'Hello, love. You're full of the joys. Treated yourself to a new car, have you?'

Lisa smiled happily.

'No. It belongs to a friend of mine. The one I went with to Spain.'

'Does it now?'

Sandy closed the door and Lisa followed her along the hallway to the bright, glass-roofed modern kitchen that ran the whole width of the back of the house.

'I've brought you some olive oil back from Spain. We got it in this beautiful little village.'

We got it? That sounded good.

'That's smashing, love, thank you.'

Sandy went over to the sink and filled the kettle. 'I thought you sounded full of the joys when you called me. But just look at you.'

She turned to face her daughter who, still smiling, was sitting on a stool at the central island unit, leaning on her elbows, with her chin cupped in her hands.

'You look so happy.'

'I am, Mum. Really happy.'

'This friend of yours, it wouldn't be serious, would it?'

'Who knows . . .'

'Really?'

Even a 'who knows' was more than Sandy usually dared hope for.

'But don't let yourself get too excited, Mum. I don't want to rush things, because I don't want to mess this up.'

Sandy didn't say so, but that sounded even more promising.

'And anyway,' Lisa went on, 'I've got other things on my mind for now. I'm thinking about setting up a business. I'm so excited about it. I got home at ten this morning and sat straight down at the computer and worked for five hours flat out getting a plan down on paper.'

'That's excellent, love.' She opened a tin and put it in front of her daughter. 'Biscuit?'

'No thanks, I'm taking care of my figure.'

'So he's a special fella then.'

'Can we talk about that later, Mum? What I really want to know right now is whether you think Richard might be prepared to flick through the plan, you know, give me a bit of advice, even though it would only be a small sort of venture?'

'Of course he would. Not only does he care about you – like a daughter, as if I need to repeat that point – but the money we've paid his firm over the years, he'd feel obliged to advise you even if you were starting a paper round.' She laughed. 'And please tell me it's not a paper round you're planning on starting.'

Lisa suddenly found something fascinating to stare at, deep in her teacup. 'Don't be silly, Mum. Anyway, I'm not really sure what sort of business I'm interested in yet.'

Sandy shook her head. 'Doesn't really matter – if you do it right, you can be in any sort of game. Business is business.'

'How about the businesses Dad's family used to be in?'

This time it was Sandy who looked uncomfortable. 'They were in scrap one minute, cabs the next . . .'

'How about the rest of it?'

'You'll hardly be following in that particular O'Donnell tradition, now will you? But I'm glad you're thinking about doing this, Lisa, it'll make use of all that studying you did. But you go along and have a chat with Richard first. He's the one to give you proper advice.'

Chapter 34

Lisa sat in Jason's car, calling her goodbyes to Sandy.

'See you soon, Mum. And I'll phone and let you know what Richard had to say.'

'Good girl. We can have lunch to celebrate and you can tell me all about this new friend of yours.'

'You don't give up, do you?' laughed Lisa.

'Never. I can't wait to get one of them trendy three-wheeled baby buggies.'

As soon as Sandy had closed the front door, Lisa took out her mobile. She made a quick call to Richard's assistant to make an appointment, and then took a breath and dialled Jason.

'Hello, you,' she said. 'I'm back. Now tell me how much you missed me?'

Fuck. 'Lisa? When did you get back?'

'About six hours ago.'

He could feel the blood pulsing in his ears. He took a breath. 'Where's the motor?'

She laughed. 'Don't worry, I haven't broken it.'

'No, course you haven't.'

Come on, you dozy cow, where is it?

'So where are you now then?'

'Right now?'

'Yes.' He was feeling fit to strangle the silly bitch.

'I'm parked outside Mum's; I came over to give her the present we bought her. She really liked it. And she is very curious about you. You'll have to come over and meet her, let her see how handsome you are.'

'Yeah, we'll have to do that.'

Jesus, all that fucking charlie packed in the motor and it was just sitting there – out in the street in broad fucking daylight.

'And I've got some good news.'

'Aw yeah?'

What the hell was she on about now? He could barely control his voice as his breathing came fast and shallow, and what was she doing – yammering on about good news? Surely she hadn't lied about being on the pill? No, course not. Much too soon to know even if she had lied. He was just panicking.

'I spent the time driving back working out what I want in a contract, what I'm going to put forward at this meeting with the Kesslers. And I think it's pretty impressive. I'm sure they'll go for it.'

Thank Christ for that.

'That's brilliant, Lisa.'

If she'd have been there, he'd have kissed her for that at least. It was going to be as good as having his own stable of door bitches. And that meant that he'd have his guaranteed route for knocking out all the cheapest over-cut gear he could get his hands on. A

177

regular run of motors coming over from Spain packed with coke and he'd be out of trouble in no time, all debts paid, well back in profit, and back where he should be – on top of the fucking world.

But he had to get that motor off the street.

'I'm going to speak to Richard first. Check with him that what I've got to say will come over as professional.'

Shit. 'Right.'

'In fact, I'm going there now. Then, if you like, you can meet me at the Kesslers' – Diamond Dan's at eight o'clock?'

'Please, Lisa, drive the motor round to my flat now. I'll shoot home right away and meet you there.'

She could feel the flush creeping upwards from her throat.

'You sound very keen to see me, Jason. Are you having wicked thoughts?'

'Too right I am. You wouldn't believe how much I've missed you.'

'Easy, tiger, I've already called Richard and he's expecting me in twenty minutes. But then I'll drive straight over to yours – I promise. I should be there by what, six? Then we can unpack your suitcase for you, and spend a bit of, you know, *quality* time together before we go to the Kesslers'.'

'Yes, but –'

'Sorry, Jason, I've got to go, Richard's breaking into a meeting just to see me.'

'But –'

'You'll have to be patient. I'll be over to yours by six.'

'Lisa!'

He stared at the screen on his mobile.

She'd ended the fucking call.

It was too late. She was on her way. Jason stabbed the speed-dial button.

'You've got to reassure her, Richard, tell her she's going to do just great. No question. And you've got to tell her fast. She's got to get over to me as soon as possible. Have you got that? *As soon as possible.*'

Richard shuddered at the horrible sensation as cold sweat trickled slowly down his spine. No one else but her mother knew that Lisa was an O'Donnell. And God alone knew what would happen if someone did uncover her true identity. Worse still, if they were to link her to her family's history with the Kesslers.

The feuds, the violence, the deaths . . .

My God, he had to put a stop to this.

Now.

'I can't do that, Jason. And, while we're at it, I don't think it's a good idea for you to see her again.'

'Don't you? And do you know what, Richard, I don't think it'd be a good idea if all your posh clients got told how you're such a fucked-up, sad-arsed, cokehead. And let's face it, mate, when your old woman finds out the things you've done for me to get

hold of the stuff – and believe me, she will – I can't
see her darling daddy letting you stay on in the family
firm, can you?'

'You wouldn't.'

'Don't be fucking stupid, Richard.'

Call over.

Richard closed his eyes, as he tasted the bile rising
in his throat.

How the hell was he going to stop Lisa seeing
Jason Carter without everything blowing up in his
face?

Chapter 35

Lisa thanked Richard's assistant as she showed her through to his office.

'I'm so grateful you agreed to see me at such short notice, Richard. And coming out of your meeting really was very kind of you, but this couldn't wait. Everything's moving so quickly. And Mum agreed that it was a good idea to show you the plan – just to make sure it hasn't got any howlers in it.'

Richard was confused. Surely Sandy didn't know about this? He'd spent the last twenty minutes racking his brains to think how he'd be able to keep her from finding out that her daughter was even contemplating having anything to do with the Kesslers.

'And what would that plan be exactly, Lisa?'

'My business plan.'

'I see.' He'd keep his words non-committal; let her do the talking, so he could try to understand exactly what was going on here.

'You seem shocked.'

'No, of course I'm not.'

Her eyes narrowed. She'd thought better of Richard.

'Yes you are. You don't think I'm up to it. You don't think that I could run a business like normal people who haven't spent their lives being protected from the real world.'

'No, Lisa, believe me, I never thought anything of the sort. I saw all those years of study, and how hard you worked. I'm sure you'd do really well.'

'Good, I'm relieved. Because I can't tell you how upset I'd be if I thought that was the case.'

Lisa looked at him. Richard had always been so kind to her, so sensible, such a nice man – if congenitally overcautious. He'd go completely crazy if he knew about the Kesslers' involvement in all this, especially after all the trouble and effort he had gone to over the years to keep her away from that world – their world, the world that had finished off her father.

He'd possibly go even crazier than her mother would if she found out.

So what the hell did she think she doing?

She sat up straight. *Come on, Lisa.* The plan wasn't to become a bloody gangster.

'This new venture . . .' She put down a copy of the business plan she'd put together. 'It's with friends of Jason's, and –'

'While we're talking about Jason Carter, Lisa, I must say I'm rather surprised by how well you're getting on with him.'

182

'So this is what this is all about – the coolness, the distance.'

'I don't know what you mean.'

'Really?'

'Look, Lisa, I just wouldn't have thought he was your sort, that's all.'

'You're not being a snob, are you? Not judging him because of where he comes from and the way he speaks?'

'Of course not. I'm just being overprotective as usual. Old habits, you know.'

'I'm glad about that, Richard, because I'm very fond of him.'

Richard stood up and walked over to the rosewood table that stood to one side of his big partner's desk. This was all far worse than he'd thought.

'Do you fancy a drink?'

'Don't you have to get back to your meeting?'

'No, come on, let's call it a celebration.'

Lisa frowned; he looked anything but celebratory. Surely Richard didn't know she was about to get herself involved with the Kesslers? No, that was ridiculous. How would he? She was being paranoid.

That was the trouble with being an O'Donnell: it left you not trusting anyone.

And that was also why she was so enthusiastic about all this. At long last she had found a man she knew she could trust – Jason. A man she was sure, when the time came, would not reject her when she told him the truth about herself. A man Sandy would adore, and would be more than happy to call her son-in-law, knowing that he would never do anything to hurt her daughter.

Chapter 36

David Kessler was clearly more impressed with the prospect of this woman supplying and organising the 'female door staff' – as she insisted on calling the door bitches – for their clubs than was his brother Paul.

Paul couldn't believe his brother was really contemplating having this total stranger – this friend of bloody Jason Carter's, of all people, this *Lisa Taylor* – running the doors. From what she'd said about her business experience it seemed to him that she barely knew her arse from her elbow, let alone how to run a door.

But he hadn't said too much during the meeting – other than bluntly pointing out the woman's obvious lack of experience – because arguing with your family in front of people wasn't what you did. And anyway, David was saying more than enough for the two of them.

He was offering her all sorts, even suggesting putting the two deputy managers from Diamond Dan's at her disposal.

Was he mad? They were their two most experienced girls, the ones who had been trusted to escort the merchandise over from France, and, even though they no longer danced, they'd been given proper, important, supervisory roles. And their time was all more than accounted for as it was, so if they were going to be sidelined nursemaiding this posh tart through her job, then who was supposed to do their work for them?

There was no way Paul was going to get involved in it, and he knew for a fact that David would go among the missing if there was even a sniff of extra stuff that had to be done – especially now they were about to oversee the opening of the new casino.

But he shouldn't have been surprised, that was his big brother David all over. For a start he only had to fancy a bit of skirt and he promised her the world. But there was a lot more to it this time. Over the years, they'd been a bit lazy about advertising or actively seeking members, and had just been more than happy when Jason Carter, a big spender himself, had brought in the punters – rich punters and plenty of them, everyone from City boys to footballers, bent law to lawyers. He seemed to know everyone, he was that sort of bloke. Trouble was, David now realised that he couldn't risk putting the bastard's nose out of joint – not yet anyway. He was a nasty little fucker who wouldn't think twice about coming up with some new gaff and persuading the punters to go there. Then the profits would take a dive until they went through the fag of getting a new list of members built up –

leaving way too much time for the old man to stick his beak in to find out what was going on.

So, for now, until they got the casino up and running and found a bit of time to get the membership sorted out, David had to keep Jason Carter sweet – and if this new tart of his wanted to have this contract . . .

Reluctant as he would have been to say so, deep down Paul knew that he had to agree with his brother – the brother who was now reaching out and shaking Lisa Taylor's hand.

'Good, we go ahead on that basis then,' said David. 'You set about getting your staff together – a regular core of at least a dozen should be your aim for now – then I can see how they operate in a few of the nightclubs and, maybe later, if all goes well, we can try them out in the other clubs and, who knows, maybe even in the new casino we're opening in a couple of weeks. It's –'

'You're opening the casino that soon?' Jason butted in, excited at the thought of all those new, money-rich tossers gagging for his goods.

'Yes,' snapped David, annoyed by the interruption. 'And you'll need a good few back-ups and all, Lisa, in case some of them lose their bottle and chuck it in, or if their kids get the bellyache and they phone in five minutes before opening time and let you down.'

He puffed at his cigar then examined its glowing tip.

'Experience'll teach you that they do that. Bloody nightmare, some of them.'

Lisa nodded, indicating that she understood, but, in truth, she was getting a bit pissed off with David Kessler. In her estimation she was probably twice as clever as he'd ever be, and yet he was speaking to her as if she were a child.

Why was she even bothering with this? She didn't need this hassle.

Paul saw the look of doubt shadow her face.

'Are you sure you're up to this, love?' he asked, surprising them all.

'Course she is,' said Jason.

'Thanks for your support, Jason,' said Lisa, perhaps more sharply than she'd intended, but now furious at Paul's condescension, 'but I am more than capable of speaking for myself. And I do understand how to run a business, Mr Kessler, and in my opinion, the nature of the business doesn't really matter. As people even wiser than you have said – business is business. And I don't see why this should differ from any other.'

Lisa stood up, ready to take her leave. No one spoke to her like that. 'But it seems I'm wasting my time here.'

And yet she so wanted to show these men she could do this.

What was she going to do?

David and Jason were now also on their feet,

standing on either side of her as if they were guarding her.

'You're not wasting your time, Lisa.' Jason had too much riding on this for him to let her walk out now.

And David wasn't about to have his little brother start questioning his judgement – not in fucking public, he wasn't.

'Let's all sit down, shall we?' David said, glaring at his brother. 'And just calm ourselves. Discuss this like adults rather than shouting over one another like a bunch of kids.'

'I never shouted at anyone.'

'*Paul.*'

David was ready to blow.

'Please, mate. Just sit down, will you?'

Chapter 37

Ana wandered into the club, with Nahida in tow, only just in time for their evening session, but for once the Englishwomen weren't waiting ready to pounce on them.

Ana was relieved to see that they were too busy simpering around the Kesslers, who were themselves busy talking to the blond-haired regular – Jason, that was his name – and a pretty, well-dressed, woman with silky fair hair.

Ana slipped by as inconspicuously as she could, not fancying being spotted and having yet another reprimand from the women for being late; being told off was becoming almost a regular event since getting out of bed had become more and more difficult.

Nahida, on the other hand, slowed down as she heard one of the Kesslers introducing the fair-haired woman – Lisa Taylor, he called her – to the two Englishwomen.

Nahida could just make out the gist of what he was saying; it was something about her taking on a business contract, and that she would be running something to do with the club.

Nahida looked at Lisa Taylor; she was not only

lovely to look at, she must be smart too.

Then, when the woman – Lisa Taylor – answered him, Nahida was mesmerised; her voice was so soft – not harsh and bullying like the two Englishwomen's.

At that moment, one of the Englishwomen turned her head to cough into her hand. When she saw Nahida standing there behind her and still in her outdoor coat, her eyes widened in fury.

Nahida was sure she was going to strike her and dodged sideways out of her reach – *knocking Lisa Taylor's drink all over her beautiful clothes.*

'I am sorry,' she managed to say before bursting into tears.

'You stupid cow!' snapped one of the English-women.

'No, leave her,' said Lisa taking the handkerchief Jason handed to her. She dabbed at her sleeve. 'It's okay, really. It's only white wine.'

Nahida couldn't believe her kindness. She reached out to touch her hand.

But that was as far as she got.

Caught up in her reverie of being saved, Nahida didn't notice the Englishwoman who had shouted at her, making a grab for her.

Gripping Nahida by the arm she marched her roughly over to the lavatories.

'Why is it always you, you lazy slut? Have you any idea how much that outfit must have cost her?' She spat the words into Nahida's ear. 'You're really going to regret this. Remember what I said? No more chances. I'm gonna pay you back fucking big time.'

For once, Nahida didn't care about her threats. The spark of hope that Ana had extinguished so cruelly had risen again in her chest.

Nahida had a new plan.

She would wait until the Englishwomen weren't watching and go to Lisa Taylor and ask for her help. She was sure she would say yes. And then she would be able to leave and find her way home – back to the tumbledown farm. And she would repair it with her own hands and make it a proper home for herself, and she would live there all alone – with no one touching her or making her do things she didn't want to. And she would grow vegetables and fruit, and keep hens, just the way her grandfather had shown her. Maybe even cast out lines for the fat oily fish that he used to grill on sticks held over the embers of the fire.

Everything would be okay. She knew it now.

When the Englishwoman rejoined the Kesslers and the others she painted on a smile, directing it at Lisa.

'Sorry about that, you try to keep these girls in line but there's always one who'll take liberties. Now can I help mopping up your dress?'

'No, don't worry about it. I just hope she wasn't too upset.'

Too upset? The woman wondered if this snooty bloody tart – who seemed to have totally pulled the wool over David's eyes – was capable of handling even herself let alone a stable of streetwise door bitches. She very much doubted it. She'd met her sort before, getting their cheap thrills from slumming it.

'If you're sure.'

Despite her smile, David recognised the animosity in the woman's voice. It was typical; just because he'd screwed her a few times she thought she owned him, and now she didn't like the attention he was paying Lisa.

Now it was his turn to conjure up a smile for public consumption.

'Why don't you lot go over to the bar and get another drink? I just want to clear up a few things, a few business details, with Lisa, then we'll come over and join you.'

Before anyone could utter a word of dissent, Jason had his hand clapped matily over Paul's shoulder, and was jerking his head in the direction of the bar, winking encouragement at the two Englishwomen, steering them forward, leaving David to close the deal with Lisa.

David watched Jason settle the somewhat reluctant group at the bar and then offered Lisa more wine.

'No thanks, I won't, not at the moment.'

She flicked her hair back over her shoulder and watched him puffing on the ludicrously fat cigar. She was becoming agitated; it was if he was playing with her, flirting as if they were on a date rather than coming to a business arrangement.

'You said you wanted to clear up a few things.'

'Yeah.' He dropped his head back and blew smoke into the air through the corner of his mouth. 'You and blond Jason.'

'What about us?'

'I'm curious. Wouldn't have thought he was your sort.'

'And I wouldn't have thought you'd be a snob.'

Lisa glanced over to the bar. Paul had disappeared, but Jason was there with the two women. He was laughing infectiously, the women now at ease and relaxed in his company. He was a popular, funny, laid-back, great-looking Jack the Lad, happy and content to be on his home ground, but he was no fool. His job alone proved that.

And perhaps if more people knew her real background they wouldn't be quite so surprised by her choice of lover.

'In fact, Mr Kessler,' she said, looking at him down her nose, 'the views I'm being offered on my friendship with Jason are beginning to irritate me. It's the second time I've had that reaction in a single day.'

'Come on, darling, it's not that I'm being a snob, believe me.'

'No? You could have fooled me.'

'Tell me, how well do you know Jason exactly?'

'Without wishing to be rude, I really do think that

194

that is my business. Now, shall we join him, or is there something else you'd like to say? Something else you might prefer Jason not to hear, perhaps?'

'No, you're all right.'

Lisa couldn't be sure, but she probably wouldn't have argued with anyone who suggested that there was a hint of mockery as David Kessler smiled at her.

Chapter 38

'This is so good of you, Jason, helping me like this.'

Lisa gripped the arms of the desk chair and swivelled from side to side, taking in the transformation of her spare bedroom into a very professional-looking workplace.

'This is brilliant. A proper office.'

'Delighted to have been of help, ma'am.'

Jason saluted her smartly and then tossed the screwdriver he'd been using to assemble the shelving units back into his toolbox.

'You really are full of surprises. So many talents.'

'Just a pity I spend so much time at work, and that I don't get the chance to use my DIY skills more often.'

Lisa stood up and put her arms around his neck.

'Do you know, there's something irresistible about a man in a pair of paint-spattered jeans and a tight white T-shirt?'

'Careful, you'll get filthy.'

'That's precisely what I was hoping,' she said, pulling her sweater over her head. 'But we'd better get you showered first, hadn't we?'

Jason grinned as he followed her into the bath-room.

'Have to be quick with the loofah though, Lis, the first of the girls is gonna be here in an hour.'

Lisa turned to face him; she was now wearing only her underwear.

'I think that'll be long enough,' she said, unhooking her bra and letting it fall to the floor.

'Right,' said Lisa.

She was facing the fifth applicant that Jason had shown through to her new office.

'Your CV is excellent, as are your references. And you know the terms.'

'Yeah, very fair,' said the striking-looking redhead. 'And you say it's definitely all above board – registered, and tax and insurance paid and everything?'

'Absolutely.'

'That's great, a real relief; I got myself into a right fix at my last gig. Had the social after me and everything. You know how it is, worrying you'll get investigated, and that they'll wind up sending the bloody welfare do-gooders round to see if you're looking after the kids.'

'You won't have to worry about anything like that if you're working for me. But there is one thing I'd like to raise before we go any further. How would you feel about doing door work at, say, a lap-dancing club?'

'No problem at all. Matter of fact, I used to do a bit of pole dancing myself, but I couldn't be doing with all that having to keep my body in shape all the time. Not after my second kid.'

'You look in pretty good shape to me,' said Jason pleasantly.

'Nice of you to say so, but I'm not exactly in the condition you need for that type of work.'

'Right, thank you, Ms . . .' Lisa looked at the CV. 'Bryant. I'll call you sometime tomorrow morning to let you know my decision.'

'Oh, okay then.' The redhead stood up. 'I must have misunderstood. I thought you said you'd tell me if I had the job today.'

'More applicants than I expected,' said Lisa without looking at her.

'Fine. Thanks for your time. I'll look forward to hearing from you.'

After letting the woman out of the flat, Jason wandered back to the office. He stood in the doorway, leaning on the jamb, arms folded, forehead creased in a frown.

'I was surprised you didn't snap that one up right away – martial arts, trained first-aider; bright as anything – she had the lot. Why wait till tomorrow?'

'You were a long time seeing her out,' said Lisa apparently distracted as she shuffled through the pile of applications. 'Was there a problem? I could hear you both talking out there.'

'Just being friendly. I've talked to all the girls who've been here today.'

'Really?' Still she didn't look up. 'I didn't notice you showing quite so much interest in any of the others.'

'Aw, I see what's going on here.'

Jason walked across the room, edging round to the back of her chair. He reached down from behind her and cupped her breasts, rubbing his thumbs over her nipples.

'You're jealous cos I said she had a good body.'

'What if I am?' She had to concentrate to keep her voice steady. 'It's just that it makes me feel vulnerable, feeling about you the way I do.'

She twisted round to face him. 'I don't want to get hurt, Jason.'

'Well, I'd better show you that you've got nothing to worry about then, hadn't I? And you've certainly got no need to be jealous of anyone, cos, believe me, I'd never do anything to hurt you, Lisa. Never.'

He bent forward and kissed her gently on the side of her neck.

'I know I'm the luckiest man in the world having you – why would I risk spoiling that?'

'I'm sorry, I'm just tired.'

She pulled away from him.

'Course you are, with all the work you've put in.'

Keep her sweet. Keep her fucking sweet.

'Here, I'll rub your shoulders.'

After a moment's hesitation, she let herself drop back in her chair.

'Tell you what, how about having a little break? A couple of nights away from all this'd do you good, before you start the really hard work? I know what, I've got to go down to my place in the country for a few days. Why not come with me?'

Slowly, she turned, reached out and took his face in her hands, and shook her head.

'You're a very patient man. And you really do keep coming up with these surprises. Your place in the country, eh? Do you have any more of them up that sleeve of yours, Mr Carter?'

He grinned. 'Maybe.'

She grinned back. 'Oh, I do hope so.'

Chapter 39

Jason made his way back from Lisa's flat in the Docklands, driving home to the Barbican through the almost empty, late-night City streets. The route, so familiar now, allowed his actions to become almost automatic, and for all his conscious attention to be focused on his phone call to Guillermo.

'Yeah, that's exactly what I want – for you to provide the same quality and quantity as the last deal. And I definitely intend to make this a regular arrangement.'

'Jason, I need you to reassure me that you have thought about this. I do not want you causing trouble for me. If I arrange this with these men, I cannot withdraw. They are not the sort of people who would allow that. You are certain you have the outlet for regular amounts of that size?'

'Look, don't worry yourself about it. Everything's taken care of this end. All you have to do is provide the gear.'

'Are you listening to me, Jason? I do not want to set this in motion and then have to let down my contacts; they are not people I would like to displease.

They are the sort who think nothing of killing someone who does no more than offend them. And if something went wrong and the money was not there to pay them, they would not come looking for you, but for me.'

'This, Guillermo, is a sure thing. Guaranteed distribution.'

He hesitated for the briefest of moments.

'I might as well tell you – I'm going to be running the door staff at a chain of clubs. It's fucking perfecto, mate.'

'I agree, that is good. That makes me feel better. But now, another, smaller detail – but still important. What about the girl driving the vehicle? I have to know who I'm working with. Will it be the same one?'

'No, that bird's got a different role in the organisation now.'

Jason heard his sharp intake of breath.

'You said she knew nothing about what you are doing. Have you been lying to me, Jason?'

'No. Course not. She knew nothing then and she knows nothing now. And that's the way it's gonna stay. But she doesn't matter. What matters is that the set-up will be the same. Me over there with a woman for a day or two then I get called back urgently and they ship it back for me, driving across the ferry with a pretty smile and nice luggage, and a motor packed to the gills. I'll be varying the motors and all

202

– different colours, and plates and that – we don't want customs getting suspicious.'

There was silence at the other end.

'You still there, Guillermo?'

'I was thinking about what you said. And I'm not sure.'

Another pause.

'Jason, there really cannot be any slip-ups. No mistakes. These people believe – and they are right – that even one little mistake can leave a trail, allowing matters to be traced back to them.'

'I don't understand why you're worrying so much.'

'What happens if the woman you bring here won't drive the vehicle back to England for you?'

'Is that really bothering you?'

'Yes.'

'Well, there's no need, mate. With my charm, Guillermo, I have women eating out of my hand. Just like that. I sweet-talk 'em, show 'em a good time, and they do exactly what I want. You'll have to come out with me one night. See how I operate. I reckon even a Latin lover like you could learn a thing or two from a smooth operator like me.'

'Not too smooth, I hope, Jason. After all, we all need to keep our edge.'

'I'm telling you, you've got no worries there, mate; no worries in the fucking world.'

*

Less than two minutes after he'd ended the call to Guillermo, Jason's phone rang again.

'Y'ello?'

'At last, I've been trying to get through for –'

'Who is this?'

Richard Middleton swallowed hard. Jason knew very well who it was.

'Sorry, Jason, I should have said, it's me, Richard. It's just that I've not seen you for nearly a week, and I was wondering –'

'Running low on supplies?'

'Actually, yes.'

'You must be desperate calling from home.'

'I'm still in the office.'

'At this time of night? You're doing longer hours than me.'

'As I said, I've been trying to get in touch with you, so I hung on here and finished off some paper work.'

As you well know from all the messages I've left on your mobile, you little shit.

'Well, then I'm sorry too, cos I won't be able to bring any gear round for you tonight.'

'Jason, please. As a favour.'

'Blimey, you sound well strung-out, mate.'

'I suppose I am. But not only for the reason you think. Jason, I have to say that I can't help feeling concerned about Lisa and you –'

'Why would that be then?'

204

'I've known her since she was a child.'

'That's nice, you sound just like a kind, concerned, old . . . uncle, shall we say?'

'Jason, I'm serious, I'm not fooling around here.'

Jason's face suddenly creased into a broad smile.

'D'you know what, Richard, you're in luck, mate. I've changed me mind. I'll be with you in about half an hour.'

As soon as the night porter buzzed up to his office to say his visitor had arrived, Richard hurried out to the waiting area.

He heard the ping of the lift arriving and then the sound of approaching footsteps – oddly metallic on the marble floor.

Jason appeared round the corner carrying a brief-case.

'You should count yourself more than lucky, Richard,' Jason said, walking straight past him and into his office. 'Cos I'm not doing any personal deliveries at the minute. I've been too knackered. But I thought I'd help you out, and take the opportunity to have a word at the same time.'

He propped the case on Richard's desk, spun the combination locks to line up the numbers and clicked it open. Taking out a thick, padded envelope he twisted round and tossed the package at Richard, who stumbled forward as he hurried to grab it before it fell to the ground.

'You see, if you don't watch yourself, mate, and don't praise me like you should – to misquote that fabulous song – if Lisa asks you anything about me, then that is going to be the last lot of gear you score off me – ever. You got that? But, of course, I can always arrange for someone else to do business with you. Perhaps someone a little less accommodating than me, but he'd still be a supplier. In fact, there's this feller I know over in Hoxton –'

'Jason, don't even think about it, you know I only deal directly with you. That's always been the agreement.'

'Always *was* the agreement, Richard. But I suppose it would be embarrassing if I did fix up another supplier and word somehow got out about you . . . Nasty. So you'd better think about that when you next come over like some old woman over me seeing Lisa, hadn't you?'

Richard stood there, clutching the parcel, a reprimanded, now repentant child.

'Well, I'd better get going. Me and Lisa are going down to the country for a few days, and I need to build me strength up with a good night's sleep cos I intend to screw the arse off her.'

He grinned. 'That'll give you something to think about when you're fucking Mrs Middleton or when your hand slips down your pants later on tonight, eh, Richard?'

He clicked his briefcase shut and walked over to the door.

'Make the money transfer into the account as usual, and don't forget –'

Jason fashioned his hand into a pistol shape, closed one eye, cocked his thumb and stared down his fingers – pointing them at Richard as if he were aiming the gun at his head.

'– you, mate, are my biggest fucking fan from now on.'

With that, he closed the door behind him and was gone.

Richard dropped down on to his chair. The little yob was actually threatening him. But what could he do about it? Say he really cut off his personal deliveries, what then? And what the hell had he done already allowing Lisa to become involved with a piece of scum like Jason Carter?

He put his head in his hands and felt the weariness flood through his body. After all these years of protecting her, he had thrown her to the bloody wolves.

If Brendan O'Donnell had still been around, Richard Middleton might just as well have signed his own death warrant.

But O'Donnell was dead – although that fact didn't actually make Richard feel much better. He was all too aware that he would never have dared cross that man if he were alive by exposing his daughter to the likes of Jason Carter.

As he carefully unstuck the envelope, Richard Middleton felt the tears pricking his eyes as he saw himself all too clearly for the self-serving coward he knew himself to be.

Chapter 40

Lisa did a deliberate comedy double take and let out a long, low '*Bloody hell!*'

She could just make out the house over the hedge through the top of the railings and, even with her limited knowledge of architecture, she could see it was what might be described as 'important', Queen Anne by the look of it – not fussy, but simple, beautiful. It was sitting at the end of a long, straight drive edged by post and rail fencing. From the size of it, it had to have at least a half a dozen bedrooms, possibly a lot more.

She drew the Saab up to the big double gates. 'Well, Jason, I have to say: this is impressive.'

Jason leaned to one side and fished a tiny, palm-sized zapper out of his trouser pocket. 'And I've got to say: I'm proud of it. I worked my bollocks off to get this.'

And then I nearly lost the whole fucking lot because of that cocksucker, Marcus.

He flicked the little gadget at the receiver and the gates opened smoothly and silently.

She drove in.

'*Blimey!*'

To the left of the drive was a meadow dotted with mature chestnut trees covered in spikes of buds that would soon become candles of white flowers, and newly unfurled, rich green leaves. And while there might have been rabbits rather than deer or cattle grazing beneath their branches, it all still looked pretty imposing to Lisa. On the right of the drive was another broad meadow gently sloping away from the house. In it were two neatly parked, very clean quad bikes housed under a wooden, bad-weather shelter.

She couldn't help but let out a delighted gasp as she neared the house and saw, set out on either side of it, twin stone pools, complete with fountains, their waters glinting in the midday sun.

She knew that the successful City boys – like the ones in Jason's firm – earned a lot, but this was amazing. More like the sort of set-up she'd have expected from someone in her father's line of work.

She laughed mirthlessly to herself. It just went to show how the world had changed in just a generation or two. Those in legitimate lines of business were taking over from the villains.

Or were the lines just blurring, with places like Diamond Dan's taking over from the old-fashioned knocking shops of her grandfather's era, and gangsters using computers to exercise their power rather than having broken-nosed, cauliflower-eared henchmen wielding coshes?

She wasn't ever likely to find out – even today women were still on the sidelines.

But at least she knew this was a man who definitely wouldn't be after her for her money.

'No butler or housekeeper then?' she teased, as Jason led her across the tiled black-and-white floor of the entrance hall.

He squeezed her hand, turned and kissed her on the forehead. 'Don't get sarky with me, darling.'

'Wouldn't dream of it, Mr Carter.'

'Good, because, of course, I have to have help down here, but I don't want you to go thinking I've got illusions that I'm some bloody duke or something.'

'Double good, because I wouldn't like you if you were like that. But what I do like about you is the fact that –'

'Never mind all this flattery lark, come on, come and see the rest of it – and how about starting with the bedrooms?'

'Only after I've told you my news. I was going to save it until we had a bottle of champagne to crack open, but I can't wait.'

She dropped her handbag on the floor and held out her arms.

'The girls we picked at the interviews – all fifteen of them – they're all in place.'

She hugged him close.

'I've done it, Jason. I've really done it. They start in three of the Kesslers' clubs next week.'

'Lisa, that is fantastic news, girl.'

He kissed her on the top of her head.

'I don't think I could be more pleased for you. How did you manage to keep it quiet for the whole journey down here?'

'I really don't know.'

She leaned back so she could look at him.

'You've believed in me all along. Even when I had doubts. You were there, encouraging me.'

Jason grinned. 'Well, we'd better celebrate then, hadn't we? And I think we should start upstairs.'

While Lisa soaked up to her chin in a bath full of sweet-smelling bubbles, Jason admired himself in the bathroom mirror as he towelled his freshly showered body.

He threw the used towel in the laundry hamper and kissed her gently on the mouth.

'I've just got to go out the back and bring some logs in,' he said, pulling on a grey cotton tracksuit. 'You stay there and relax, then I'll knock up a bit of dinner.' He winked at her. 'You need a square meal after all that exertion.'

Jason unlocked the door using the state-of-the-art electronic keypad and let himself in. What looked from the outside like an ordinary outbuilding was, in fact, more like a sterile operating theatre crossed with a particularly boring kitchen – plain white tiles, bright overhead strip lighting, brushed metal worktops, microwave oven and an assortment of stainless-steel tools.

He checked the calibration on a small set of scales and began weighing out a measure of sodium bicarbonate. He'd get the first batch going and then cook up some more a bit later on when Lisa was asleep.

Crack wasn't usually Jason's thing and, he had to admit, he was a bit fazed by the scary bloke from Dalston he was going to have to do business with, but if he could just hold off Marcus for one more week, he'd have given himself the breathing space in which to earn enough dough to pay off his full debt to him.

Then he could relax.

And he'd be back in the nice tidy world of charlie before he knew it.

Chapter 41

Jason put a Miles Davis CD in the player, threw another log on the fire, poured two large glasses of brandy, and then sat down close to Lisa on the leather chesterfield.

They sipped their drinks and stared into the flames. It was a cosy, dark-panelled room at the back of the house, lit by the firelight and by the lamps on the rosewood tables that stood at either end of the sofa. The room had the same tall sash windows as those at the front, and French windows that opened out on to the grounds. All the curtains had been left open, but it wasn't possible to see much outside: it had gone eight o'clock and the gathering twilight and the lowering sky were blurring hard edges into vague, amorphous shapes, and tricking the eye into misunderstanding distance.

'It's not quite like being in Spain, is it?' he said, putting his arm around her shoulders. 'Look at it out there.'

'Don't be so negative.' Lisa leaned into him and curled her feet up underneath her.

'Nothing could spoil my mood – nothing. I think those storm clouds rolling in are amazing, really atmospheric – like something out of a nineteenth-century novel. And, as for the company, it's the best I could ask for. Truly, Jason, the very best.'

She snuggled closer, resting her head on his chest. 'And this place's not bad either.'

'No, I suppose it's not bad for an Essex boy,' he laughed, touching his lips to her hair. 'But then I do have very good taste. Especially in women.'

She lifted her face to return his kiss, when a loud banging startled them both.

'Was that thunder?'

'No, it was the bloody great metal knocker that I'm gonna go and rip off the front door.'

Lisa sat up straight, startled as Jason slammed his glass down on the sofa table, spilling it over the polished surface as he leapt to his feet. Images of Hoxton Marcus flanked by steroid-fuelled henchmen were making his bowels threaten to let him down.

'And I wanna know who the fuck's coming down here uninvited at this time of night.'

Before he had a chance to find out, there was the sound of hurrying feet scrunching on gravel, and then two figures appeared outside the French windows.

It took a startled Lisa a few moments to realise that it was a youngish black woman, maybe in her early twenties, standing there with a mixed-race child who looked to be about six years old. They both had the sides of their hands pressed to their foreheads, their faces close to the glass, as they peered into the room.

The effect was like watching mime artists pretending to look out to sea.

Lisa turned her gaze back to Jason; of course she couldn't read exactly what was going on in his mind, but she could tell from his expression that his immediate feeling was one of relief – very swiftly followed by fist-clenching, white-knuckled anger.

He strode across the room, wrenched open one of the glass doors, and stood square on the step to block the woman and child from entering.

'Go round the front, Shaylee. Now.' His voice was low, menacing.

'Jason, for Christ's sake, at least let us in. We've been on the train then on a bus for bloody hours. It's cold out here, and Alfie's freezing, fit to drop he is. Look at him. And it's gonna start pissing down in a minute.'

'I said: go round the front.'

'I'm fed up with you ignoring us, Jay. And I've got bills. Bills I can't pay. If I don't get some money tonight –'

'*Round the front.*'

Jason almost smashed the French windows shut and, without a word to Lisa, strode out of the room.

Lisa gulped at her brandy as she heard Jason and the young woman shouting at one another. The woman screamed something about Jason not being interested, and then Jason snapped back that she was lucky he was giving her anything and she knew what

216

she could do if she didn't like it, and who did she think she was turning up like this.

Even though Lisa couldn't make out all of their words, the anger and the accusing tone were both clear enough – as was the sound of the massive front door being slammed, very firmly shut.

It was less than ten minutes since the woman and child had appeared at the French windows and yet Jason was already back in the room with Lisa, pouring them both another large brandy.

'I'll put on some more logs,' he said stiffly, handing her the glass. 'It's cold out there tonight.'

Lisa sat there, staring into her glass.

'Maybe it'll brighten up tomorrow,' he added.

'Maybe,' she said, standing up. 'But I won't be here to find out; I'm going home.' She wouldn't demean herself by asking about the woman.

'Lisa, I know how it must look, but –'

'I'm going home, Jason. Now.'

He pointed at her glass. 'Just as you told me once, you can't drive, you've been drinking.'

'I'll call a cab.'

'Lisa, please.'

He couldn't let her go, not now, not with everything so close.

'I love you, Lisa. I wouldn't ever do anything to hurt you. Stay, please. I'll explain everything and we'll drive back in the morning if you still want to.'

'I don't want to hear your explanations.' She swallowed down the brandy. 'I presume you've got a spare room in this place.'

Chapter 42

The weather not only hadn't improved by morning, it had actually got far worse, and as Lisa drove them along the motorway back towards London, the rain was beating down on the soft top of the Saab like an overenthusiastic percussion section racing to the end of a score.

'Do you mind if we stop for a few minutes?' Jason asked, squinting through the windscreen as the wipers failed to deal with the spray thrown up by yet another huge lorry ploughing along in the middle lane.

'I phoned work earlier and said I was gonna be in, but I'd better give them another to call to let them know I'm gonna be late, cos I don't think this is gonna be an easy journey.'

'No.'

'No you don't mind if we stop, or no you don't think the journey's gonna be easy?'

'Please, Jason, we'll stop, okay. I'll do what you want. But just don't keep talking and asking questions, I'm not really thinking straight at the moment.'

'No?'

'No. I've got a headache.'

Lisa gripped the steering wheel tighter, her knuckles staring proud through her pale skin.

Jason didn't like the way this was going at all.

Why did Shaylee have to go and do that to him last night? Bringing the fucking kid out like that. She'd pulled that sort of stunt too many times for him to carry on being so fucking understanding. If she ruined this for him, he'd bloody kill her.

Her and the kid.

He'd bury the pair of them, and wouldn't think twice about it.

At the next services, Lisa eased on to the slip road and joined the queue of cars and vans whose drivers had decided that downing a hot drink and a fry-up was a far more appealing prospect than aquaplaning along the motorway.

As she pulled into a parking space, Jason took off his seat belt and reached across to the back seat for his briefcase. He caught the look on Lisa's face as he opened it.

'Yeah, that's right – three mobiles. I'm an even busier man than you thought.'

He laughed and shrugged, constructing the story as he spoke.

'And yes, they're all pay as you go. I've got this old girlfriend in the Met, see. She's a bit of a nightmare, always trying to get in touch with me.

Drives me nuts, I'm telling you. Just won't accept it's over.'

Lisa could feel the tears pricking at her eyes. 'You make your call, Jason, I'll go and get some coffee.'

'Have you got an umbrella?'

'There's one in the boot. But I'll be fine.'

'Let me get it for you.'

'I said I'll be fine, Jason.'

When Lisa came hurrying back towards the car, Jason was relieved to see that there were two paper cups of coffee wedged into the cardboard holder she was carrying – at least she was thinking of him, even if she wasn't saying much.

He jumped out and helped her into the driver's seat.

'See her?' she said, wiping the rain from her face with the back of her hand. 'With the older man.'

She was actually chatting to him – this was better.

'What her?'

He lifted his chin towards a strikingly tall, painfully thin young woman, who had her arm linked through that of a squat, puffing, much older man, making a dash across the car park in the sheeting rain towards a low-slung Porsche – it wasn't clear how they were going to fit into the thing.

'That's her. You're not going to believe this, but when I nipped into the loo, she was in one of the cubicles with the door open and she was snorting cocaine – I promise you – in broad daylight. Didn't give a damn who saw her.'

Thank fuck for that – she was speaking to him again.

'You know what it's like nowadays, Lisa. When people go anywhere it's –' he patted his jacket then his trouser pockets as he chanted rhythmically – 'Hash, cash, coke, keys. They're all at it.'

'Not everyone.'

'No, not everyone, I agree, but believe me, that's all a lot of people want. And I mean a lot of people. It's got so it's what's expected. Let's face it, people are always gonna find a way to get off their heads and, for now, charlie just happens to be the flavour of the month.'

'Not for me, it's not.' She handed him one of the cups.

'So you don't then?'

'No, I don't. And I don't like people who do. Drugs cause trouble.'

'You sound like you're speaking from experience.'

'Sort of. There were some distant family problems.'

'I thought it was just you and your mum and some disfigured old aunt in Ireland.'

'It is. Now drink your coffee before it gets cold.'

He put his hand on her thigh; he wasn't about to let her lower the shutters again.

'I suppose you want to know about last night.'

'Why? It's your private business. Why should I be concerned?'

'Look, Lisa, I know how it must have looked. You know I love you – I've told you – and then that had to happen. I mean, it's not exactly usual, is it, a woman and kid turning up like that?'

'What you do is up to you.'

'Don't be like that, Lisa. I want to tell you. I want you to know the truth.'

She said nothing.

There was a lot riding on this. He had to make it sound good. More than good. It had to be convincing.

'Shaylee – that's the bird's name – she used to work for me. Did a bit of cleaning over at my flat in the Barbican, and a bit of clearing up down in Sussex after parties and that. But now I can't get rid of her. Thing is, I suppose it was my fault. I was good to her, see. Too good. But then – and this is why I'm telling you, now I know you feel the same way about these things as I do, I'll tell you the truth – she got into drugs. In a big way. I'm telling you, Lisa, it's bloody tragic. It's fucked her life right up.'

'But she's got that little boy.'

'I know. And that, believe me, is the hardest part of it. I just don't know what to do. I mean, what would anyone do? How do I decide? Should I keep giving her money or live with the fact that I know full well that if she's stuck for cash she'll just leave the kid somewhere, dump the poor little sod with Christ knows who, and go out on the game to pay for the drugs.'

'That's terrible. And when you think there are people who'd kill to have children.'

'I know, and that's me included, Lisa. That's exactly what I want for myself one day. To settle down with a nice little family to call my own. You know, us against world. Give them a better start than I ever had.'

Lisa turned away and looked out of the window, not wanting him to see her tears.

She was such a fool; she had very nearly blown it. And all because of her stupid lack of trust in people.

He squeezed her thigh as he took a swallow of the tepid brown drink that was masquerading as coffee.

'Like I said, Lisa – it's tragic. Really tragic.'

More like magic, he thought, hardly able to suppress his laughter at how easy it was to con a bird that reckoned she was in love with you. He'd give her a right seeing-to tonight – give her a nice warm glow – then he'd get back down to the country tomorrow, finish off his work down there, and then – oh yes – he was gonna treat himself. He hadn't had a proper spend-up for a while now. A new motor maybe. One like the limited-edition Porsche that the odd couple over there had just squeezed themselves into – that looked the right business. Very appealing. And now he was as good as guaranteed plenty of dosh coming in – and on a nice regular basis – surely he could hold off Marcus for just a bit longer.

Course he could. He was well on form, full of fucking fire.

Chapter 43

Nahida wound herself sensuously around one of the poles on the central podium.

Every evening she had to make the same difficult decision: should she dance as sexily as she could and hope that the Englishwomen would leave her up there on the podium as a come-on to the customers to encourage them to spend more money on private dances? The women sometimes did that – thinking they were punishing her by depriving her of the men's tips. But it also meant risking a punter being so turned on by her that he wanted her – *and only her* – to go upstairs with him. The alternative was to dance as inconspicuously as possible, giving out the message that she wasn't interested, that she wanted to be left alone. But if she did that it meant risking the Englishwomen starting on her again. And she was already in enough trouble with them.

Ana was lucky, she didn't worry herself with such dilemmas; she wasn't going to waste her energy on the podium and that was that. She just brushed off the Englishwomen's complaints by saying that she preferred going upstairs to the private rooms, because she could earn more money. And in truth the

Englishwomen didn't mind, because Ana wasn't fussy who she went with, and that could be very useful; most of the local girls grumbled and complained and even threatened to leave if a punter was much older or more unpleasant than usual.

Nahida really envied the local girls having such freedom to choose.

As she swung herself around the pole, balanced on the ball of one foot, her hair flying out behind her, Nahida watched as Ana made the trip upstairs for what must have been the third or even fourth time this evening; her eyes were glassy, her skin pallid.

Nahida didn't know how Ana could do it so willingly, even with her need for the drugs, but no matter what she did, or how she behaved, she had been a good friend to Nahida – her only friend – and had helped and protected her so many times. Ana was now the closest thing that Nahida had to family and she would give anything to be able to help her in the same way.

But all Nahida's hopes about Lisa Taylor being her saviour – no, *their* saviour – had amounted to a big disappointing nothing. She had been in and out of the club, but on each occasion she had been accompanied by either one of the Kesslers or the Englishwomen, and Nahida hadn't had a single chance to speak to her in private.

The music stopped briefly as the track changed. Then another pounding beat began.

The bosomy redhead who was grinding her crotch against the pole next to Nahida hissed at her over the music.

'Here, d'ya see him? That bloke who just came in?'

Nahida glanced over her shoulder towards the door. 'Grey-haired man?'

'That's him,' said the redhead. 'He's only a famous lawyer, the one who does all them human rights cases. He's always in the paper.'

'I don't understand.' Nahida didn't miss a beat as she took another look at the distinguished-looking man who was greeting one of the Englishwomen as she helped him off with his overcoat.

'Yes you do. He helps people, people in trouble. Poor people and that. Uses the law.' Her voice was sneering. 'The fucking hypocrite. He don't help us, does he? If I don't work every single night this week *and* next, and earn plenty of tips, then I'm not gonna have enough to pay me mortgage again this month. He wants to sort out the fucking human rights of the cost of childcare, that's what he wants to do. Not spend all his time helping all these bloody foreigners. No offence, Nahida.'

'He helps foreigners?'

'Yeah, too right he does. Loves all them asylum-seeking ponces.'

The Englishwoman had taken the man's coat and was going over to the cloakroom.

228

This was her chance; Nahida didn't even wait for the music to stop.

She stepped carefully off the podium – despite her excitement she knew the heels could be lethal – and made her way over to the man who was now sitting at one of the tables with an equally refined-looking man in a dark suit; they were talking easily as if they knew one another.

'Excuse me, sir.'

She could barely keep her voice steady, but knew she had to make her English clear, had to make him understand her.

'You are lawyer?'

The man looked at her and smiled, then at his companion. 'My fame has spread before me.'

'You help foreigners?'

Now his friend was smiling too. 'Especially if they look like you, he does.'

'That is wonderful!'

Nahida leaned forward holding out her arms, her see-through top revealing her breasts spilling out over the cups of her push-up bra.

'I am foreigner. I need help. The men – the Kesslers – they brought me here. My passport is not real. I want to go home to my country.'

The lawyer's smile faded. He turned and looked at the other man, raising an enquiring eyebrow.

The man shook his head. 'Not on your bloody

229

nelly. I prefer to keep my kneecaps intact if it's all the same to you.'

'My thoughts exactly.'

Without looking her in the face, the lawyer took his wallet from the inside pocket of his jacket, slipped out a fifty-pound note and, before a shocked Nahida could move away, he had his hand under the scrap of material covering her lower body and had tucked the money into her G-string, his fingers deliberately seeking out her pubic hair.

Now he looked directly into her eyes.

'Make it a good dance and you keep that. Make it even better and I'll take you upstairs.'

As Nahida made a run for the lavatory, stumbling on her heels, crashing into tables and shoving furious, semi-naked dancers out of her way, she could hear the men's laughter chasing and mocking her.

Chapter 44

As Jason ushered Lisa into the celebrity-favoured, Covent Garden restaurant, she scanned the room. For once, there wasn't a single famous face in sight – well, not one that Lisa recognised, anyway. But Lisa did recognise something familiar about the scene – it reminded her of something her mother had shown her over ten years ago.

Because, apart from the designer dresses and the hairdos of the women – the majority of whom were seriously assisted blondes with poker-straight bobs and deep brown complexions that spoke of too much time spent in the tanning booth – the scene could have come from any one of the photographs taken in restaurants and nightclubs that her mother had, finally, shown her on her eighteenth birthday. It was the same day that Sandy had at last told Lisa the truth about her family – the O'Donnells – and the terrible blood feud they had had with the Kesslers for two generations, a power struggle over who ran what in the East End.

That day Lisa also found out that all the money she had inherited had been earned as a result of the O'Donnells' many successful 'businesses' – criminal businesses that had spread a web over the whole of east London, out into Essex and even abroad.

These people could so easily have been in those photographs.

In other words, she was looking at a room full of a lot of rich men who were being ostentatious with their wealth, and generally ignoring the mostly younger women accompanying them. But while most of these men were probably engaged in similar sorts of businesses to the Kesslers, those businesses were probably all legitimate and above board like the clubs and casinos. Even if they were the kinds of businesses she probably wouldn't have become involved in – had Jason not been so enthusiastic and reassuring.

She had a lot to thank him for.

'They must certainly have some influence, being able to hire this whole place for the evening,' she said, clasping Jason's hand as he led her through the maze of tables to where David and Paul Kessler were sitting on either side of their father – the obvious guest of honour for the evening. 'From my experience of coming here, it's difficult enough getting a table for two on a Saturday night, never mind for two hundred.'

Jason kept his eyes front, but dipped his head so she could hear his whispers.

'It's not every day that old man Kessler has a birthday party, and what Daniel wants Daniel pretty much gets. Now smile nicely, and get his present ready to hand over to him. Makes you laugh really, but even with all that dough he must have in the bank, when they gave me the invitation, I was still warned we should bring a gift along cos apparently he acts like a sulky little kid if he don't get one.'

'Some people never grow up.'

'You're right, I suppose. But you won't say that to his face, will you, Lis?'

'Hello, Mr Kessler. We'd like to wish you a very happy birthday and many happy returns and all.' Jason flashed his perfectly bleached teeth. 'And perhaps I can introduce you to Lisa Taylor. Lisa, this is Daniel Kessler.'

'All right, darling,' said Kessler without much interest, fiddling with his huge pearl tiepin.

Lisa struggled to find some appropriate words of polite reply, but couldn't help a guilty pause before she spoke – *Mr Kessler* . . .

Why hadn't she told Sandy that she was doing business with this family?

It wasn't much of a question.

Lisa hadn't told her, because Sandy would have stopped her from doing it, that's why. Simple. And it had felt more important for Lisa to do this – and if she was honest with herself, to please Jason – than to be straight with her own mother. She didn't find it a very nice thing to admit. But, hey, she was a grown-up, wasn't she? She had to make her own decisions.

Lisa finally held out her hand in greeting.

'Mr Kessler. Happy birthday.'

It was odd, but standing there meeting this oddly compelling man, Daniel Kessler, somehow made the situation more real, more unavoidable to skirt around the reality of it – much more so than when she had just been dealing with his sons – she was an O'Donnell doing business with the Kesslers, her father's enemies. There was no getting away from it.

This man was part of the world that her father had inhabited – ruled – for many years: a violent, cruel world, from which she had been sheltered all her life by those who loved and cared about her.

Now here she was, offering her hand in greeting to this living link not only with that world, but with Brendan O'Donnell himself, her father.

The actuality both troubled and – disturbingly, but undeniably – fascinated her.

Had her father been like this man? Had he possessed this same confidence, this arrogance that was both unsettling and attractive, no matter in how brutish or unreconstructed a way?

She was standing there, staring at him – her hand out and with a smile on her lips, if not in her eyes – but Kessler was making no attempt to shake that offered hand, instead he looked at it as if surprised to find it empty.

'Oh, yes. Of course.'

Flustered by her thoughts and her unaccustomed

gaucheness, Lisa held out her other hand.

Eagerly, Kessler took the small, turquoise carrier bag from her, precious stones glittering in the rings on each of his little fingers, and gold flashing from the heavy gold chain and watch on his wrist.

He plunged straight in, pulling out the tissue-wrapped offering.

He tore off the paper to reveal a gold cigar cutter with a curling letter D fashioned from diamond chips set into the gold – the piece that Jason had had to argue long and hard with Lisa to persuade her that it was not showy and vulgar, but was a perfect choice.

Kessler slipped the cutter into his jacket pocket.

Jason looked relieved.

'So,' Kessler said, looking Lisa up and down with an expression that gave nothing away. 'You're Lisa, are you? I hear from my sons that the girls are doing well at the clubs.'

'Yes, they're all very –'

Cutting across her, Kessler turned to the young blonde by his side.

'Clean napkins,' he said, as if Lisa didn't exist. 'Not enough on the table. Get the fucking maître d' over here sharpish. Can't stand not having enough clean napkins to wipe me hands on. Looks fucking cheap. And I hate that. It's a fucking show-up. In the old days they'd have been piled fucking high.'

He dropped back in his chair and sniffed loudly.

'No one's got any class nowadays.'

235

With a meaningful widening of his eyes directed at Lisa, Jason took her by the arm and shepherded her firmly away.

'Audience over, thank goodness,' he said as he pulled out a chair for her at a table on the far side of the restaurant. 'You did well. He doesn't usually bother saying very much, especially to women.'

'I'm sorry, Jason, but in my book that wasn't much of a conversation. *The girls are doing well.* Thank you so much, Mr Kessler. You are so very generous. But how about the fact that I've had those girls in place for almost a month now, and there's not been a single hint of trouble in any of the clubs we're covering? Nothing. And he didn't even think to mention that *I was doing well* providing such good staff in the first place.'

'Surely you know enough about blokes like him, Lisa, to be able to ignore his behaviour. He's from another world.'

Jason jerked his head towards where Kessler was still holding court.

'Look at him. Even his clothes give him away. He's not changed his style since Gawd knows when, cos he's one of the old school. The ones who don't know how to treat a woman, because they couldn't ever admit that they just might be as good as they are. He's exactly like them idiots I have to work with, only they think no one – man or woman – is as good as them.'

He raised his glass.

'To the day when I'll be free of the bastards.'

He took a long pull on his drink.

'You don't know how lucky you are working for yourself. And making such a success of it, no matter how much that old git chooses to ignore the fact.'

'You're right, I am free, and I am lucky,' Lisa said, at last managing a genuine smile. 'And you're also right that he's no different from those men you work with – except he probably wears more jewellery.'

Chapter 45

Kessler took out the gold cutter, weighed it in his hand, and then set about preparing a cigar. He addressed his sons without looking at them.

'That Lisa, she's a pretty girl. Classy and all. One of you should get in there, and see if she's got a nice-looking mate for the other one of you; it's about time you two settled down and gave me and your mother some grandchildren.'

Paul threw a warning look at his brother. *Don't start*. But David wasn't so easily silenced.

'You've got grandchildren, Dad.' His voice was flat, restrained.

'I mean real ones, not bastards. What son would bring bastards home to his mother and father? Get married, that's what you've gotta do. Just look at your Uncle Sammy and your Uncle Maurice. It was okay them messing around when they were boys, but now they're in their sixties they look at me and I know they're jealous. Family, that's what a man needs. And a woman indoors to keep a nice home for him.'

Kessler looked about him. 'Your grandfather would have hated all this nonsense that goes on nowadays. Fucking women getting involved in

238

business. What's happening to the world? We wouldn't have tolerated it, not in my day we wouldn't. We knew how to do things. We acted like real men. Them O'Donnells were mad fucking Irish dogs, so what did we do? We put 'em down. Over. Settled.'

Paul stood up.

'Dave, I want to go and make sure the maître d's sorted out them napkins and knows when to start serving and that he gets everything just right for Dad. Come with me and make sure I remember every-thing?'

Paul and David stood outside on the pavement beside the grand art deco entrance to the restaurant.

It was an unusually warm, early-June evening, and they were eyeing the young women as they walked by in their flimsy summer dresses and flesh-revealing, low-slung trousers and cropped tops.

Paul handed his brother a cigarette.

'Promise me you won't start tonight, eh, Dave? We've been hard at it enough these past few weeks getting the casino up and running without giving our-selves another headache. I don't want him anywhere near that place till it's running like clockwork – when he won't be able to find anything to complain about. You know if there's the slightest problem he'll make it an excuse to start sticking his beak in. And with this big order coming over from Vito and the Bosnian boys, the last thing we want is Dad getting busy and screwing things up.'

'You amaze me, Paul, d'you know that? I ain't stupid, I don't want him getting busy either, but how can you keep so calm, and not get wild with him? He is such a fucking hypocrite. And a liar. From the way he talks you'd think he'd personally gunned down them O'Donnell arseholes. And as for family, it's so important, so he tells us. But there's him – he can't wait to get rid of Mum, get her out of his sight, always sending her off with her sisters on another fucking cruise. He never sees her. Just wants her out of the way so he can get stuck into his latest little whore. Look at that one sitting in there with him. She don't even look legal. Fucking trollop.'

'I've not heard Mum complaining.'

'Have you ever asked her what she really thinks, Paul? How she feels about the old bastard and how he treats her?'

'Dave, don't do this.'

David drew fiercely on his cigarette.

'He only got together with her in the first place cos he wanted kids to carry on his businesses. And now he's got us, we have to worry all the time that he'll start interfering, cos he thinks he can run things like he did in the fucking *good old days*. What does he want us to do, get out the sawn-offs and do a few banks cos that was how they used to fucking do it? Way he talks you'd think he was Al Capone.'

He ran his hand agitatedly through his hair.

'And everyone knows the fucker's not even married to Mum.'

'Don't get yourself in a state, Dave. We've known since we were kids that it's always been one rule for him and one rule for everybody else. So what's new?'

'D'you know what, Paul? It don't matter that I know all that, it still makes me sick. The sooner we take over the businesses completely the sooner I'll like it. Just looking at him makes me want to punch him in the face.'

'Well, if we carry on doing as well as we have been, and carry on expanding, then why should he get busy? There'll be nothing to argue with, will there?'

'D'you reckon?' David threw his barely smoked cigarette into the gutter.

'And anyway, Dave, I thought you said you fancied that Lisa. Would it be such a bad idea settling down? And it would hardly present much of a problem nicking her off of a dumb little Essex barrow boy like Jason Carter.'

'I could certainly do with a bit of entertainment to take my mind of that old bastard in there.'

David clapped his hand over his brother's shoulder.

'And I'm going to start by offering her the door at the casino. Birds like her like to be taken seriously, treated like they've got a bit of brain in their heads.'

He winked at his brother.

'D'you know what, Paul? I'm in a much better mood now. I'm so good at handling women, I frighten meself at times.'

Chapter 46

'I'm so pleased for you, Lisa. This employment agency idea was obviously a good one.'

Sandy looked around at the office in her daughter's flat that now showed no signs that it had ever been a rarely used spare bedroom.

'My little girl running a successful business; it makes me very proud.'

'What, did you think I'd run an unsuccessful one?'

'Don't be daft.'

Sandy held out her arms and pulled Lisa close to her; she couldn't put her finger on it but there was definitely something odd about the way she was acting. She had to be careful, didn't want to sound too nosy or Lisa would just clam up – even as a child she had been headstrong. Typical O'Donnell.

'When you didn't ask me over to see how you were doing, I dreaded that it had all gone wrong for you.'

Lisa craned her head back so she could look her mother in the eye. 'I wanted to wait until I was sure it was working, Mum. And it is. I'm doing really well. Even better than I'd hoped.'

'With everything you've got, you could have spent

the rest of your life sitting on your backside, but you haven't. You've studied and now you're grafting. You're a good girl, Lisa. It's just a shame old Eileen O'Donnell's not still around to see what a good job I did on you. Even she wouldn't have been able to disagree with that.'

Sandy let her daughter go. 'Now, how about a cuppa tea?'

She followed her daughter up the stairs and sat looking out over the river while Lisa put the kettle on.

Maybe it was something to do with this new man. Perhaps he'd let her down or something.

'You should have someone to share all this with, you know, babe. It's such a pity living in this beautiful place all by yourself.'

'You live by yourself,' Lisa called from the open-plan kitchen in the corner of the room that took up the whole of the top floor of the duplex.

'I'm a tough old bird who's got used to my own company. There were only ever two men I wanted in my life, the two who really mattered to me – Barry and Brendan – and both of them buggers wound up letting me down, made me suffer, but out of all that, I got you, the most important thing that ever happened to me. And I don't want you to go missing your chance to have the same. You know how pleased I am about all you've achieved, Lisa, but don't let it stop you settling down with someone. You girls leave it so late nowadays.'

Lisa abandoned the tea-making and went to sit on the sofa beside her mother.

'You weren't exactly a teenager when you married Dad and had me.'

'Well, my life wasn't exactly normal, was it?'

'And mine is? A false name and no family I can ever talk about.'

Sandy shifted uncomfortably; she was aware, every single day of her life, that her daughter hadn't only inherited the O'Donnell money, she'd inherited the curse of their history as well.

'So tell me, how about that bloke you went to Spain with?'

'Who knows?' Lisa felt her cheeks colouring. 'I hope something might come out of it. But, typical me, you know how I never trust anyone, always feel suspicious because of *the family*. Well, I nearly dumped him a couple of weeks back. I thought he was messing me around.'

'You okay with him again now?'

'I hope we're a lot more than okay, Mum.'

'That sounds good.'

'It is. And while I don't want to make any assumptions, I really think Jason might be the one.'

'Really?'

Sandy didn't get it; if she was so happy – the employment agency, the new man – then why was she acting like she was standing on top of a wasps' nest with an open jar of jam in her hand?

'Really.' Lisa nodded. 'I've fallen for him. He's so open. No edge to him at all. And he's done well, but hasn't tried to reinvent himself. He's happy with who he is. A straight, decent person – just like you.' She let out a long slow breath. 'It just worries me that I've been leading him on, lying to him about who I really am. And I can't bear the thought that if I tell him the truth, he might leave me. Hate me for lying to him, and despise the sort of man who fathered me.'

So that's what was getting her down.

'I know how tough it is, love, but it's been for the best, believe me. You can't begin to imagine how your life would have turned out if it had ever been leaked to the press. I saw some of the stick Eileen went through when the papers got hold of her story. It would have been all *Villain's Secret Daughter Exposed*. All that sort of crap. You'd have been tortured morning, noon and night by photographers and reporters.'

'I know all that, Mum. And that's what scares me – his reaction. I want to be honest with him, and yet I don't want to drive him away.'

As Lisa stared down at her lap, Sandy could see the strain in her daughter's face.

'Have you spoken to Richard about this?'

If she had, maybe that was why Richard had been avoiding taking Sandy's calls – he was trying to put off discussing what Lisa should do. The day when Lisa would meet someone so special she would want to tell him the truth – the day Sandy and Richard both hoped for and yet both dreaded.

Lisa's head snapped up. 'Why would I speak to him about it?'

'Because he cares about you, that's why.'

Sandy put her arm round her daughter's shoulders.

'Lisa, you just remember, I'll always be here for you, darling – whatever happens. That's a promise.'

Chapter 47

'Mr Kessler, it's for you.'

The bikini-clad barmaid at Diamond Dan's handed the phone across the counter to Paul.

'Paul, it's me, Jason. Is Lisa in tonight?'

'No, she's over at the casino tonight. Checking how the new staff are doing.'

Result!

'Aw, that's a right shame, that is. Cos I'm on me way over to Dan's with some mates, and I was hoping to introduce her to them. Show her off, you know. And show her the new motor I've just bought. Lovely it is. Boxster special edition. Very sweet.'

Paul put down the phone and turned to his brother.

'That was our friend, blond Jason. He's bringing in some mates. Wanted to know if Lisa was in, so he could show her off to them. And going on about how he's bought himself a new car.'

David shook his head contemptuously.

'He's a piece of fucking work. I don't know how a girl like Lisa got herself hiked up with that idiot. I tell you, Paul, it's gonna be a pleasure taking her off him.'

David leaned forward for the barmaid to light his cigarette.

'But you know how important his rich mates are, Dave; and when he's in the mood he knows how to spend and all. Even if he is a dickhead.'

'Yeah, I ain't stupid. But I'll have to leave it to you to smile at him while you're taking all his dough tonight, bruv, because while they're here partying, I fancy taking a stroll over to the casino to check on his bird.'

Nahida watched as the blond man called Jason came into the club – sometimes Lisa Taylor was with him – and the Englishwomen were nowhere to be seen.

Please be with him.

Since the lawyer had laughed at her, Nahida was becoming increasingly desperate. Ana, who had once given Nahida strength, was now depending on Nahida for almost everything, and was taking most of her tip money from her as well. All she seemed to think about was when she could inject herself again, and if she had enough pills, or something to smoke.

Ana was a mess, and Nahida was now prepared to try almost anything to get them both away from the club and everything associated with it. She would find a way to repay her past kindness.

For weeks now she had been waiting for the opportunity to talk to Lisa Taylor about the situation, persuading herself that although the man had refused even to listen to her, a woman would be sure to help them if only she knew the truth.

But the only people with the blond man were four other men.

Nahida watched them, numb with disappointment, and then one of the Englishwomen appeared.

Jason handed the woman some money, as he whispered something into her ear.

The Englishwoman smiled and pointed over at Nahida.

'Her, go on, take that one,' Nahida heard her say. 'She'll be up for it; no better than animals, that lot. Just make sure that it's you who takes her upstairs, and that you go into the far room along the landing – the one with the heavy door. Then I'll get the music turned up a bit louder.'

'You say she's up for it, but is there a little hint in what you're saying that you're expecting a bit of fuss from her? Am I right?'

The woman looked sheepish.

'Don't worry,' he grinned, fondling the woman's backside, 'the fella'll enjoy that.'

Nahida wasn't sure what was happening when the blond man took her up to the room. She was even more confused when four other men joined them. Then they all started to take off their clothes.

She realised then what they were going to do to her

250

– or she thought she did – and she tried to run for the door, to get away, but Jason threw her down on the bed and started ripping off her outfit.

She began to scream, but one of the other men put his hand over her mouth and told her that she had better be quiet or he'd slap her.

During two frenzied hours, Jason and the others forced themselves on her again and again. They raped her and they forced themselves into her mouth making her gag. One man threw her over on to her stomach and, as he entered her from behind, she thought he was going to rip her apart. All the while they were laughing at her, spitting on her, and one of them had urinated on her.

Now she lay alone on the bed in the upstairs room – silently, no longer even crying, just overwhelmed with feelings of pain and shock and a crushing sense of bewilderment.

It wasn't that a man would do so many bad things to her – Ana had told her in sleep-disturbing detail about what the soldiers had done to the girls and women back home, and she had seen for herself, with her own eyes, what men were capable of doing since she had been forced to work in the club – but she really couldn't understand how not one of those men had tried to stop the others from hurting her. Instead, they had just urged each other on, encouraging one another to hurt her even more and to humiliate her.

The Englishwoman had said she was no better than an animal.

Was that true?

Did her life really matter so little?

Chapter 48

The next morning, Nahida stood by Ana's bed trying to rouse her. It was eleven o'clock, the time Nahida usually got up, but a full three hours before the time that Ana ever surfaced for her breakfast of strong coffee and whatever drugs she had managed to eke out to give her a first hit for the day.

Nahida had not slept and could wait no longer to speak to her.

'Ana, please, wake up, I am sorry for this, but I can't carry on.'

Ana rolled over and peered up at Nahida through puffy, red-rimmed eyes that had, just a few months ago, been so beautiful and full of mischief.

'What?' She yawned, not bothering with the nicety of covering her mouth. Her breath was sour.

'I can't carry on, Ana. Not after last night.'

'Are you still going on about that, Nahida? You mustn't let it touch you in your head. What does it matter if it's one man? Two men? Five men? And why was it so bad for them to push themselves into your mouth and your arse? They are pigs, worth nothing.'

Ana levered herself up on to one elbow.

'And I bet they tipped you well. Those sort always compete with each other, showing how many notes they can give us. And at least we are able to sneak out some of those tips. My friend tells me that some clubs body-search the girls before they leave – every night. And they are given just enough food to survive on. They would think you were lying if you told them we have a cupboard of our own with coffee and sugar and food. They are beaten if they complain – you would be black and blue.'

'Ana, concentrate on what I'm saying. I told you: they attacked me. I *am* black and blue. Look at me. How they hurt me.'

Ana flopped back on her pillow, throwing her scrawny arm across her face and sighing dramatic-ally. Her skin was pale and clammy.

'You have to stop letting it get to you or you won't survive.'

'I told you, I can't carry on. I'm leaving here. Now.'

Ana's hand shot out from under the covers and grabbed Nahida by the wrist.

'Don't be so stupid. You can't leave.'

'But I have to.'

'You can't. If you try to leave they will only come and find you and then you will really know what it is to be hurt. They might even kill you.'

Ana glanced at the clock on the packing case that served as her bedside table.

'Why have you woken me up at this time?'

She yawned again, making her eyes water.

'Go and make me some coffee, Nahida. Now I'm awake I'm going to keep an eye on you. Because you are going nowhere.'

Despite it being such a sultry afternoon, Nahida wore her coat to the club.

It was very close to opening time, and the two Englishwomen were standing by the bar, watching her, trying to outguess one another as to what on earth she thought she was up to.

Whatever it was, she was definitely making no effort to get ready; she was just loitering around the door to the tiny lavatory where the girls put on their outfits and made final touches to their make-up.

One thing was clear, she couldn't take her eyes off the entrance to the club. It was actually as if she was waiting for someone. But, apart from the other dancers, who would someone like her know?

One of the women was just about to go over to her and threaten her with yet another warning, when the door opened, Lisa Taylor walked in and Nahida made a dash for her, blocking her way, and opening her coat wide like a pair of unfurling insect wings on a newly hatched pupa.

The two Englishwomen wouldn't have been more surprised if Nahida had burst into joyful laughter and offered to buy them both a drink.

The one who had been about to have a word with Nahida began to move towards them, but her companion stopped her.

'Hold your horses; let's see what this is all about,' she whispered. 'I knew there was something funny about that snobby cow, Lisa.'

Despite being totally startled, Lisa was the first to speak.

'Is there something I can help you with?'

'Yes! The man with the blond hair – your friend.'

Now Lisa was confused as well as startled.

'Jason? What about him?'

Nahida ripped off her coat and let it fall to the floor. She was wearing a skimpy vest and buttock-displaying batty-rider shorts. Her arms, legs and throat were dappled with the bloom of deep bruising that hadn't yet come fully to the surface.

'Jason and four other men. They did this to me. They did other things, and made me do things to them. They hurt me. They raped me. In my mouth, and my arse. And they laughed and pissed on me.'

'Don't be so ridiculous. You must have him mixed up with someone else.'

'All the men who come here think we are nothing.'

Nahida put her hand on Lisa's arm and began to cry. 'They think we are not human.'

Lisa shook her away.

'Get off me.'

Lisa wanted nothing more than to shake this girl, to

stop her from making these accusations, but she couldn't bare the thought of touching her. From the look of her, she probably didn't even keep herself clean.

'Look, you chose how you wanted to earn your living, and –'

'No, please, listen to me, you are wrong. I do not choose this work. They make me do it. And I hate it. I will do anything else. Anything. Please. Help me.'

She had her hands together as if in prayer.

'This is nothing to do with me.' Lisa stepped round her and moved towards the bar. 'And I think you should be careful who you tell lies about in future. Now, I'm sorry, but I'm busy.'

Nahida grabbed at Lisa's sleeve.

'But you don't understand what goes on here,' she sobbed.

Lisa, her eyes wide, tried to pull away from her.

At that point, one of the Englishwomen went and dragged Nahida away, while the other one, the one who had organised the previous night's 'entertainment' for Jason and his friends, led Lisa over to the bar, speaking to her in a lowered, shocked tone.

'I can see from your face that something's upset you, Lisa. She's a real stirrer that Nahida. Her and that other foreign girl, her mate, Ana, they've been a right pair of nuisances since the first day started here. But for some reason a lot of the customers like them.

I suppose it's because they're prepared to do things the others draw a line at. Pair of dirty little whores.'

Lisa's mouth was feeling very dry. She hadn't thought herself naive, had believed that she knew exactly what went on in these places, but she really hadn't imagined that there would be violence.

'What sort of things?'

The Englishwoman snorted unpleasantly. 'You name it, love, they're bloody up for it. Like animals they are.'

'She didn't seem *up for it*. She was covered in bruises.'

The Englishwoman pasted on a smile.

'Look, this is a respectable premises. And we have respectable customers here – just like in all the other places David and Paul run. But her sort, they – how shall I put it politely? – they make private arrangements with people who pay a lot for something a bit more specialised. There are some weird sods out there. And what the girls choose to do in their own time is their business. Nothing we can do about it. But if she's got the cheek to start saying it's down to our members then she'd better watch her mouth.'

She looked at her watch, and managed another, albeit rather thinner, smile.

'You'll have to excuse me, Lisa, it's time to put the show on the road.'

Lisa watched the woman going round the club lowering the lights, then checking the girls as they lined up for inspection, and finally issuing last-minute orders to the bar staff.

The other Englishwoman was nowhere to be seen and nor was the young girl who had just asked for her help.

Lisa swallowed hard. Why would that girl have done that, made those accusations about Jason? The only answer was that she really was confused – probably from too much drink or too many drugs. Lisa wouldn't let herself get sucked into the madness of her paranoia. She had already nearly ruined things with him once, over the misunderstanding about Shaylee, almost losing him because she had mis-interpreted his kindness to that girl and her child. She could just imagine how he'd react if she even mentioned that someone had accused him of doing something as vile as this.

Lisa made a decision – her life was going too well to let some drug-crazed girl's rantings spoil things for her now.

Chapter 49

As was usual, when she awoke, Ana had no clear recollection of how she had spent the two or three hours before she had gone to bed. She yawned noisily and scratched at the tiny scabs dotted in the crook of her elbow.

The flat was very quiet; Nahida must be in the kitchen or in the little bathroom.

'Nahida? Where are you? Are you making coffee?'

No reply.

Ana looked at the clock.

Shit!

It was nearly half past four. Surely Nahida wouldn't have gone to work without waking her.

She closed her eyes, maybe she was punishing her because she hadn't been kinder when she'd asked for her help. But she couldn't worry about that now.

She snatched up the dress that she'd worn the night before – a tiny halter-necked scrap of material – from off the cracked lino and hurried through to the bathroom.

She looked in the mirror and immediately closed her eyes at the sight of her ravaged skin and puffy eyes, her dull, over-bleached hair and cracked lips.

She was going to have to get her life together. She couldn't keep using the rubbish she was buying in Commercial Street – look what it was doing to her. She had to be able to afford better stuff, and she had to get it when she needed it.

She would have to work harder, that's all; earn more tips. And she would ask Nahida to give her more money. She was a good girl, she wouldn't let her down.

With her face plastered in even more make-up than usual, her hair sprayed stiff with cheap lacquer, and her head full of questions about why Nahida had gone to work without her, Ana stumbled her way along the steamy streets to the club.

'Look what the cat's dragged in at last,' sneered one of the Englishwomen. 'And where's your mate?'

Ana blinked as if someone had just shone a light in her face.

'Nahida isn't here?'

'Bright, this one, in't she?' said the other English-woman. 'No, she's not here. After she started leading off last night, I sent her into the lavs to wash her face and no one's seen her since. She has, I suppose you could say, fucked off out of it. But I can't say I'm surprised you haven't noticed, cos look at you, you're in a right bloody state. I've been meaning to have a word with you about getting your head sorted out for weeks now.'

Ana could feel her legs begin to shake, and her knees turning to a wobbly mass that threatened not to support her. Nahida couldn't have gone, Ana needed her – her and her money.

'You must call the police. You must find her.'

'And why would we bother doing that? It's more than obvious what she's been up to – working on the side, going off with Christ knows who. If you ask me, she'll have been murdered likely as not. That's the risk they take when they do that. They don't know who they're dealing with.'

The other Englishwoman nodded.

'And even if a body is found, what d'you think they're gonna do? Who's gonna care about another dead skaghead? An illegal Eastern European whore? Go on, tell me, who's gonna give a shit?'

'Exactly. Everyone'll just be glad that it's happened to one of you lot and not a decent British girl.'

Ana felt sicker than she had in days.

'But how about the Kesslers? Won't they wonder what has happened to her? Want to go and find her?'

The women both laughed, and one of them said: 'Darling, they'll be shipping in some fresh meat very soon, so I don't think they're going to be too upset about losing one little foreign tart. Do you? Go on, be honest with yourself. Face the truth. In fact, when you think about it, it's probably saved them the time and effort of getting rid of her themselves.'

The two women walked away, still speaking, making sure that Ana could hear every word.

'I heard David saying it was about time they got in some new ones. And when you see the state of her, that Ana, who can blame them? She looks like one of them adverts they have for diseases and that. Nothing but skin and fucking bone. And that hair of hers. What a bloody mess that is. How can she expect to carry on working here when she looks like that?' She laughed nastily. 'I mean, who'd want to have her hanging about the place? It's enough to make the customers' dicks go limp at the sight of her.'

'I'll give her another week, tops, before they get rid of her.'

'I still don't see why they don't stick with decent British girls.'

'Me neither, but perhaps this'll teach them a lesson. Who knows? And who cares for now? Cos we've got better things to do – like getting this place opened up before the punters start kicking the bloody doors down.'

The other woman laughed. 'Don't you mean blow the bloody doors?'

Ana staggered over to the lavatories and vomited into the sink, making the other girls squeal at her as they leapt out of the way – but she didn't even register their anger.

She clung on to the cool porcelain, her head

bowed, concentrating on trying to stop her heart from bursting out of her chest.

Ana had heard the words from the woman's own mouth – Nahida had probably been murdered, and *it had saved the Kesslers the trouble of getting rid of her themselves.*

Was that what really happened when they brought in new girls? She had thought they sent the ones they didn't want in the club over to the place they called Forest Gate – to work in the saunas.

What could she do now? Now that she didn't have Nahida to care for her and give her money? She would have barely enough to buy what she needed.

She knew that the supply she got from the girl who worked in Commercial Street was only a recut portion of her own fix – the fix that was supplied to her by her pimp – and that she'd been having to buy more and more of it to top herself up, because it was so weak. But if she couldn't afford even that supply, she would soon look even worse, and then the Kesslers would definitely *get rid of her.*

She had to leave this place before that happened.

She would work tonight, get as many tips as she could, and then, tomorrow, she would go to see the girl on Commercial Street, ask her to get her some work there. She knew the pimps took everything off the girls, but at least they gave them their fixes.

And the men in their cars didn't seem to care that much about who they went with.

Ana splashed water on her face and straightened up.

She had decided – that's what she would do.

Chapter 50

David and Paul Kessler, dressed in jeans and T-shirts rather than their usual sharp suits, were sitting in the back office of Diamond Dan's. It was a small, overcrowded room – no space that could be used for profit was wasted on administration.

Being mid-morning, they were alone – the cleaners had left and no other staff had arrived yet – and that was exactly the way they wanted it. This was a conversation they definitely didn't want to share with anyone.

'I'm telling you, Dave, first that foreign girl buggering off, and everyone claiming they haven't got a clue where she is, and now this. Lisa's got to be responsible. It stinks to high heaven. Something's going on and everything points to her.'

'Everyone has a bit of a weed now and again.'

'A bit of a weed? Look, I said all along we should never have let an outsider come so close. But we did and now this is what happens. Even you've got to admit that it's got to be more than a coincidence that in the six weeks she's had her staff in here the money's suddenly gone right down. And nearly every time one of the dancers asks a bloke if he wants a bit

266

of gear, she's been blanked. Nearly every single time.'

Paul flicked over another page of the coded ledger that recorded their 'special' income from the club, waggling a cheap, plastic ballpoint pen that he'd picked up in a bookie's back and forward between his fingers.

'And you do you know what'll happen if we don't get this sorted out, and get it sorted out very soon – Dad's going to start noticing something's wrong, and all hell'll break bloody loose. And if that's not bad enough . . .' He stood up, pulled a copy of the *East London Chronicle* from the back pocket of his jeans and handed it to his brother. 'Now even the fucking government wants to get busy.'

David gave the headline a brief glance.

'So what's new? It's only all the usual old fanny. I don't even have to read the article to know what it'll be about. They'll be going on about Albanians and sex workers, and sex workers' rights, and kerb-crawlers and communities, and what they're gonna do about it all. I can just hear the fucking hypocrites – *Look at us, see us regulate it all, see us make the streets safe for nice old ladies*. Like they never go to whores. And what's it really all about? I'll tell you – raking in more taxes. That's what. Reminds me of how Grandad used to go on about the Irish and the blacks, yet he was more than happy to work with them if it meant a profit for him. Hypocrisy, see, Paul. Some things just don't change.'

267

'You don't seem worried that they're going to make it legal and nick all our trade off us.'

'Because they'll never do it, that's why. They're just testing out *public opinion*, that's all. Like they'd give a fuck about that if they really wanted to do something.'

David threw the paper in the already overflowing bin.

'Look at the state of this place. And why isn't there a fan in here? I'm bloody sweating.' He stood up and started pacing around the tiny, stifling room.

'Because we don't have to work in here, Dave, that's why. And cos we don't care about the ones who do. Now can we get back to business?'

David stopped pacing, spun round, and smacked his hands flat on the desk; he leaned forward, so that his face was only inches from his brother's.

'Come on, Paul, this is stupid. We've gotta be barking up the wrong tree. You've seen enough of her to know she's not the sort.'

'Not the sort? Start thinking with your brain instead of your prick for once, will you? And *then* tell me: who is the sort? You've seen the customers we get in here: barristers, doctors, big-bollocks financiers. But that don't stop 'em coming to Dan's to poke a bit of stray before they go home to their old woman and their kids and their Labradors, now does it? So why should a posh voice make that cow any

268

more straight than anyone else? If you can call what she does straight.'

'How d'you mean?'

'Do you really think them birds working for her pay tax and insurance? That they're not all on the social?'

David shrugged and dropped his chin, unwilling to meet his gaze.

'I can't stand this, Paul. If Dad finds out, he'll go potty.'

'And would you blame him? We've been a right pair of mugs.'

David tapped agitatedly on the desk. 'We take our fucking eye off the ball for five minutes, while we concentrate on opening the bloody casino, and this has to happen.'

He raised his head and looked at his brother. 'And I know neither of us even dares say it, but let's face it, mate, Dad's gonna be the last of our worries. If the figures are as bad as you say, we're not gonna have the cash to pay for this next load from Miami, and I don't reckon them Bosnian muckers of Vito's are gonna be keen on taking a credit note off us, do you. So what the hell're we gonna do, Paul?'

'For a start, I'd suggest we go through the figures again – properly this time, nice and calm, day by day, so we have the full details. And then, when we've got the evidence right there – so she can't wheedle her way out of it – we have a word with Miss Taylor, and

269

we ask her what her fucking door bitches have been getting up to, that's what.'

David dragged his fingers down his face.

'One of the oldest tricks in the fucking book and us two idiots have fallen for it. I'm telling you, if Dad ever does find out, he's just gonna love this. He'll want to take everything over again and treat us like a pair of kids. He won't let us make a single move without him saying yes or no to it. And he'll think he can go steaming into that Eastern European lot like he did with the Irishmen in the old fucking days, and we'll all wind up being chewed up by the crabs and eels on the fucking Essex marshes. Dead as fucking doornails.'

'And that, Dave, is why we have to sort it out before he does find out. Now come on, pull your chair over here and let's start doing the figures.'

David didn't move. 'I feel sick, d'you know that? And more fucking stupid than I can tell you.'

'Yeah, we've not been too bright, have we?'

Chapter 51

Knowing that the warm, sunny weather would bring the lunchtime crowds to the riverside restaurants by Tower Bridge, Lisa had arrived early at Le Pont de la Tour to make sure that she had a table on the riverside terrace ready for when her mother arrived. She'd brought a book with her for company, but she hadn't read a single word. How could she concentrate? This wasn't going to be one of their regular gossipy lunches. No, it was going to be far more than that – it was going to be a confession.

A partial one at least.

As always, when something was troubling her, Lisa's first instinct was to talk to Sandy. And today there was plenty troubling her. Okay, at the time, she had dismissed the lap dancer's claims that Jason had had anything to do with hurting her, but there was no denying that the girl had been hurt by someone – badly hurt – and she had been adamant that it had happened to her in the club. And the girls did all seem to know Jason . . .

Much as she had tried to push it out of her mind, that little bit of doubt was still there picking away, niggling at her, asking difficult questions.

Lisa had always known that the girls were really tarts rather than just dancers, but what had happened to that girl was far worse than anything she had imagined going on there. And, since the girl had disappeared, it was playing on Lisa's conscience that she had done nothing to help her. Nothing. Even though she had pleaded with her, Lisa had simply closed down, refusing to believe that Jason could possibly have been involved, that he was above such vile behaviour. But the fact that he had let her, a woman he said he loved, become mixed up with such a club in the first place, what did that really say about him?

Lisa took off her sunglasses and pinched the bridge of her nose.

Was it really possible that she had been blinded by her feelings for him, by some deep need to find someone to share her life with?

'Hello, babe.' Sandy came up behind her daughter and kissed her on the top of her head, and then she handed her linen jacket to a waiter.

'I know I'm late, Lisa, but you expect that of me, don't you, babe, and on a beautiful day like this, and with that view, it couldn't have been too much of hardship waiting.'

Sandy settled herself in her chair and stared at the table. 'Not trying to make me go on the wagon at my age, are you, love?'

'Sorry?'

'Where's my vodka and tonic?'

'Mum, I need to talk to you.'

'That sounds serious.'

Lisa dropped her gaze to the tablecloth and said it, quickly, briefly, before she lost her nerve.

'My agency. It's not an ordinary one. It's for female door staff. And one of the places my staff are working, it's a lap-dancing club.'

She pressed her fingertips to her temples, still staring down at the table top.

'Don't say anything, just let me finish. This isn't easy for me.'

'I'm not bloody surprised. You do know what –'

'Mum, please. I know everyone says they're meant to be fine – if you don't mind that sort of thing – and I was told all the girls loved working there, that they earned good money and were well looked after. That it was no different to earning a living as any other type of dancer. But I'm not stupid, I knew this one was a front for a brothel, but . . .'

She could hardly bring herself to say the words that she'd been rehearsing since Sandy had first called her to ask her out to lunch.

'Mum. I've done something really stupid. I don't think all the girls want to be there. And one of them said she'd been gang-raped.'

'Oh, Lisa.'

Shaking her head, Sandy took her daughter's hand.

'After all I told you about me and your dad, and all

273

the crap he got me stuck with. How could you have let this happen? Getting involved with clubs.'

'I thought it'd be okay. That I was tough enough to handle it. That it would be, I don't know, exciting, I suppose.'

'That's my fault; I must have made it sound exciting when I told you about the O'Donnells. That's what's given you the taste for this. It was me. But, darling, it seemed the right thing to do at the time. I thought that if you knew what really happened, what it was really like, then you'd realise how horrible it all was, not glamorous like you see on the telly and in the films. Me and Richard handled it the best we could. It was part of us trying to protect you from the past, to stop it being able to hurt you. I thought we were making you strong – like when we encouraged you to get an education – it was all about giving you a choice about who you could be. But now you've been sucked into that crappy little world we thought we'd saved you from.'

Lisa closed her eyes.

'This is not your fault, Mum. Or Richard's. I'm not a kid any more. And I feel so ashamed. I've been a complete idiot.'

'You're right. You have. Aw, Jesus, just think what'll happen if anyone finds out who you really are. The papers'll think it's bloody Christmas.'

Lisa so wanted to be able to ask her mother what to do, but she couldn't expect her to sort this lot out. She was on her own this time. She was the one who would have to work out what to think about Jason and that young foreign girl, and she was the one who would have to do something about the door staff – she couldn't expect those women to stay working there if there were customers capable of doing that to a girl.

She had to put a stop to all this right now. She'd go and see the Kesslers, pull out of the contract and, who knows, maybe even find out something more about Jason and what had happened to that girl.

She'd been so self-satisfied, so smugly sure that her life was all going so perfectly, and now look at it.

Shit, it was all so complicated.

'I'm going to work out this mess, Mum, I promise you.'

'I know you will, Lisa, and I'm sorry I snapped at you like that. I know you'll do what's right.'

'And I'm sorry too, Mum, more than you'll ever know. Look, I've lost my appetite. Do you mind if we make this another day?'

'Of course I don't mind.' Sandy picked up her bag. 'Now, what can I do to help?'

'Thanks, but I've got to sort this one out alone. It's my responsibility. So don't waste a lovely day like this, you stay and have something now you're here.'

'Go on then, you go. And I'll order meself that vodka and tonic.'

Lisa stood up, stuffing her sunglasses and book carelessly into her tote bag.

She kissed Sandy on the cheek.

'Lisa, promise me one thing, love – be careful. And if you do need any help, you call me or Richard, okay?'

Lisa nodded, biting back the tears of humiliation and anger, and the shame about lying to her mother.

Lisa waited until she was halfway up the steps leading to Tower Bridge before she dared key in the mobile number David had given her. If her mother did somehow find out that the Kesslers were involved she didn't think she'd ever be able to face her again.

'David, it's me, Lisa. Lisa Taylor. Do you think it would be possible for us to have a meeting?'

'Yeah, sure.'

He turned to his brother, pointed at the phone, and mouthed, *It's only her.*

'Tell you what, no time like the present, eh, Lisa. Me and Paul are at Dan's at the minute, so make it straight away, and the three of us'll be nice and private. We can have a chat before the staff start turning up.'

'I'll be there as quick as I can. Have to go, I've just seen a cab coming.'

Call over, David put his phone down on the desk.

'Well, well,' he said, staring at it. 'Now what do you think this is all about then?'

Chapter 52

Less than twenty minutes later, Lisa was speaking into the door intercom outside Diamond Dan's Gentlemen's Club.

'Hello? David, Paul? It's Lisa Taylor here, for our meeting.'

No one answered, but she heard the metallic click of a lock being released. She thought nothing of it, but as she swung the outer door inwards, she was met with total darkness.

They must be in the back office, probably watched her come in on the CCTV.

She put out her hands and felt her way forward.

'Hello? It's me, Lisa. Can someone turn on a lamp or something, please? I can't see a thing.'

Suddenly the room was flooded with bright light.

She blinked and drew her chin in tight to her chest. She tried to shield her eyes with her hand, but someone grabbed her arms and pinned them behind her back.

Tall and fit as she was, Lisa couldn't move; whoever was holding her had her in a grip that she had no chance of breaking.

'What's going on?' she yelled, not sure if she was more angry or afraid.

'You've got some balls, girl, I'll give you that.'

The voice came from behind her.

She kept her head down and opened her eyes just wide enough to see David standing in front of her. The voice from behind must have been Paul's.

David had his arms folded and was shaking his head.

'Oh dear, oh dear,' he sighed, as if he were the headmaster, and she was a favoured pupil, a pet, whose bad behaviour had let down not just him but the whole school.

'Take her through to the back office, will you, Paul? We don't want to be disturbed.'

So it was Paul holding on to her; maybe that meant that there were just the three of them. Maybe. But as to what was happening, and why – she had absolutely no idea.

'I said, what's going on?' she repeated out loud, still struggling to break free, but well aware that Paul was far too strong for her.

David walked past her; she heard him behind her, locking the mortice on the front door.

'Will you answer me?'

'Let's just say there are some questions we want to ask you,' he said, sliding home the big brass security latches at the top and bottom of the jamb.

'Questions? What about?'

278

She planted her feet and twisted her head round to talk to him as Paul tried to march her towards the office.

'I said – what questions?'

'You'll find out soon enough,' said Paul. 'Now just move, will you, or I'll bloody drag you into the office. Kicking and screaming if I have to.'

'If you hurt me, everyone will know it was you. Lots of people know where I am.'

She knew she was talking like a character in some cheap cop show on the TV, but what else could she do? Other than hints about the violence in the stories her mother had told her about the family, she had no experience of anything like this.

'I promise you, it would be a big mistake to hurt me.'

'Why on earth would we hurt a nice young lady like you?' David asked, his tone of mock offence at such a suggestion making him seem even more menacing.

'Here, Paul, don't tell me she's gone and done something wrong. Something we might take exception to. You've not, have you, Lisa? Because that'd be terrible that would, wouldn't it, Paul? That'd make us really unhappy.'

'No, I haven't done anything wrong, and that's why I want to know why you're doing this to me. I demand to know –'

'Bloody hell,' David interrupted her, 'what is it

with birds, eh, Paul? Don't they ever know when to fucking shut up?'

He stuck a finger in her face.

'Now you just button your fucking lip. I'm gonna ask you some questions and then you can fucking talk when I fucking say so. You got that?'

Lisa nodded.

Chapter 53

It had been just two days since Ana had left the club, but she was already spiralling down to depths that she had never known before. She had never experienced such fear and anxiety, such cold and outright terror – not even back home when she had had to flee for her life.

All she could think about, focus on, was how she could get her next fix.

At first it had seemed as if everything was going to be fine. When Ana had turned up on the patch where she worked, Teri, the prostitute who supplied her with drugs, had taken pity on her and had agreed to take her in. Ana had even thought at first that one of the other street girls might have seen Nahida, might know where she was staying.

But Ana soon realised, even in her befuddled state, that the other girls couldn't give a damn about Nahida or her whereabouts, and that things at Teri's were far from ideal.

If she wanted to earn better money, Ana had to look good, but having to sleep on the single, greasy arm-chair that, apart from a ripped and stained mattress, made up the furnishings in Teri's tiny, grubby flat was hardly going to help. And the semi-derelict, graffiti-covered tenement block sandwiched between Commercial Street and Brick Lane was not even a safe place to sleep. The flat in Hackney, where she had lived with Nahida, hadn't been exactly palatial, but at least there hadn't been gangs of children setting light to the overflowing bins every night as they tried to smoke them out, and older kids calling out vile names and hurling abuse at Teri and the other girls as they stood waiting for the kerb-crawling customers on the street corners and in shop doorways.

Worse than all of that was the fact that – for the moment – she had no money. Not a single penny left. Teri was being as generous as she could – and even in the state she was in, Ana was still aware enough to know that the woman owed her nothing – but when she had pleaded with her to introduce her to her pimp, Ana had been faced with a brick wall of refusal. And no matter how Teri had tried to dress it up with kind words, it was a total obliteration of all Ana's hopes.

'I'm not being funny or nothing, Ana,' Teri had said, in her smoke-coarsened Liverpudlian growl, 'but you look dead rough, girl. Why don't you have a rest for a few days, get yourself together? And then I'll see what I can do for you.'

Ana had wanted to shout at her, make her see that she had to get her work with her pimp – it was all she had left – but she had to be careful: if she upset Teri she had nothing.

Not even a greasy armchair, in a rat-infested slum.

'And look, love, to be dead straight with you, the other girls won't be very welcoming, even if he does agree to take you on. They can be right vicious cows when they get the nark with someone. And you might look a bit, you know . . . tired – but you're younger than most of them, and with a bit of slap to cover the bags under your eyes and to give a bit of colour to your cheeks, you'll make them look like right minging old crows. You see, you've not got saggy tits and stretch marks on your belly like they have – like I have and all, I suppose,' she added with a good-natured chuckle. 'And, believe me, they won't take that very well.'

Teri took a deep swig from the can of strong lager she'd been holding, swiped the back of her hand across her mouth and handed it to Ana.

'And, there's something else you should know, and all,' she went on as Ana drank from the can. 'This area belongs to the Kesslers.'

Ana nearly choked on the lager.

'That cannot be true.'

'On my life, it is. They took over the whole territory years ago from this right hard Irish family. The O'Donnells they were called. I'm not sure of the full story – you hear all sorts round here – but some-thing kicked off between them and the O'Donnells and then the O'Donnells started fighting among themselves, and while the Irishmen were busy

shooting one another, the Kesslers took the opportunity to move in.'

'These people let the Kesslers do this?'

'They weren't here to stop them, were they? The
ones in charge of the O'Donnells rubbed each other
out. It all happened somewhere over in Spain so they
say. And, from what I've heard, the others just
disappeared, got out while they could. Anyway, at
first, the Kesslers used to run the girls themselves,
with their old man overseeing everything, but, what
with them running the clubs and stuff, it's all subbed
out now, with blokes being allowed to work their girls
round here if the Kesslers say so, *and* if they pay them
their dues on the dot and remember to show respect
by not taking any liberties. Cos I'm telling you now,
Ana, the Kesslers don't take any prisoners.'

Teri took a few moments lighting a cigarette.

'See, Ana, I'm telling you this, because if the word
got round that you'd done a runner from one of the
Kesslers' clubs, any of the blokes here would have
your arse back round there before you could so much
as offer them a blow job by way of showing them
how grateful you'd be if they didn't. They wouldn't
risk upsetting that family. No one would.'

She reached out for the can.

'So, what you gonna do then, Ana?'

Ana shook her head. 'I don't know, but I have to
have money.'

'Yeah, it's a right bugger that fivers don't grow on

trees, eh, girl? But I was thinking, you could try a bit further away – say Whitechapel. For a start there'd be less chance of anyone recognising you down there. Although you'd still have to be careful of the other girls; they don't like new people moving in.'

Ana nodded, her mouth was dry, and the sweating was getting worse.

'Thank you. I will go to Whitechapel away from you and where you work. But please, help me, Teri. I need my fix. I promise I will pay you when I have worked. But I can't work unless I have fix first. Please, Teri. I will pay you everything I owe you. Soon. Very soon. You have my word.'

'Go on then,' said Teri, with a sickly half-smile. 'I'm just too soft for me own good, me. Always have been. That's me trouble. And how I got into this game in the first place – couldn't say no to a boyfriend who owed his dealer a lot of dough. But this is the last time you get anything off me for no money, all right? I just can't afford it.'

'Thank you, Teri, thank you. I promise I will pay you very soon.'

'Yeah, yeah, ne'mind all that, just let's get this over with and then I'm going back to bed for a couple of hours.'

She swallowed the last of the lager.

'This bloody heat's really getting to me.'

Chapter 54

An hour later, Ana was fully made up and dressed to thrill. But she wasn't standing where Teri had told her to, at the top of one of the few remaining Victorian alleys that still lead off the Whitechapel Road, just as prostitutes had done since the time when Jack the Ripper had terrorised the women of the East End. Instead, she was skulking around much closer to home – or rather Teri's home – by Spitalfields Market at the top of Lamb Street, watching the spot across the main road where Teri usually worked. It was still burningly hot, despite it now being late afternoon, and she was finding it difficult to stay alert with the drug still fresh in her veins. Her thick foundation and blusher were beginning to dissolve and slip as they mixed with the trickles of sweat bleeding from her hairline.

She forced open her eyes, holding them wide, and licked at her lips, feeling the stickiness of her lipstick, as she scanned up and down Commercial Street. There was the usual busy mix of people – business suits striding purposefully along despite the heat; trendies posing outside the bars in their latest scruffily outlandish outfits; heavily veiled Muslim women shuffling along in sandals, loaded down with carrier bags of shopping and babies; and young Asian boys on bikes wearing hoodies and tracksuit bottoms calling out to one another in accents as phoney as the labels on their baseball caps, that sounded as if they originated in the Caribbean rather than in east London or Bangladesh.

But despite the throng of people, and her thick head, Ana still managed to pick out four working girls. They were standing in a straggly line by the kerb, smoking the black-market cigarettes they bought in Brick Lane, and scoping the passing traffic as they waited for the stream of customers who would soon be pulling up in their cars, looking for a quickie before facing the rigours of the rush hour as they made their way home to their wives and families.

Her thoughts wandered back to Nahida. Was she standing on a street corner somewhere, desperate enough to earn money to do what she had always hated? Or maybe she just couldn't take any more and was floating face down in a river, released from all of this for ever.

Forcing herself to concentrate on what she was about to do, Ana shook herself, and then stood poised like a nervous greyhound waiting in the traps, knowing she would have to act fast if this was going to work.

She saw the first car slow down – a battered silver-grey Nissan Bluebird – and waited for the driver – his face concealed by the peak of his baseball cap pulled down low over his eyes – to duck his head as he assessed the girls standing on the pavement.

He stopped by a hefty brunette. Her hair was caught up in childlike bunches tied with tatty red ribbons, and she was wearing a tiny shoestring-strapped vest and a micro-kilt made from some stiff, cheap material that had left a criss-cross of pink scratches on the wobbling expanse of her bare, orange-peel thighs that were displayed almost to her crotch.

The driver wound down the window on the passenger side and leaned across to speak to her. The brunette folded her arms and rested them on the roof of the car; she looked down at him with a mouth-only smile, making sure her heavy, braless breasts were on full show.

Even in her bewildered state, Ana knew this was her chance; the chance she had to take before she lost her courage.

She rushed out into the road, making a dash for the other side of the street, weaving through the hooting traffic and ignoring the foul-mouthed curses being hurled at her as cars and trucks swerved and skidded around her.

She pulled open the back door on the driver's side of the Nissan, jumped inside the car, and gasped hurriedly: 'I do whatever you want. For five pounds less than her. And I'm prettier.'

288

It was difficult to tell if it was the customer or the prostitute who was the more surprised, but it was obvious who was best pleased by the unusual turn of events.

'Sorry, darling, she's right, she is prettier than you,' said the driver, slipping the car into first. Then he looked approvingly at Ana in the rear-view mirror. 'The blokes at work are never gonna believe this in the morning.'

As he spun the car round in a wild U-turn – setting off another round of tooting and shouting – so that he was facing in the right direction to head for the spot he favoured near the site of the old goods yard, Ana twisted round and looked out of the back window. She couldn't hear the other girl's words, but her meaning was more than clear.

That would be the first and last time that Ana would be allowed to pull that particular stroke on Commercial Street. And if she wanted to keep working – and her head on her shoulders – it would have to be the unknown streets of Whitechapel from now on.

Chapter 55

Lisa felt like nothing more than curling herself into a ball, making herself as small as she could, less of a target from she didn't know what; but she forced herself to sit determinedly upright in the swivel chair behind the desk in the back office – the chair that Paul Kessler had practically thrown her on to. She wouldn't let them see she was cowed, even though Paul and his brother were staring down at her, their faces stony, their shoulders set, their hands grasping the edge of the desk – a nightmare vision of lawyers conducting a Kafkaesque cross-examination demanding to know the truth.

She wanted to shift in the chair, to smooth down her skirt that had ridden up over her thighs – the exposed flesh making her feel even more vulnerable – but, she reasoned, to start wriggling and fidgeting would make her seem as if she felt discomfited, sitting there with them looming over her.

Discomfited, who was she kidding? She was bloody terrified, and not least because they weren't saying anything.

Why weren't they saying anything?

The silence was really beginning to get to her.

She took a gulp of air – barely able to swallow it down.

'My mother is expecting to meet me in less than half an hour.'

'Cut the crap.' It was David. 'We know you've been conning us.'

Lisa felt her stomach lurch. They'd found out who she was.

'You really had us for mugs, didn't you, you bitch? We had you down as someone who just wanted to do a bit of business with us, for a fair amount of dough. More than a fair amount as it happened, because me, silly nuts, took a shine to you. But the game's over, darling, we've seen right fucking through you.'

Surely they wouldn't blame her for things her father had done. But looking at their faces, she wasn't so sure.

She had to do something; play for time so she could think what to do.

Do something.

'I'm sorry, I don't understand.'

'What's not to understand? We've got the measure of you, you lying cow. We. Know.'

'Look, this is ridiculous, I genuinely have no idea what you're –'

'Please, do us a favour.'

This time it was Paul speaking. He looked about him impatiently.

'It's bad enough you trying to cop our business

off us, but do not, and I mean do not, treat us like mugs. Unlike my brother here, I'm not usually an aggressive man, but if there's anything I hate, it's having the piss taken out of me. And it's all so bloody obvious now – that is exactly what you've been fucking doing. Soon as we started concentrating on the casino, you made your fucking move, didn't you? And we let you.'

Paul threw up his hands in frustration at his own stupidity.

'And while we're at it,' David took over, 'what do you know about them two Eastern European birds disappearing? Tell me you're not running knocking shops on the side and all, are you?'

'They've *both* disappeared? When?'

'Please, just try and remember what Paul said about taking us for mugs. That dumb act might work with your sort, sweetheart, but I'm warning you, if you don't start talking about who's involved, and the exact ins and outs of how and what you've done to us, you are going to be very sorry indeed. That pretty face of yours is going to be rearranged so that even the Commercial Street punters wouldn't give you the fucking time of day. Now, I'm telling you this for nothing, I want names, and I want them now, spelt out for me, because every single person who's been involved in this is going to pay – personally – for even daring to think they can have one over on the Kesslers. It is going to become public knowledge that

292

no one – *no one* – can do this to us. They can't even think of upsetting us without paying the price. And I do not intend making a prick of myself by blaming people who've got nothing to do with it. Because I am not going to look weak. I am going to take back control of this situation. Have you got that?'

Now Lisa was totally confused – did they know she was an O'Donnell or not? He made it sound as if they still believed she was Lisa Taylor, the *posh bird*.

'What do you mean "my sort"?'

'What?' David looked at his brother to see if he could make any sense of what she was saying.

'You said something about – I can't remember the exact words – but something like "this dumb act working with my sort". What did you mean?'

It was now David's turn to show his frustration, which he did rather more violently than his brother. He swept his arm across the desk, sending everything crashing to the ground, then he reached across and grabbed Lisa so roughly by the collar of her neat white shirt, that it ripped off, coming away with half of the front panel, exposing the swell of her breasts over the lacy half-cups of her bra.

She recoiled from his touch and then gasped in shock and pain as he slapped the back of his hand across her cheek.

'Stop it,' she screamed.

'You think that hurt? Believe me, that was just a fucking tap. So, if you don't want worse, start talking.

293

Is it all the door bitches you've got shifting charlie through the clubs? Or just –'

The pain of the blow to her face was nothing compared to this. 'Me, dealing in drugs?'

'Halle-fucking-lujah. She's admitted it at last.'

'I've admitted nothing, I just thought you'd found . . .'

'Thought we'd found what?'

'Nothing.'

'Now you really have made a mistake.'

David walked out of the office into the main body of the club and came back with a bottle of red wine, holding it by the neck.

'D'you want some of this, do you?'

Lisa shook her head, trying to steady her breathing and to ignore the stinging in her cheek. 'No. I think I'd be sick.'

David looked at Paul. 'Is she for real?'

Then he smashed the body of the bottle on the edge of the desk, leaving him covered in red wine and holding what was now a jagged weapon that he thrust towards Lisa's face.

'I wasn't offering you a fucking drink, you saucy mare.'

She screamed again and held up her arms to protect herself.

'I am giving you one last chance to tell me the truth or you get this in the face and then, guess what, you'll find yourself having a car crash and all to explain away the fucking wounds. Please, Lisa, don't make me do that to a pretty girl like you – much as I'd enjoy it.'

Chapter 56

Back home, even during the worst of the troubles, Ana had never slept in the street before. Yet here she was in London, the capital of Great Britain, a place she could only ever have dreamed she would see, curled up under layers of flattened-out grocery cartons, in a stinking, urine-soaked alley in White-chapel that was full of rubbish, scurrying rats, and other noises and smells that she couldn't even begin to identify – had she wanted to.

She wasn't huddled under the cardboard to keep warm, the night air was almost steaming it was still so hot, but to disguise the fact that she was there. She might have been tougher and more experienced than any eighteen-year-old had a right to be, but she had no intention of letting the ragbag of drunks and junkies who seemed to make up most of the night-time population of the area know she was there. Even the cheap, ill-made clothes she had been given to wear in the club, including the halter-neck dress that she had now been wearing for the past three long days, looked like haute couture compared to what they had wrapped and draped around them.

But it was the stench of them that was the worst.

When she had crawled out of the container on the back of the lorry after the horrendous first part of their journey, Ana had sworn to herself that she would never be dirty again, and she had kept that promise. Until now.

She couldn't stomach the thought that she would become like these creatures.

If only she had enough money, she would go to Teri, pay her debt, and get another fix, and then she would be fine, she would be able to work, sort herself out.

She had tried to work, but after only one punter – five pounds for a blow job against a big blind wall topped with razor wire that fenced in a big, old-looking building that she realised must be a school when she heard the children laughing and singing as they played their games on the other side – she had felt so overwhelmingly tired that she just had to find somewhere to rest.

She hadn't meant to, but she had fallen asleep under the cardboard. Carefully, she lifted one of the layers and looked up and down the alley.

No one there.

Ana undid the ties of the halter neck and pulled down her top to check that the five-pound note was still tucked safely into her bra.

If she hadn't felt so bad, she would have gone and seen Teri anyway, seen if she would help her – as a friend – until she had done more business. But she did feel bad. Really bad.

Doing more business was her only option.

She smoothed down her hair, not wanting to imagine what she must look like, and tottered on her high heels towards the light coming from the street lamps on the main road.

Ana stood at the top of the alley and looked up and down the broad thoroughfare.

A few cars, an empty taxi with its light off – the driver heading home, not even bothering to try and find a fare in this area – and then an ambulance speeding out of the hospital opposite – siren off the street was so empty. Even the drunks had vanished.

She leaned against the rough brick wall, her hands hanging loosely by her side, eyelids drooping with exhaustion.

She should have kept them open.

'Hand it over,' a man's voice demanded from behind her, from somewhere deep in the alley.

Ana spun round to confront whoever it was who had spoken to her, but she misfooted herself on her high heels, and stumbled towards him at speed, arms flailing as she tried to right herself.

'What the fuck are you doing?' The man was alarmed, not expecting such a reaction. 'Just gimme your mobile or I'll chiv you, you whore.'

Ana managed to stop the momentum by throwing

herself sidelong into the wall, and finally brought herself to a halt. But as she stared into the pitch darkness of the alley, she couldn't make out anything other than a dark shape looming in front of her; the man, on the other hand, could see her silhouetted clearly against the street lighting at the mouth of the alley, giving him the advantage.

'I said, gimme your mobile, cunt.'

His voice was now very close and Ana could see him in enough detail to know he was a gangly, skinny man, with deeply sunken cheeks, and a wild halo of matted hair. He could have been any age.

'I don't have mobile.'

'Lying bitch.'

A filth-ingrained hand shot out and tried to grab her, but Ana wasn't giving up her five-pound note – all she had in the world – that easily.

She turned and threw herself back towards the mouth of the alley, running as fast as she could, and straight out into the road.

The night bus hit her before she had even realised she had left the pavement.

And the young doctor standing smoking on the hospital steps opposite hadn't even had time to shout for her to stop.

Chapter 57

'You're a fucking O'Donnell?'

Lisa, chin in the air, teeth clenched, nodded. It might have been a moment of madness admitting it, but she had really thought he was about to stick the bottle in her face: the world and the men who inhabited it – that she had found so fascinating – were suddenly only too horribly real.

David looked at his brother. 'She must be Brendan's kid.'

'Come on, Dave. She's making it up to sound hard, and you're being paranoid believing her.'

'Am I? How would someone like her come up with that name unless she was something to do with them?'

Paul shrugged. 'There's plenty of books she could have read.'

'Think about it, Paul. Think about when Dad used to tell us all them stories when we were kids and he was pissed up and getting all sentimental about the *good old days*.'

'You obviously listened to him more than me. I just used to cock a deaf 'un, when he started. Bit like you did when I said we shouldn't have this scheming cow coming anywhere near the clubs.'

300

Lisa watched in silence as the men argued, trying to figure out a way to get out of this.

'I'll ignore that for now, Paul, and just say that perhaps you should have listened a bit closer when Dad was spinning his tales. Cos he reckoned that after Luke blew his and Brendan's brains out, the only one of the O'Donnell mob he was ever worried about was the bird Brendan had got married to. He said she was smart. That she had it in her to carry on the businesses if she had a mind to.'

'A bird taking over all the businesses?' Paul glared at Lisa who was doing her best to resist throwing up. 'Leave off. Who'd let a woman get away with that in them days?'

'I'm telling you, I can't remember her name, but this particular woman set up one of the first escort businesses this side of the West End. Had all the trade from the City and east London. But then she fell out with Brendan over something and she disappeared with their kid. And this bitch has gotta be that kid. And now she's got it in her head that she's fucking gonna take everything over.'

He grabbed Lisa by the hair, dragging her towards him over the broken glass on the desk, soaking her in the red wine.

'I don't want to take over anything,' she said, her face contorted with pain.

'Oh no?'

He yanked harder on her hair.

301

'*No*. I only got involved in the first place because of Jason. I knew nothing about how clubs are run, how to go about setting up an agency for door staff. Nothing. Not without him helping me with the recruiting and registering and . . .'

As the words tailed off in her mouth, Lisa knew exactly what she had just done: she'd not only implicated Jason in all of this, but she had at last admitted to herself the truth about him. The truth she had been denying for all too long.

David pushed her back in the swivel chair. He spun it round so fast that her head snapped back and she thought she was going to pass out. She closed her eyes, took a deep breath and then looked up at him; she had to calm him down.

'Jason couldn't have known what was going on. He's got too much to lose. You know how bad his upbringing was. Yet he's achieved so much at work, he'd never want to –'

'Do what?'

'He'd never risk everything he's worked so hard for.'

David burst out laughing, but he didn't sound in the least amused.

'What crap has that arsehole been feeding you?'

'He worked his way up from nothing, and he –'

'Stop right there, you silly mare. His poor background is actually very plush, spoilt Essex boy with a big house and private schools. Daddy was a

302

stockbroker. And young Jason only started working in the City when his old man forced him to after he was chucked out of the last of those very posh schools that had finally had enough of him and his little two-bob scams and his bullying all the younger kids.'

'No. You're lying.'

'Well, ask him, you silly whore. He's proud of it. Tells everyone – except the *laydeez* of course, cos they don't like that sort of thing do they. And it's important to that little prat to impress 'em.'

Lisa no longer felt the pain of David's blow, only the pain in her gut, the pain of betrayal. The final, undeniable proof. Jason had been using her all along. Taking her for the worst type of needy fool, and that's exactly what she had been. But no more. She'd have that bastard for this – one way or another. And then she had one or two questions for Richard Middleton.

She needed to play for time.

'At least let me talk to him. Let me be sure.'

David looked at Paul.

'What d'you reckon?'

Paul considered for a moment.

'So long as we keep tabs on the pair of them, it's probably not a bad idea. This is serious stuff, Dave, and we want to be certain we've got the right person this time.'

He jerked a thumb at Lisa.

'Only a couple of minutes ago, I was sure it was her. But now I really don't know. If she is involved, knowing Jason, he'll be more than willing to drag her down with him. So what's the odds?'

David turned back to Lisa.

'Fair enough, you can go and see him, but if you don't want to end up going on the missing list, you just remember we're going to be close by. And you can remember this and all – you are doing a job for us, not helping that wanker get away with it. So any sign that he's trying to have it away on his toes – you're both in trouble. Got it?'

Lisa nodded.

He stuck a finger right into her face.

'In fact, Lisa Taylor, or O'Donnell, or whatever your fucking name really is, if you're not lying about this – and for your sake you'd better not be – and it is him and not you who's been having us over, then we are going to expect you to bring us Blond Jason's head on a fucking silver platter.'

Chapter 58

Despite the oppressively humid weather, Hoxton Marcus, his dark hair curling down on to his shoulders, was wearing his trademark black, theatrical-looking suit with its long, flaring jacket and drainpipe trousers. He was leaning against the rough, bare brick wall, arms folded loosely across his bony chest, at the back of the latest trendy bar to spring up on the Kingsland Road. Geographically the bar could have been part of the Kesslers' empire, but in terms of who frequented it, it might as well have been in another galaxy. People who drank here would no more go to the sorts of places owned by the Kesslers than they'd have been seen in anything other than the latest outfits created by the young indie designers working around Spitalfields and Brick Lane. The same could be said of the Kesslers' booted and suited customers who wouldn't give the trendy bars a second look, dismissing them as half-finished dumps full of weirdos.

'So,' breathed Marcus, his voice velvety and languid, just a touch effete, matching the decadence of his appearance. 'You say that young Master Carter is back on the scene and spending lots of money again.'

'I'm only telling you what I've heard, Marcus.'

His companion spoke in a strangulated mockney, the latest accent taken up by the trustafarians who lived in the lofts and warehouse conversions in and around the Shoredtich Triangle – in the homes flogged to them by enthusiastic estate agents who couldn't even begin to afford living in the area themselves, and who despised their clients for many more reasons than their affected speech.

'And I'm not stirring or nothing, geez, you've got my solemn word on that, but I just thought you'd want to know, that's all. What with you putting the word out that he's in debt to you and no one's to let him have any gear or anything. So it didn't seem right to me.'

Marcus sighed wearily, unfolded his arms and took a red-enamelled cigarette case set with a mother-of-pearl cross of St George from his inside pocket.

'I appreciate the information, but what would make me a far happier man would be knowing whether the gentleman in question has any intentions of paying back some of the money he owes me.'

'Can't help you there, Marcus. Law to himself that one. Always ducking and diving. Here, there and everywhere. You know Blond Jason.'

'Unfortunately, yes, I do know him. And I also know that I was a fool to be so kind and generous to the ungrateful little man.'

Warming to being in Hoxton Marcus's good books

– a useful place to be when you wanted to buy yourself some marching powder but had no cash in your pocket because the next cheque from your trust fund wasn't due for ten whole days – the man began building up his part.

'He's well taking the piss, if you ask me, Marcus. And that doesn't make you look good, does it. You know what I'd do if I were you, I'd –'

Marcus's eyes narrowed slightly. 'Don't even think about being me.'

'Sorry.'

The man squirmed, not daring to speak until spoken to, while Hoxton Marcus smoked.

At last.

'I would be interested in finding out where all this money has suddenly come from. So far as I'm aware, most of the City boys aren't due their big bonuses for months yet. And with all the debt he must be in, it's rather a puzzle.'

The other man relaxed. This was his chance to play his ace.

'Word is, Marcus, he's found a nice little niche for himself. A good little earner that's raking it in.'

'Really? And what sort of *earner* would that be?'

'Distributing gear through this string of clubs. Lap-dancing joints and a new casino.'

'So, he's gone wholesale, has he?'

'Yeah, but it's not straightforward, Marcus. See, the clubs, they belong to these geezers called Kessler.

And the thing is, they don't even know he's moved in on 'em yet, cos he's not being exactly public about it. I only found out about it because I know a girl who works at one of the Kesslers' clubs as a door bitch.'

And who won't let me have any more charlie till I get my cheque, the miserable, evil witch, he thought but knew far better than to say out loud if he wanted to hang on to the chance of Marcus being rather more generous with him.

'Kessler. I've heard the name, of course, but can't say I've ever taken much interest in their sort of trade. Not my thing. Too downmarket.'

Marcus studied his perfectly shaped nails. He wasn't going to show it – that wasn't his way – but he wasn't happy about this. He'd never had to consider the Kesslers' presence as any sort of competition – theirs was a different world, a world his clients wouldn't be seen dead being part of. Except for one – Jason Carter. With him coming into the equation he couldn't be so sure any more. Carter was one of those rare people who seemed to be at ease in any environment, a social chameleon, and if he had enough gear to supply that many clubs, his ambitions might just start expanding in a way that could affect Hoxton Marcus's very nice way of life.

Marcus blinked slowly. If he wasn't careful this could turn into some embarrassing old-style turf war with Blond Jason thinking he could run the whole show.

'Who would know about these people, these Kesslers?'

The other man thought for a moment.

'There's this old bloke I've met a couple of times in the boozer where he drinks, over Spitalfields way. Pete Mac they call him. And when he gets pissed – which is just about every time he gets a glass in his hand – he goes on about how he was this hard nut, a right well-known face in his day. It's all to do with him being part of this big, tough Irish family – the O'Donnells. They had a feud with the Kesslers. A lot of people got hurt. It was over territory, that sort of a row, you know.'

'I know,' said Marcus flatly.

'Well, soon as people buy him a few drinks he just can't stop talking about it. He loves it, reckons he's still some sort of gangster or something. What he doesn't realise is that half the time they're ripping the piss out of him.'

Marcus took a long draw on his cigarette.

'I'd like to meet this Pete Mac.'

He looked at his watch.

'Nearly two o'clock. Will he be there now, do you think?'

'Marcus, do bears shit in the proverbial?'

'There really is no need to be vulgar.'

Chapter 59

With the flat being so high up in the landmark tower that looked out over the City and far beyond, Jason didn't bother drawing the curtains in the bedroom of his Barbican apartment, and so the strong, afternoon sun was filling the room with bright summer light, making it as warm as a tropical beach.

But that wasn't the reason that Jason's body was covered in a film of sweat as he straddled the bucking female body stretched out beneath him.

He was, in his typical, competitive way, proving that he was the best sexual partner a woman could wish for, and that no one else – no one – could claim to come anywhere close to having his masculine prowess.

That sort of thing was important to Jason Carter.

After she had climaxed with a series of shuddering orgasms, he rolled off her and stretched out for the waiting spliff in the ashtray on his bedside table.

Propping himself up on one arm, he lit up and then turned back to her. He ran his hand rhythmically up and down her body, stroking her heavy breasts, and tracing the outline of her full round hips, his hand pale against her black skin.

'I always knew I was your best girl, Jay. I am your girl, ain't I? Tell me I am. Go on. Please, Jay. Make me happy. Just say it.'

He pulled his hand away and fell back on to the pillows.

'Don't start whining, Shaylee.'

'I'm not whining, I was just saying. Asking you to be nice to me for once.'

'Well, fucking don't. What's wrong with you? You always have to go and spoil things. I don't know why I put up with you. Why I even let you back in here.'

'Am I allowed to say anything?'

'Long as it's not more fucking moaning.'

'It won't be, Jay, honest.'

She smiled and took the spiff from his hand and inhaled deeply – Jason could always be relied on to only ever have the best dope.

She gave it back to him. 'I just want to talk to you about our little Alfie, love him. See, I was wondering if you'd let me have a bit of money for his new school shoes. He's growing like anything these days, Jay. Gonna be a right beanpole, he is. You'll have to see him again soon or you're hardly gonna recognise him. And he's getting to be a right little devil.'

She nestled closer.

'Just like his daddy. And d'you know what would be really great, what would really help? If you could find a bit extra for us, you know, to see us through the school holidays when he breaks up. And that won't be long. The weeks are flying by. And I know what'll happen, he'll be wanting to go out for the day and go to the pictures and that, and have extra sweets and stuff. That's all you get out of him at the minute – can I have this? Can I have that? Can we do this? And can we do that? And can I have these new trainers like the other kids have got? The ones that footballer wears – you know, Jay, that young bloke they're all talking about, the one with the ears. And he wants one of them new hoodies – the one with the designer name on the front. Honestly. His age, and he's into fashion.'

Shaylee waited a moment, gauging Jason's mood. She had all this prepared, but she knew she had to be careful how she spoke to him. He could flash from angel to demon before she knew what was happening.

'Here,' she said, all bright and smiley, as if she'd just had a brainwave, 'd'you know what'd be really great, Jay? What'd really make our little un's day for him?' She sat up and looked right into his eyes, her face shining. 'If the three of us went away somewhere. Together. On a proper holiday. Like a real family. He'd love to be able to say he'd gone away with his mum and dad. Be really something special to tell all the other kids on the estate. Maybe we could even go abroad somewhere. I know he'd be really made up if we did that.'

'Have you finished?'

He needn't have said anything; the look on his face was enough to deflate her.

'Yeah. Sorry.'

His mobile began ringing; the personalised tone that told him it was Lisa calling.

'Look, Shaylee, me wallet's on the side in the kitchen. There's, I don't know, about three hundred and fifty quid in there. Take the three hundred and leave me the rest. Go on. Go and get it. I've gotta take this call.'

Naked, Shaylee padded through to the kitchen. Silently celebrating a bigger victory than perhaps, deep down, she'd ever dared to expect.

Jason closed the bedroom door behind her.

Chapter 60

'Lisa. Hello, darling. I can't tell you how good it is to hear from you. You won't believe this, but I was just daydreaming about you and me. Thinking about what I'd like to be doing to you on this lovely sunny afternoon rather than being stuck in here in the office. It is very hard indeed – pun fully intended – to concentrate while I'm sitting here at my desk, when all I've got on my mind is you. I just hope the others don't work out why I've got this pained expression on my face.'

Lisa stiffened. *I won't believe this?* Well, he was right about that, the rotten, stinking liar. She'd already tried him on his work number, and his horrible cow of an assistant had taken great pleasure in saying she was surprised that Lisa didn't know he wasn't in today.

She took a deep breath and let it out slowly to steady herself.

'You still there, Lis?'

'Yes. Sorry. I'm still here. The line was breaking up, that's all. Listen, Jason, I've been thinking about you too. And I really want to see you. Soon as you can.'

'Something wrong?'

The door opened, and Shaylee, smiling happily, came back into the room; she was about to speak, but Jason frowned angrily, shook his head and put a finger to his lips

'No, nothing wrong, Jason, just urgent. Very urgent. Can you . . .' There was a slight pause, as she summoned up, with great effort, the effect of sounding as if she wanted him desperately. 'Get away from work?'

'Sure I can – if it's that important to you.' He liked the sound of this. 'That'll be no problem at all.'

'That would be fantastic. I really can't wait. It's been days since we've been able to be alone together, what with me being so busy at the casino. And I don't want to be too explicit over the phone, but this warm weather, it's making me feel – you know.'

She looked round at David and Paul Kessler who were stretched out on her sofas with drinks in their hands, as if they were welcome guests rather than two thugs who had not only threatened her but had actually hit her. She knew she had no choice, but she was feeling so shell-shocked by the bombardment of lies and revelations – and fear – that she felt like doing nothing more than crawling into bed and going to sleep, to hide away from the hideous truth that she knew was going to be revealed, here in her own home, the place she had believed was her haven.

'Jason, can you come here, over to my flat?'

'Give me half an hour to finish what I'm doing?'

'Great, I'll see you in half an hour. But make it sooner if you can. Promise me.'

'You're on.'

She knew it would be agony waiting in the flat with those two brutes staring threateningly at her, but at least it would give her some time to try and pull herself together, to think what she would say to Jason once he got here and how she would say it – and to get changed into something not ripped to shreds, and to layer on some make-up to disguise the bruise that she could feel growing on her cheek.

Jason ended the call and made sure he locked the keypad.

'Hurry up and get yourself dressed, Shaylee. I've got a meeting to get to.'

'But –'

'Don't get me wild, Shaylee, or I'll have that dough back off you. All right?'

'All right, but can't I have a shower first? I'm really hot and sweaty.'

'If you have to.'

'Thanks, Jay.'

She held out her arms to him.

'Wanna come in the shower with me? Alfie's going round his little friend's after school to play for a couple of hours, so I haven't got to go for ages yet.'

Little Alfie was actually going to be letting himself

316

into their flat on the run-down estate with the key he wore round his neck on the cheap, rolled-gold chain that Shaylee had bought by the inch in Ridley Road Market, and that she'd passed on to her son when the yellow metal had started flaking off, making it look even cheaper than it was. But she didn't think that sounded like the sort of thing that would impress Jason.

'No, you're all right, Shaylee, I've got to get going. Business to attend to. You can use the shower in the other bedroom.'

He walked through to the main bathroom.

'If I've left by the time you've finished in there,' he called out to her over the sound of gushing water, 'remember to make sure you slam the front door behind you.'

Jason was showered, dressed, fortified and boosted up with coke, and down in the underground car park in less than fifteen minutes, leaving Shaylee warbling away, writhing under the water, pretending to be Jamelia, superstar, performing in front of an adoring audience, rather than Shaylee, single mum, desperate for just one man's approval.

As he drove his new car through the busy streets of the City, heading along London Wall, Jason smiled smugly to himself as he caught the sight of heads turning to watch in what he took for admiration and envy as he passed by, Usher blaring and booming from his sound system.

Heading south and then east towards Docklands, he used the palm of one hand to steer, the fingers waggling in time to the music; while, with his other hand, he ran his electric shaver over his chin.

He had to look nice for the lady . . .

Knocking off two birds in one afternoon. A black one and a white one. How bad could that be? Maybe he'd have to get himself a Chinese sort to add to the set.

He laughed out loud.

No one could accuse Jason Carter of not being a supporter of diversity.

And no one could accuse him of not being back on top of the game.

He was a winner, and he was loving it.

Chapter 61

The warm weather had encouraged most of the drinkers to spill out of the pub and on to the pavement on the corner of Hanbury and Commercial Street. There was the regular odd mix of age, type and ethnicity that made it such a popular venue for locals, City workers and the bohemian newcomers to the area alike.

Not so keen to be out in the sunshine, because of his pale, freckly skin, and his already sunburnt scalp that showed through his thinning, once-vibrant red, but now dull, yellowish hair, the sweating, portly figure of Peter MacRiordan – known to everyone as Pete Mac – sat inside the pub on a bench that ran sideways on to the door, catching what little breeze there was to be had.

He had a half-finished pint in one hand and a roll-up in the other, and was holding court to two scruffy-looking young men, one of whom was sketching Pete Mac's flabby face on an A4 pad with a stub of pencil.

'Are you saying you really knew the Twins? Actually spent time with them?' The artist, pencil poised in the air, spoke in an almost reverentially hushed tone.

'Knew 'em?'

Pete Mac swigged down the rest of his beer and slammed the glass down on the little round wooden table.

'I had to give the pair of 'em a slap many a time to keep them in line. Trouble with them, see, was that they just wanted to be fucking celebrities. I'll put you straight about them two – all they were interested in was going to parties and being seen hanging about with film stars and that. They weren't real hard men. Not like my family, the O'Donnells, they weren't. We're the ones they should have made a fucking film about. Not them prats.'

'But I thought they ran the East End back in those days.'

'That's what you *would* believe if you only read the papers, but I lived through it, mush. *We* were the ones who really ruled the manor. Everyone knew how to behave when the O'Donnells were around.'

'You know,' the artist turned to his equally awed companion, 'this would be great material for a new video installation. *Peter MacRiordan: The true story of Pete Mac, East End Hard Man*. We'd get gallery space no trouble.'

'Brilliant idea.' The companion stood up. 'Another drink, Pete?'

'Don't mind if I do, son. And I'll have a whiskey chaser and all this time. A double. And tell the girl it's for me and she'll make sure it's a Jameson's. Then we can discuss terms for this video of your'n.'

While the young man was away fetching the fresh round of drinks, Hoxton Marcus, who had been standing listening in the doorway, slipped silently into the pub and took the man's chair. Marcus's sycophantic trustafarian companion stood behind him.

The artist looked at Marcus, curling his lip in challenge.

'Do you mind, this is a private conversation we're having here.'

Marcus turned his head and stared at him. This was gruesome enough without having to deal with idiots.

'Take my advice: go.'

'No. Why should I? We've been buying him drinks all lunchtime.'

The artist looked over to the crowded bar to check his friend's progress with the order. He was at the back of a considerable queue. He turned his attention to Pete Mac.

'Tell him. Go on.'

'Makes no odds to me who buys me drinks,' he said, looking knowingly at Marcus, seeing something in him that the younger man couldn't, because, despite his years of drinking, Pete Mac still had enough nous to recognise a genuine hard man, a real alpha male when he met one.

'Matter of fact, I'm a bit pissed off talking with poxy kids, so go on, sling your hook. I fancy having a chat with the grown-ups.'

With mutters of protestation, but no wish to get involved in anything that might mean physical violence, the artist slunk away to the bar and told his companion they were leaving.

Marcus's tame trustafarian immediately moved into his seat.

'Not yet,' said Marcus, without taking his eyes off Pete Mac.

'First go to the bar and tell the girl we want three pints of whatever the gentleman here is drinking, a bottle of Jameson's and three glasses.'

'But I'm a bit –'

Marcus turned to face him, wallet in hand. 'Take it out of that. But remember, I know exactly how much is in there. Oh, and don't push in the queue like a lout, will you?'

Chapter 62

'So, Mr MacRiordan,' said Marcus, pouring a large measure of Jameson's into Pete Mac's glass, 'tell me a little about yourself. I'd be fascinated to hear your stories about the old days.'

'Mr MacRiordan? Please. Marcus. Mate. It's Pete Mac. That's how everyone knows me. I'm famous for me name, ain't I?'

'Pete Mac. Interesting nickname. That's one from the old days, I'll bet. Come on, tell me all about them. And let's start with how you came to be associated with the O'Donnells.'

He watched Pete Mac slug back the whiskey; waited and filled his glass to the brim again.

'So, Peter. These O'Donnells.'

Free-flowing booze and talking about himself as hero of his own story – Pete Mac was a pig in shit heaven.

'Well, as you can see, I've always taken good care of myself.' He winked as he patted his massive belly. 'Bit of a tough guy, me. You know. Well respected by everyone round here. And well looked after by the little woman indoors. That's my Pat. She's a right good girl. Good Catholic. Always kept a nice clean home – we live over in Jubilee Street, have done since we got married – and she's always had me dinner waiting on the table. Proper meat and veg and all, none of this pizza shit everyone lives on today.'

Marcus forced back his impatience with this mouthy fool.

'But the O'Donnell connection?'

'My Pat. She's Gabriel O'Donnell's daughter. That's my link to the family.'

'Right. I see. So you'd be able to tell me the truth about some rumours I've heard. Stories about a feud. Between your family and another local family.'

'That'd be them Yiddisher arseholes. The fucking Kesslers.'

Marcus leaned towards him.

'I think that was the name I heard.'

Pete Mac drained his glass and held it out for a refill.

'You one of these fellas writing a book, are you? I've had plenty of them hanging around over the years, but they never want to divvy up the money the way I do. Reckon they deserve the lion's share. And it's my fucking story they're telling. The bastards.'

Marcus poured the whiskey until it reached to almost the brim of Pete Mac's glass.

'I assure you, I have absolutely no interest in writing a book, I just have a scholar's interests in the old days in the East End. You know how we new-comers like to romanticise the place, create legends.'

324

'Well, we *were* legends. Proper tough nuts. Faces. Not like some of the little poofs you see round here nowadays, dealing their bits of shit to one another. We'd have swiped them out of the way like fucking ants.'

'You were saying about the Kesslers.'

'Aw yeah. Them.'

He scratched his stubbly chin, and leaned closer to Marcus – a conspirator sharing a secret, and with breath that could have stripped paint.

'Fact is, I still keep an interest in what's going on, see – family things. We used to run this manor. Every inch round here was ours. And I couldn't believe it when I heard the other day that my little niece, bless her – not that I see her too often nowadays, but I keep my ear to the ground, you know – has set up a business for herself working all the doors on the Kesslers' clubs. Her grandfather, old Gabe, would have slapped her face for her if he'd have been alive. And as for what her father would have had to say, I can't even think about that.'

'Your niece?'

'Yeah, young Lisa.'

'She's running the doors? Are you sure it's her? Not someone called Jason Carter?'

'You've been talking to someone who don't know what he's on about, mate. My Pat – my old woman – was out shopping up West and bumped into Sandy O'Donnell. More like Fanlight fucking Fanny if you ask me, with all her dough and her diamonds. But she was so proud, she couldn't wait to tell Pat how –'

'Wait a moment, Peter, I'm becoming confused here. Sandy O'Donnell is your niece?'

And Pete Mac's rapid intake of whiskey wasn't helping in the clarity stakes.

'*No*. Keep up, mate,' said Pete Mac, his initial assessment of Marcus as being a man due some respect all but forgotten. 'Sandy is Lisa's mother. And Lisa's dad was my brother-in-law – Pat's brother – Brendan. Brendan O'Donnell. He was a right nasty bastard, him. God rest his soul.'

'So you say it's this Lisa O'Donnell who runs the doors for the Kesslers.'

'Now you're up to speed. But what Sandy was full of, what she was bragging about, was how Lisa's got this smashing bloke. Reckons they're gonna settle down together. Get married even. Now *that* is where Jason Carter comes in – or so my daughter, Caty says. She works in the bookies where Jason Carter goes. In the City, near the Barbican. Shocking my girl has to go out to work, grafting all hours, when there was all that money left.'

'You were saying about Jason Carter.'

'Yeah. Well, my Caty heard him bragging about his posh girlfriend, Lisa Taylor.'

'Taylor?'

'Young Lisa goes under that name. She don't use O'Donnell. Never has done except when she was around old Eileen, her old bag of a grandmother. The girl's got no pride in her background, see. If you ask me, it's a real pity. But that's the influence of that cow of a mother of hers. Fucking Sandy.'

'Let me get this right: your niece is Lisa O'Donnell, but goes by the name of Taylor. She runs the doors for the Kesslers. And she is Jason Carter's girlfriend.'

'Got it in one, mate. And I had you down for a right dozy bollocks, when you kept asking questions.'

Marcus resisted the urge to punch the fat old fool in the face.

'Complicated family.'

'Yeah, but I like to keep up with it all. Family. I reckon it's important to know your own history. It's who you are, innit?'

'I couldn't agree with you more. Now tell me, Peter, do you suppose that the Kesslers know this young woman's true identity.'

'I shouldn't fucking think so,' grinned Pete Mac. 'But I'd like to be there to see the boys' faces if they ever do find out. In fact, I'd pay good money to see the look on their old man's mush – that's old Danny Kessler – if he gets to hear about it.'

He guzzled down the last of his pint.

'He'd do his fucking nut. He'd have them boys hung, drawn and quartered, mate, for letting an O'Donnell anywhere near his businesses. He's as hard as nails, that man. He'd have them boys hurt without thinking twice about it. Money, that's all he's ever cared about. Horrible man. He's hated our family all his life, and he don't care much more for his own.'

'No interest in telling him yourself then? Maybe enjoy causing a bit of mischief for the family you had a feud with?'

'No thanks.'

'Why?'

'Because I haven't got a fucking death wish, that's why. Danny Kessler might be horrible, but Lisa's mother, Sandy O'Donnell – she'd kill me stone dead.'

'How would she find out who told him?'

'Listen to me. That woman has not survived being married to Brendan O'Donnell and wound up with all that dough – that was my Pat's and my Caty's by right – by being an idiot. She's one hard bitch, I'm telling you. Clever and all. And she idolises that kid of hers, treats her like she's a fucking princess. And with all that money Sandy's got, she would be more than capable of getting someone very seriously damaged. And she's still got plenty of contacts from over the years.'

He shook his head.

'No, I wouldn't wanna cross her.'

Chapter 63

Lisa opened the door to find Jason standing there grinning at her.

'Hello, sexy. Blimey, I love that dress. My very own lady in red, eh? You look absolutely gorgeous, girl. All I'd have to do would be to slit them little straps and I reckon it'd fall right off.'

He bent forward to kiss her on the mouth, but she turned so that his lips only brushed her cheek.

'What's up? Thought you couldn't wait to see me.'

Lisa could feel herself shaking; she'd been rehearsing what she'd say over and over again as she'd waited for him to arrive, but she could still barely get out the words.

'Something's happened. While you were on the way over. Something awful. It's the Kesslers,' she said, knowing that the brothers were only yards away from her, lounging around in her sitting room at the top of the stairs, listening to every word she and Jason were saying.

'They've pulled all my staff out of the clubs. And the casino.'

'All of them?'

She nodded. 'I can't believe it. It seems some of

329

the girls have been bringing drugs into work, selling them to the customers. David Kessler rang me, wanted me to go in and see him, but he sounded so angry I said I wouldn't go round there until he told me what it was all about. Eventually he gave in and told me over the phone. But Jason, he thinks it's all my doing. That I arranged it all.'

She put her hand to her mouth, acting out the scene the way she'd planned it – as if her life depended on it. And for all she knew, maybe it did.

'If I'd gone to see them, I don't know what would have happened. I just thank God you're here with me now. Jason, what should I do?'

She looked into his eyes, but he was giving nothing away. Nothing. The Bastard.

He tapped his knuckles on his chin, looking about him as if there might be an answer to the problem right there in Lisa's hallway.

'Do they know where you are?'

'I don't know. He called me on my mobile.'

'When did you speak to them?'

He couldn't stand still, he was moving around clicking his fingers, and then slapping the back of one hand into the palm of the other.

'Forty minutes ago. I don't know; maybe less.'

'The door bitches, have they spoken to them yet?'

'Jason, please stop questioning me. I've told you everything I know.'

330

She sat down on the stairs, barring his way, just in case he decided he needed a drink and wanted to go up to the sitting room to get one.

'And my head's completely spinning with all this.'

'We've got to find out if they've spoken to them, Lisa.'

Slowly, Lisa stood up.

'Why, Jason? Why is that so important?'

He stopped fidgeting and looked at her.

'Don't play the innocent with me, Lisa. You're not thick – you've got to have known what's been going on.'

'No, I didn't actually, Jason. So why don't you tell me? Go on, tell me. What *has* been going on?'

'Look, I don't know why you're so upset, you had no interest in that side of the business, so I –'

'*That side of the business?* It was you, wasn't it? And this whole thing has been a set-up. You made me fall for you, then, when you had me exactly where you wanted me, you bloody used me. You bastard.'

'Leave off, Lisa; we're both adults here. And, let's face it, I never heard you objecting when I was shtupping you. In fact, the way I remember it, you were begging me for more. Couldn't get enough of me. So what's your problem?'

'Did you ever think anything of me? Did we ever mean anything, the two of us?'

331

He began fidgeting again.

'*We* are neither here nor there, love. The problem we have right now is the fucking Kesslers.'

'How right you are, Carter.'

It was David; he was walking down the stairs towards them, his right hand behind his back.

Jason made a run for the door.

'I wouldn't do that if I was you, mate.'

David shoved Lisa aside and grabbed Jason by the shoulder. His right hand was now in front of him, held at chest height – he was holding a gun and it was pointed directly at Jason. He smiled and tipped his head towards the stairway.

'Now, let's all go up to the living room and have a little chat, shall we?'

Lisa steadied herself against the wall.

'Please, David. Don't do this. Think what you'd be starting up again. All the trouble you'd be dragging up.'

David tapped Jason on the shoulder with the gun.

'Don't suppose you know what she's talking about, do you, Carter?'

'No idea,' said Jason, sounding far cockier than he felt.

'Shall I tell him, Lisa? Or will you?'

Lisa closed her eyes for a moment and then looked at Jason. 'My name isn't Lisa Taylor.'

'What's that gotta do with anything?'

'I'm Lisa O'Donnell. Brendan's daughter.'

'You're fucking what?'

David's smile grew.

'Seems like it's both of you been keeping little secrets.'

Chapter 64

Less than an hour since leaving his flat, Jason found himself back at the Barbican, but this time he had David and Paul Kessler and Lisa O'Donnell – *how could she have kept that from him?* – standing beside him as he unlocked the door.

'Move yourself, Carter,' urged David, jabbing Jason in the back with the gun. 'Cos if you don't hurry up and let us have a look round for evidence of your little caper, I might get twitchy. And you don't want your neighbours coming home from work tonight to find you plastered all over the landing, now do you? I don't know if you've ever seen someone shot before, but my God it makes a right old mess, especially when it's in the head: blood, skin, bone, gristly stuff and bits of brain all over the fucking shop.'

Jason managed to hold his hand steady enough to open the door, but as he stepped inside the flat, what he heard had him forgetting all about his fear of David Kessler and his gun.

He sprinted along the corridor into the sitting room and grabbed the television remote control off the arm of the sofa.

'What the fuck d'you think you're doing?' he yelled.

Shaylee, who had been stretched out watching *Countdown* on the wall-mounted plasma-screen television, jumped to her feet. She was wearing what looked like a man's shirt and very little else, although there was a pile of rumpled clothing on the floor by the sofa.

'Oi, you! I was watching that.'

'You were watching that? *Watching that?* Who the fuck d'you think you are? And what the fuck are you still doing here?'

'Aren't you gonna introduce me to your friends, Jay?'

'Yeah, come on, Carter,' grinned David – the gun now discreetly behind his back – clearly enjoying Jason's discomfort. 'Introduce us to the lady.'

'This is Shaylee,' he said, spitting the words through his teeth. 'And I am not very happy to see her here.'

Shaylee. That's who she was. Lisa knew she'd seen her before. She was the young woman who'd turned up at Jason's place in Sussex that night, with her little boy in tow.

His bloody cleaner?

Jesus, he really had taken her for a mug.

'I'm really sorry, Jay,' Shaylee went on, 'but I fell asleep after I had me shower.' She giggled. 'I'd better be getting off soon though; Alfie'll be coming home from his little friend's house and there won't be anyone there to give him a kiss and cuddle.'

David Kessler kicked her clothes towards her.

'You can do better than that, darling, you can fuck off right now.'

Lisa was trembling with fury. What sort of an idiot had she been?

Shaylee threw off the shirt, apparently unfazed to be standing there naked in front of strangers, and began dressing in her own things.

'I'll take your shirt home and give it a rinse through,' she said, pulling on her skimpy lacy thong.

Jason snatched up the shirt and threw it on the coffee table.

'Don't bother.'

'All right, suit yourself.'

She did up the zip of her skin-tight jeans, and slipped her feet into her knock-off Tod loafers.

'I'll ring you later, Jay, and you can tell me if you've thought any more about taking me and Alfie away on holiday. He's so proud of his dad, it'd be –'

'Just shut it, Shaylee. Don't you reckon you've fucking said enough?'

'What? I thought you'd be chuffed he thinks so much of you. Come on, give us a kiss goodbye, and I'll get going.'

That was too much for David Kessler. He burst out laughing.

'It's a wonder your nose ain't a fucking foot long,

Carter, cos from the look on your face, Lisa, it seems that this might be yet another little secret young Jason here's been keeping from you. Whatever are we going to find out next, do you suppose?'

Chapter 65

With Shaylee bundled out of the door – to the echo of Jason's hollered threats about what he'd do to her the next time he saw her if she didn't keep her mouth shut for once – Paul Kessler began searching the flat, while his brother kept the gun pointed at Jason who was sitting on the sofa next to Lisa.

Lisa didn't know if she was more terrified of what the Kesslers might do to her, or by the thoughts of what she wanted to do to Jason.

Paul took his time, doing a thorough job, but his efforts were still fruitless. He came back into the sitting room, his hair flat to his skull where he'd been sweating with the effort of hauling furniture away from walls, and tipping out chests of drawers.

'Nothing, Dave. Not a bloody thing. And I've gone through the lot. There's no money here, no charlie, no scales, not even a contacts book. Well, nothing except a bit of dope.'

David levelled the gun at Jason's temple.

'Well, you are a tidy boy, aren't you, Carter? Or maybe it's because you've got another place on the go. A place where you keep anything incriminating. So, tell us then, where's your other gaff? You've got

338

to have somewhere to sort out distribution if you're handling the amount of gear I reckon you are.'

'I haven't got the first idea what you're talking about, David. I'm not distributing anything. And no, I haven't got anywhere else. All right?'

'What, not even some handy little lock-up in the East End somewhere? That'd be my favourite bet. What d'you reckon, Paul? A lock-up?'

'It's definitely an idea, Dave.'

'No. I swear to you. On my life.'

'It's your life I'm thinking about, mate. You start telling the truth or you're a dead man. Cos me and Paul don't like liars, do we, Paul?'

'We certainly don't, Dave. We don't like liars one little bit.'

Lisa, who had been sitting there next to Jason with her head buried in her hands, leapt to her feet.

'For Christ's sake, Jason. Can't you see it's too late? That it's time to stop lying? Having secrets. Treating people like they're fools. *It's too fucking late*. If you don't tell them, they're going to kill us.'

'Lisa –'

'No, Jason, I've had enough. I've seen through you. Don't you understand? I've seen you for the liar and fraud you really are, and I won't let it go on any longer. I want an end to all this. And I don't want to die because of you.'

She turned to David. 'He's –'

Now Jason was on his feet beside her, grabbing her by the shoulder – David and the gun ignored.

'Lisa, no. You can't do this to me. Stop now. You don't know what you're doing.'

'Don't I?'

She shoved him away from her, and turned to look David in the face.

'He owns a place in Sussex. And I can tell you exactly where it is, because the bastard had the front to invite me down there – when he was pretending I was his girlfriend. And all the while he's been carrying on with that little tart he just had the gall to throw out of here as if she was at fault.' She looked about her, searching for something. 'Find me a piece of paper and I'll write down the directions.'

Paul dropped down on the sofa.

'No need for that, darling. You can show us. Cos you're coming along for the ride.

'But –'

Paul turned to David and shrugged. 'She didn't think we were going to just let her go, did she?'

David shrugged back. 'I dunno. But I do know that once we've sorted out this little fucker . . .' He pointed the gun at Jason's head. 'It's her turn next.'

Then he pointed it at Lisa.

'Bang!'

Lisa screamed.

'Bring her down to the motor, Paul.'

340

David stepped closer to her.

'And don't even think about trying to have it away, love, or I'll happily put a bullet in the back of that pretty fucking head of yours quicker than you can ever run.'

'Hark at the big brave man, scaring a woman.' It was Jason, his tone was flat, contemptuous. 'That's just about your level.'

David tutted as if disappointed.

'Don't be fucking stupid, Carter. I know what you're doing: trying to make me lose my temper, so I take my eye off the ball. But it won't work. I am not letting my guard slip for one single minute. We've got you. And it's all over bar the shouting.'

Jason nodded at Lisa.

'I've just noticed the bruise on your face. I suppose these heroes did that to you and all, did they?'

David raised his arm in the air.

'You cheeky little fucker.'

Jason wasn't quick enough to avoid the blow as David whacked the butt of the gun down on his shoulder.

But he certainly felt the pain.

Lisa gasped.

'Jason, just tell them what they want to know.'

'Shut up, Lisa. Haven't you said enough? Caused enough fucking trouble?'

David laughed. *'Tell us what we want to know?'* he mocked her. 'That's a good one. Cos he's gonna tell us everything, darling. Every single, solitary thing. Believe me, you can lay money on it.'

He turned to his brother and winked.

'Trust me, I know. I'm a Kessler.'

Chapter 66

David drove his dark blue, 7 Series BMW down to Sussex with the gun on his lap and Jason by his side in the passenger seat.

Paul sat in the back seat behind Jason with a knife in his hand and Lisa by his side.

Apart from David's barked requests for directions and Jason's wearily resigned replies, there was no sound other than the low drone of the engine, the Bob Marley CD playing at an almost inaudibly quiet volume, and Lisa silently weeping – not only a woman betrayed, but maybe a woman about to lose her life.

'Bloody hell.'

As he stood by the metal gates, while Jason keyed in the code, David stared through the railings up along the drive towards the house standing in the distance.

'You have done well for yourself, Carter. I reckon your reach into the trade must be bigger than me and Paul thought. So tell me, who else's territory have you moved in on, you naughty boy?'

343

'Actually, that's where you're wrong. This is all legit, and I've got the paperwork to prove it.'

The gates glided open effortlessly.

Jason's chin was in the air – he was proud of his achievements, glad that Kessler was impressed. 'I bought this place a few years ago. As an investment. Only had to use two years' worth of bonuses.'

'Shame you got greedy then, eh, Carter? Just think of all the grief it would have saved you if you'd stayed legit and not started sticking your nose in other people's business.' He turned to his brother and laughed. 'And your business up other people's noses.'

The four of them were standing in the hallway.

'Do you know, Carter,' said David, nodding his approval, 'I think I might be taking this off your hands – in part payment for all the trouble you've caused me. This is a very nice place. Mum'd love it, wouldn't she, Paul?'

Jason shook his head, sighing, jaded, knowing he was a defeated man, but he still refused to lose face, still had to have a dig, get in the last word.

'Why am I not surprised that you wanna please your mother?'

'You what?'

'You heard. Aw, and not married, are you, David?'

'I'll show you not fucking married.'

David stepped back, putting all his weight on his

344

back foot, and then lunged forward, punching Jason squarely in the face, splitting his nose and spraying blood all over the black-and-white-tiled floor.

Lisa cowered against the wall. Until today she had never experienced physical violence, and couldn't believe the casual way these men could hurt people.

David rubbed his stinging knuckles.

'You really thought you could have one over on us, you stupid fucker? On us? We're the Kesslers, mate; the fucking Kesslers; the scary men. Perhaps that'll remind you. Now where's the booze? I want a drink before we get started.'

Holding his hand to his face, trying, but failing, to staunch the bleeding, Jason led them through to the panelled room at the back of the house without a word.

Lisa did as David Kessler told her, mechanically pouring drinks for him and his brother from the decanter on the tray set on the sofa table next to the chesterfield; but her attention was elsewhere – focused on the French windows where Shaylee and Alfie had appeared that night during the storm.

The French windows that opened out on to the grounds, that stretched away to the woods and the road beyond.

Two rounds of very large brandies later, the Kesslers had Jason tied to a chair with Paul holding a knife to his cheek.

Lisa stood in the corner next to the French windows.

She chanced casting a glance at the lock.

The key was there.

'Come on, Carter, I'm getting fed up with this.'

Paul drew the blade down Jason's cheek. The flesh opened up like a mouth and a fresh trickle of red oozed out, mingling with the rusty, coagulated blood from his nose.

'I'm telling you this for nothing: think yourself lucky it's me standing here with this knife in my hand, that it's me you're dealing with and not me brother. Cos he's got a right temper on him, haven't you, Dave?'

'I have, Paul. And I've also got a very low boredom threshold.'

David grabbed Jason's hair and jerked his head back.

'So just tell us what the set-up is here, where you do the business, or I'm gonna use that knife to slice your bollocks off.'

'Fuck off,' croaked Jason, his voice a strangulated wheeze.

David, still dragging Jason's head back, looked over his shoulder at Lisa.

'You. Get over here. Now. Undo his flies and get out his meat and two veg. Cos I'm gonna start carving and I need an assistant.'

She shook her head. 'No.'

346

'What did you say?'

'I said – no. I'm not having any part of it.'

'Shame, cos you might have been a bit more gentle than me.'

With that, David went to grab Jason's crotch, but Jason doubled over, tearing his hair from David's grip.

With his busted nose, and his head almost between his knees, Jason could barely get the words out, but he wasn't about to let anyone anywhere near his scrotum.

'Just let me go, and I'll show you what you want to see.'

'And what's that?'

'Everything. It's all over in one of the outhouses – the whole cutting and distribution set-up. The whole fucking lot. Okay? That satisfy you?'

'That's a bit more like it.'

David took the knife from Paul and cut the plastic ties that had fastened Jason's wrists to the arms of the chair.

It wasn't entirely clear to Lisa what happened next, or how it happened, all she knew was that Jason was launching himself from the chair at David. And that this was her opportunity.

As Jason grappled on the floor with David, and Paul stood over them, yelling at his brother to watch the gun, Lisa threw herself towards the French windows.

She'd kicked off her shoes and was already across the terrace and on to the grass, running towards the woods, when she heard Paul shouting furiously.

'Fuck it, that bitch has only legged it.'

Then Jason's voice. 'Leave her. She didn't know anything about it.'

Then David laughing wildly, as if he'd just been told the funniest joke he'd ever heard.

'Fuck her; we'll have her later. But it's a bit late for you to start doing the decent thing, innit, Carter?'

Then Jason again. 'Lisa, if you can hear me, call Richard. He'll know what –'

Then she heard a noise, a noise that she thought could only have been a gunshot.

She kept on running.

Chapter 67

Barefoot, and with her arms and legs scratched from running through the woods, her hair caught up with fragments of twigs and leaves, and her dress ripped from waist to hem, Lisa stood by the road side – bent double, gasping for breath, head down and hands gripping her thighs.

As she tried to steady her breathing – even five times weekly visits to the gym were no preparation for this sort of punishment – she was pleading with the God that she had not prayed to since her grandmother, Eileen O'Donnell, had died. Her mum had told her that she didn't have to go to Mass ever again after that, not unless she wanted to.

And she hadn't wanted to – going to Mass was just another part of being controlled by the O'Donnells, the family her mother had rejected. The family *she* had rejected.

But now here she was doing a deal with that God – a deal to the effect that if He sent her a car before the Kesslers caught up with her, she would go to Mass as many times a week as He wanted. Even become a fully paid-up nun if that's what it took.

Then she heard it: a distant rumble that might just be a vehicle coming her way.

Please, God, please.

She straightened up, hardly daring to hope, but it was definitely getting closer.

With suddenly renewed energy she ran out into the middle of the road and threw her arms out wide. There was no way she was going to let this thing pass her by – milk float, school bus, road digger – no matter what the bloody hell it was she was going to stop it.

But before she had time to think through what she was doing, an articulated lorry appeared from round the bend, huge and menacing on the narrow country road in front of her.

The driver sounded his horn repeatedly, gesturing furiously for her to move out of the way, but, chest heaving and blood pounding in her ears, Lisa stood her ground and the lorry was forced to come to a screeching halt.

It stopped finally just a few feet away from her.

The red-faced, middle-aged driver flung open his door.

'Are you out of your flaming mind, you silly, daft girl?'

His soft Sussex burr toned down the effect, but he was obviously beside himself, his face growing more scarlet the more he yelled.

'I could have run you right over. And how would I

have felt then, eh? Tell me that. What words would I have used when I got home to the missus and had to tell her I'd flipping well killed someone? Get that image of my wife's face stuck in that head of yours, you selfish person. Then think before you ever pull a daft stunt like that again.'

Suddenly, it was as if the driver's batteries had been disconnected – he just stopped speaking.

He looked her up and down, visibly appalled, as he began to appreciate the state she was in.

He jumped down from his cab, unbuttoning his shirt as he did so, and then went over to her and draped it carefully around her scratched and bloody shoulders.

'Goodness me, my little love, it looks like you've been run over already. Are you all right then?'

Lisa started weeping.

'Please, let me get in your truck. I need a lift. Take me anywhere, anywhere will do. I've just got to get away from here. Please, I've got to get away.'

The driver sat in his seat, bare-chested but very upright, looking ahead at the road, casting the occasional, paternal glance towards Lisa.

'That's some bruise you've got on your face there, my little love. Fancy telling me how you got it, do you?'

'No. No. Not if you don't mind.'

'Course I don't mind. And I don't want you to

351

think I'm interfering either, but did your husband or boyfriend do that to you?'

'No, I think my boyfriend might have just saved my life.'

'Saved your life, eh? Well, there's a thing that doesn't happen every day of the week.'

He threw her another glance. She was still trembling.

'But perhaps you've said enough for now, eh? And, let's be truthful here, you don't want to go telling strangers all your business, now do you? So why don't you try to have a little sleep? Get a bit of rest. We won't be in London for well over an hour, maybe even longer if the traffic's a bit dodgy.'

Lisa dropped her chin until it was nearly touching her chest; she pulled the man's shirt tightly about her.

'You sound like my mum,' she whispered through her tears. 'When we were coming home from the seaside when I was little. *You have a little sleep* she used to say.'

'Now don't start crying again, my love; I hate to see a woman upset. Here, why don't you use my mobile phone? There it is, there, in that holder. Go on, give your mum a ring. Mums always know what to do at times like this. Well, my missus does. She always sorts out the girls.'

'If you don't mind, I'll call her later, but thank you, you're being very kind.'

352

'Kind? Why shouldn't I be kind? I've got daughters myself. A bit younger than you, they are. But I'd still like to think that someone would help them if ever they needed it. You know, if they found themselves in some sort of trouble or other.'

He reached into the storage compartment in his door.

'Here, have a mint. A bit of sugar in your blood'll do your nerves good. They taught us that years ago, at school. Funny the things you remember.'

Lisa took one of the sweets.

'And you do know that if it *was* some man – if you could call him a man – who did that to you, I'd be more than happy to turn this rig right round, right now, and go back and teach the rotten so-and-so a lesson he'll never forget.' He shook his head in wonder. 'I can't tell you how much I hate bullies. They're cowards, if you ask me, every last one of them. And the only way to deal with cowards is to face up to them.'

As they stopped and started through the south London traffic jams, and the driver spoke to her in his soft, kind voice, Lisa came to the conclusion that he was a wise man, and in many different ways, not least of which was his belief that she should ask her mother for help. And when he dropped her outside Sandy's house, by the time Lisa had climbed the steps to the front door, she had decided that was what she was going to do.

But first she had to tell her mother everything.

Well, almost everything.

Chapter 68

'D'you know what, girl, I'd have known you anywhere. Even after all these years, from right across the room I could see it was you. How are you, darling? Well, I hope.'

Sandy twisted round in her chair, vodka and tonic in hand, and faced Daniel Kessler.

She looked him up and down.

Older? Of course he was. Heavier too, but he was still an imposing-looking man standing there smiling down at her. And he was still doing the same old thing: playing the schmoozer – everyone's big-hearted, easy-talking friend.

'Hello, Danny. Thanks for agreeing to see me. You know how much I appreciate it.'

'An invitation to have drinks in a smart place like this,' he said, an expansive gesture taking in the plush but discreet hotel bar Sandy had decided on as comfortable but private, 'and with a lovely woman like you – how could I say no?'

He sat down, choosing the armchair directly facing her.

'And, I have to say, I'm more than a bit intrigued. What would Brendan O'Donnell's widow want with the likes of me – a simple Yiddisher boy just trying to keep his head above water, doing a bit of honest business, keeping the wolf from the door?'

'You might wanna fasten your seat belt, Danny, cos I think you're gonna be in for a bit of a bumpy ride.'

'My boys are letting what happen in my clubs?'

A hovering waiter backed away tactfully as Kessler fought to keep his voice down as he spat out the words through gritted teeth.

'You're telling me they're what?'

'You heard, Danny: they let Carter move in and take all the trade off 'em. Every single, solitary bit of it. From right under their lazy bloody noses.'

'No. You're living in a fantasy land, girl. For a start: how could you know what's going on in my businesses?'

'That is exactly why I'm here, Danny. I found out what was going on. After they thought my daughter was somehow involved, and your sons . . .' Sandy knocked back the remains of her drink and smacked the glass down on the table. 'Your sons, David and Paul, fruit of your sodding loins, fucking kidnapped her.'

'They what?' He pointed to the empty glass. 'How many of them have you had?'

'Three, and believe me, I am still more than stone-cold sober. And with the mood I'm in I don't think

356

it'd be possible for me to get drunk however much of that stuff I swallowed.'

She leaned forward in her chair, gripping the arms.

'I want you to listen to me, Danny. I might only be a woman in your eyes, which I know counts for fuck all with blokes like you, but I've got money. And plenty of it. And that buys me power. And not only that, I've still got some very good friends from the old days, friends who don't think very much of your family and who wouldn't need asking twice to settle some outstanding scores for me. And they probably wouldn't even want paying for the privilege.'

He half rose from his seat, the sweat breaking on his brow.

'Are you threatening me?'

'I said: I want you to listen to me, Danny. And I would if I was you. All this happened just two days ago – two days – so I am still feeling very raw. But I figure that your boys must be running around like blue-arsed flies by now, working their bollocks off trying to sort out all the problems they've realised they've got in the clubs, the problems caused by this scumbag Carter, before you get wind of what's going on. But if you don't want even more problems – and believe me, I'd bring you more problems and trouble than you'd ever believe was possible – then you tell them that they don't go anywhere near my daughter ever again. *Ever*. Have you go that? It's over. Finished. Because I'm not like you, Danny, I love my

357

child – the child I carried in this body of mine for nine months. She means everything to me. And I wouldn't think twice about laying down my life for that girl, so, take this as gospel, I wouldn't even blink if it meant having to put your head on the block to take care of her. And I advise you to take my word on this and all – if anyone goes near her, if anyone so much as upsets her, then all fucking hell will break loose. And you, Danny, will lose everything. All right? I'll not only get you hurt, I'll get the lot of you put inside, and then, when you get out, I'll fucking kill you.'

She opened her handbag, took out two twenty-pound notes, screwed them up and threw them on the table in front of him.

'You can keep the change,' she said, and walked away.

Chapter 69

It was that time of the year when there was an increasingly pronounced chill and dampness hanging in the air, the moment when autumn finally gives way to the beginnings of winter. It had been a lovely, cloudless afternoon, but now the sun was low on the horizon and twilight was moving in, and a patchy mist was gathering in the manicured Gardens of Remembrance swirling around the neat rows of memorial plaques. In contrast to the grey outside light, a warm yellow glow lit up the tall chapel windows of the crematorium.

Inside the chapel, a service was taking place.

At the front was the coffin bearing the mortal remains of Jason Carter resting on the catafalque, while the packed congregation sat squashed, shoulder to shoulder, listening to the organist playing Fauré's *Requiem*.

At the back, Lisa was sitting, tucked away – black pashmina covering her distinctive long fair hair – in a space she had found next to the chapel attendant. The attendant was preparing himself for the committal – getting ready to press the button to draw the curtain that would screen the coffin from their sight – the end of the service and the congregation's final goodbye to Jason Carter.

Despite knowing what her mother had done for her, she still didn't want to face the Kessler brothers – who she had known would insist on being there in a public display of their innocence.

She had thought long and hard about attending the service, but in the end she felt she had no choice – she had had to come. Once, she had really thought she loved Jason, but then she had hated him, and then . . . Then he had sacrificed himself for her.

Perhaps.

But he had told her so many lies, played her and everyone else for such fools, how would she ever know what he really thought of her?

She snapped open her bag as quietly as she could and took out another tissue. Not really sure whether her tears were for Jason or for herself.

The tap on her shoulder made her gasp.

But it wasn't Jason returned from the dead or even the Kesslers. Jason was still safely in his coffin and the Kesslers were sitting two rows from the front, she could see their heads and their shoulders, massively menacing in their dark overcoats.

She looked up and immediately recognised the young black woman she had first seen that night at Jason's house in Sussex – the young woman who had been so at home in his flat in the Barbican.

'Mad, innit, Jay being dead,' Shaylee whispered as

she shoved her way into the tiny space between Lisa and the chapel attendant. 'Cos the coppers have taken all this time releasing the body, it's like it ain't real. Like it's not Jay any more. D'you know what I mean? More like he's gone away and this is nothing to do with him. And hark at that bleed'n row they're playing and all.'

The chapel attendant and Shaylee exchanged narrow-eyed glares. Funeral etiquette and silent mourning clearly didn't concern Shaylee over much.

'That music's *definitely* nothing to do with Jay,' she went on. 'They should have played a CD; something nice like Whitney signing 'I Will Always Love You'; not this shit.'

She stopped talking long enough to unwrap a piece of chewing gum and pop it in her mouth.

'D'you see about this in the papers and all, did you?'

Lisa just stared at her.

'No need to look at me like that. His family are hardly gonna invite us, are they?'

'Us?' Lisa couldn't maintain her dignified silence any longer – she really didn't much like being included in the same category as Shaylee.

'Yeah – Jason's birds. I mean, look at us. Must be at least a dozen of us here.'

Frowning, Lisa scanned the packed rows of pews. She hadn't really noticed before, but there did seem to be a lot of young women sitting by themselves.

One or two of them, regardless of the cold, were wearing off-the-shoulder tops – showing their bra straps and elaborately tattooed backs. The favoured hairstyle was straightened bleached blonde or very dark hair caught up high in spiky ponytails. Lisa thought she recognised a few of them from the clubs.

No sign of anyone who looked as if they could have come from his office though. There was one group of men in appropriately sober suits, but she guessed – rightly – that they were police officers. Even out of uniform there was something about them they couldn't disguise.

Shaylee was off again. 'See them two sour-faced mares – them two up the front? That's Jay's wife and his mum.'

'*His what?*'

'Yeah, up there. The two with the hats on. The ones who look like their clothes come from out of the ark, and that someone's shoved a poker up their arses. Jay married that ugly mare when he was eighteen. To try and please his family, so he reckoned. But I can't see his mother ever being pleased with anything. She hates everyone, she does. Especially me – racist old cow. Won't even admit Alfie's Jay's son.'

Another exchange of pointed looks with the chapel attendant.

'You all right, nosing?' Shaylee challenged him, before turning back to Lisa.

'And that's why I wanna get what's mine. No, not

mine, I wanna get what's Alfie's. What's his by right. And I want you to help me.'

'Help you? Why would I help you when you were making a fool of me, carrying on with Jason behind my back?'

'What makes you think you're so special? He made a fool out of all of us.'

Lisa bowed her head; she hadn't even known he was married. Even his funeral was full of his lies.

'Just look at them all. And these are the ones who could be bothered to drag their lazy arses all the way out to Essex. Gawd alone knows how many more there were.'

Lisa shifted uncomfortably.

'I don't know why you think this is anything to do with me.'

'Because *you* got conned by the rotten git into thinking you was the only one what mattered, just like the rest of us. But look, Lisa. It is Lisa, innit? You're the sort who could do this, and I'm not. Just look at yourself, you look the right business. But me, I'm sitting here at the funeral of my little boy's father in a dress I bought off a stall down the market.'

'I don't think this is –'

'You got kids, have you? No, silly question. Seems I was the only one stupid enough to think it'd make a difference if he had a kid with me. But I was wrong. And now I'm stuck with it – with my little Alfie. You remember, you saw him that night down in the

363

country. I named him after Jay's dad – Alfred. My little un's grandad. He died before I got to know Jay, but I thought it would be nice, you know, for Jay. But I was wrong about that and all. He didn't give a monkey's. And now, daft cow that I am . . .' She rubbed her middle. 'Now I'm having another one. And this is Jay's and all, God help me. And while I'll admit I ain't been the best of mums to Alfie, this has all been a real shock, I'm telling you. I'm on me own now, and I've gotta make this work somehow. And that's why I need your help. I wouldn't stand a chance in hell trying to fight a posh old bag like Jay's mum. Can you imagine what it'd be like in court? Instead of treating me like the mother of her grandchildren, she'd have me looking like some right little slag. But after how they've treated me, that family owes me. So go on, Lisa, please, help me.'

At those words, Lisa felt a wave of nausea come over her as images of the young Eastern European lap dancer, the one who'd worked at Diamond Dan's, filled her head. She had once begged Lisa for help, had actually shown her the physical evidence of what she said Jason had done to her, but Lisa had refused to help her, even to believe her. She hadn't even wanted to listen to what the girl had to say. And then she had gone missing; and God knows what happened to a girl as young as that alone in London. She probably hadn't lasted the summer.

Shaylee leaned in close to Lisa, but kept a defiant

gaze fixed on the chapel attendant.

'Bloke outside, driver of one of the cars, told me the police were taking photographs of people as they arrived. Did they get you?'

'No. I slipped in after the service had started. Not long before you.'

'He was earwigging 'em. Said they had the right hump cos they reckon they know it was them Kessler brothers who did him, but they just can't prove it. And they'd love to get something on them, cos they're like part of the underworld. Proper gangsters. All the papers are saying how it was a *gangland murder.*'

Lisa looked nervously about her, but Shaylee didn't seem bothered.

'I'm not so sure if I believe it though. We all know Jay could be a bit of a rascal at times, but he wasn't a bad man. Not really.'

Quite unexpectedly she grabbed Lisa by her hand.

'But he did have money, Lisa, and that's my Alfie's. By right. So, please, please say you'll help me get it for him.'

'Maybe we can talk later.'

Shaylee smiled and Lisa could have cried even more bitter tears, not for her or Jason, but for Shaylee – one child already and a baby on the way, and not much more than a kid herself.

At that moment, Lisa knew for certain she hated Jason Carter.

Chapter 70

The moment Lisa saw the chapel attendant reach for the button, she signalled to Shaylee that she wanted to get by. She wasn't surprised that when Shaylee stood up for her to pass, she then followed her out.

'Someone you don't fancy bumping into?' asked Shaylee, buttoning her cheap, thin coat up to her neck as she shivered in the now icy wind.

'No. Of course not,' said Lisa, taking the pashmina from her head and shoulders and handing it to Shaylee. 'I just want to get home, that's all.'

'Yeah, right,' said Shaylee, winding the soft, warm wrap around her neck. 'We all do. Especially before the Kesslers and the law start appearing on them steps. Now, where's your car? You can drop me off at the tube, if you like.'

A pause.

'Unless you don't mind dropping me back to Hackney.'

Lisa unlocked the new Mini she had taken to driving after selling her Saab – too many memories of Jason.

'So, what d'you reckon?'

'Hackney's not too far out of my way; not a problem.'

'No. Not that. Are you going to help me?'

After only a slight pause: 'I'll see what I can do.'

They got into the car.

When Lisa checked the rear-view mirror she saw the congregation appearing on the steps, and her hands began to shake. Why had she come here?

'That's fantastic.' Shaylee leaned over and kissed her on the cheek. 'Are you doing it for Jay?'

'No, definitely not for Jason. For two other reasons. One, because someone once did something for me.'

Lisa felt her heart gradually begin to slow to something approaching an almost normal pace as she pulled out of the gates and on to the road.

'It wasn't long ago that someone helped me, someone who didn't even know me. A stranger. And he said some things I'll never forget – decent, kind things. He said he hoped that if ever his daughters needed help, there'd be someone there for them. And that bullies are cowards and you have to stand up to them. But it's also because I once turned my back on someone who needed my help, and that's something I'm going to have to live with for the rest of my life. So yes, I will help you. In fact, after I've been to see him, I think I know someone else who'll want to help you too.'

Lisa knew someone all right: Richard Middleton.

'Ta, Lisa, that is so nice of you. I can't tell you what it's like having someone on my side for once. It hasn't happened very often, believe me.'

'That's okay.'

Lisa had spoken to Richard just once since Jason's death, and, by the end of the conversation, he knew that he was in her debt, that he owed her – more than owed her – for getting her mixed up in the nightmare world of Jason Carter. And now Lisa was going to call in that debt. If he didn't want to face Sandy, and risk losing everything – Richard was part of the story that Lisa had not told her mother – then he would have to help her do whatever it took to make things right for Jason's son.

Lisa pulled towards the junction, looking for the sign that would direct them back to the centre of Upminster – she could find her way back into town from there.

She leaned forward, checking that both ways were clear on the unfamiliar road. As she looked to her left, she was surprised to see tears rolling down Shaylee's face.

'Don't look at me like that, Lisa. He might have been a rotten bastard cheater, but I did love him, you know.'

'I know.' Lisa patted her leg. 'Didn't we all.'

Chapter 71

Lisa and Shaylee were well on their way back to London; the police had taken all the photographs they could be bothered to take and had headed for the nearest pub; and with there being no more services planned for that day the crematorium was almost empty. But there was a small huddle of men still standing outside the chapel: David and Paul Kessler, and an assortment of so-called friends, hangers-on and minders – there for appearances' sake.

As they chatted and laughed – mostly at David's jokes at the dearly departed's expense – another man, very tall and dandified with long curling hair, joined them uninvited.

He positioned himself directly in front of David Kessler.

'I believe this is the moment where people usually shake on it.'

David kept his hands firmly in his pockets.

'Yeah? D'you reckon, mate. Shake on what?'

The man sighed, his expression pitying.

'To declare that may the best man win. Because, Kessler, I'd say it's all up for grabs now, wouldn't you? Blond Jason's gone, and even though he went still owing a lot of people a lot of money, he left me something very special: he showed me how being a bridge can be so very useful.'

David smirked at the others. 'A bridge? Is he for real?'

'I can see I need to explain more simply for you. He showed me just how easy it was to move in on your patch, a patch in which, I must admit, I previously had no interest. But as you're so complacent, lazy, and because you think you can run everything by sitting there doing nothing, you are very easy pickings. Your sort are old-fashioned, Kessler. No business acumen.'

'How do you know my name?'

The man raised his eyebrows and sighed.

'Because I have the means to find out such things. That's how. Now, a word of advice: I'd watch my back if I were you.'

David frowned. Who was this weirdo? He looked like something out of a horror movie and yet he was talking like he was some fucking big bollocks. David didn't like strangers knowing more about him than he knew about them – it made him uncomfortable.

'Look, perhaps I was a little hasty, it's been a difficult day.'

David held out his hand.

The other man looked at it, making no move to touch flesh to flesh, making it very clear that this was about him, that he was the one controlling the situation.

370

'As I said, Blond Jason has gone now.'

The man began to walk away.

'And look what happened to him,' David called after the man, shaping up, shoulders turned, fists clenched ready to punch out like some little kid in the playground. He felt pathetic even as the words left his mouth.

Paul clapped his brother on the shoulder.

'Take no notice of that ignorant bastard, Dave. Blokes like him should learn to have a bit of respect and learn how to conduct their fucking selves.'

Stung by his own ineffectiveness, David raised his voice to a holler. He was spitting as he shouted, the spittle forming little bubbles in the corners of his mouth.

'Yeah, respect, that's what people should have. And it's what we fucking deserve, not being treated like tossers by that poofy-looking cunt.'

Slowly, Hoxton Marcus turned and pointed at David Kessler – stabbing his finger just the once.

'What did you call me?'

'You heard, you cunt.'

'I'm sorry to say that I think I did. You might live to regret that Mr Kessler.'

With that he walked away.

Chapter 72

'Hang on, Paul, I'm not gonna leave it there. I'm going to have a word with that arsehole before he goes. No one talks to me like that. Especially not in front of my friends.'

'Do you have to, Dave? Can't we just shoot off? He's no one. Some chancer, that's all.'

'I'll be one minute.'

Paul raised his hand in warning to silence any comments from the other men.

'Look, I'll come with you. I don't want you doing anything stupid, this is too public.'

'What? You treating me like a cunt and all now? Course I won't do anything stupid.'

He turned to the now embarrassed-looking group of men.

'And you lot can fuck off out of it and all.'

The men melted away – glad to have been dismissed, however abruptly – leaving Paul to stand there alone smoking yet another cigarette, waiting while his brother went off to shout at a stranger.

'We'll be locking the gates soon, sir,' said a sallow-faced man in a long dark coat, who had appeared from somewhere behind him. 'Always lock up at dusk at this time of the year. I know how hard these days can be, seeing off loved ones, but everybody else has gone home. So would you mind?'

Paul wagged his head non-committally.

'And if you wouldn't mind putting out your cigarette end in the appropriate receptacle.' He tutted looking down at the smoking debris scattered on the ground around Paul's feet. 'It would be much appreciated.'

Paul bobbed his head again. The stupid fucker didn't know how lucky he was that he hadn't just said that in front of David. Paul got pissed off sometimes with his brother's temper, but there were times when he totally understood why he lost it – times like this, for instance.

He had just turned to get rid of the butt *in the appropriate receptacle* when the unmistakable sound of a gunshot split the air.

He threw the cigarette end on the ground.

'Fuck it, Dave, what have you gone and done now?'

He started running, knocking the startled crematorium attendant out of the way, slowing down to a relieved trot when he saw that David was already in the car, sitting behind the wheel, ready to go.

Paul wrenched open the passenger door and threw himself in.

'Come on, Dave. Move it, mate, or we'll have the law back here quicker than –'

373

It was then that he saw something in his brother's hand; it was one of the order-of-service cards – and it was spattered with blood.

'For fuck's sake, Dave. Are you out of your mind? What d'you think you're doing with that? There's gotta be fucking forensics all over it.'

Paul pulled a handkerchief from his pocket and gently took the card from his brother's hand.

As he did so, David slumped forward, his head hitting the steering wheel with a dull thwack.

Paul looked from the card, to his brother and back again.

Written in an elegantly looping hand on the back of the card was a message in black ink:

No one calls me a cunt.

As Paul cradled his dead brother in his arms, he heard the sound of police sirens growing louder.

Postscript

The young woman, not much more than a girl really, walked towards the elegant frontage of the famous London hotel. She could see the lights of a Christmas tree twinkling in the grand foyer, its star reaching right up to the double height ceiling. Beside the tree was a pretty girl, about her own age maybe, wearing a lovely dress made from some magical, floaty material that shone and glittered in the lights. She was being squeezed hard by an old man with fat wet lips and dried food stuck on his chin.

And she was so glad it wasn't her.

She walked straight past the doorway and ducked down an almost hidden alleyway that ran alongside the hotel.

The night air was crisp and wintery, with a cold wind driving up from the river along the narrow thoroughfare, tossing the litter and leaves around in skittering swirls about her feet, but she hardly noticed the mess tonight, she was too excited.

Up until now she had been working in the bowels of the hotel in the steaming, overpoweringly hot kitchens, scouring the greasy, stinking sludge from the pots and pans, cookers and wall tiles, and then scraping it into the big metal skips outside the back doors for the men who spoke no English to take away to some unknown destination.

But tonight she was going to be allowed to work with the cleaners, the ones who worked upstairs in the main hotel, and who wore smart overalls and rubber gloves, and who used vacuum cleaners and dusters. Good work, not filthy and rank like in the kitchens.

She had slipped out into the street earlier because she had to pretend that she was coming in from outside – acting out a lie, as she was scared that someone would find out that she was living in the hotel and tell the supervisor and get her sacked.

Well, she wasn't in the hotel exactly, not in one of the fine rooms or one of the suites upstairs, she was living in a damp, musty smelling storeroom-cum-changing room known by everyone as the Cleaners' Depot.

She and Bisa, a skinny African law student, who had become her special, dear friend when she had shown her the depot – unbelievably in London, a free place to sleep! – would wait every night until the others had gone home, rushing off to catch their night buses, and then they would slip inside the storeroom, quiet as ghosts. There they would settle down among the bottles of bleach, the rags, mops and buckets, ignoring the scratching of mice and the scuttling dart of fat cockroaches, and thank their gods for their good fortune.

Because this was their home.

Bisa would study, sometimes reading out loud to her in a quiet whisper from her books, telling her about what people did to each other in the name of the law, the amazing amounts of money that people would just throw away over matters of pride and anger, while she fell asleep listening to the stories of the madness, and Bisa's beautiful African voice.

There was no way she would let anyone take all that from her. And that was why she didn't feel guilty about her lie.

At the end of her shift, the tall, stooping black man – Bisa had told her he wasn't African – came by to check her work.

She stood there, her heart ready to burst from her chest, pleading with the spirit of her grandfather to watch over her and make everything all right.

The man spoke.

'You have worked well tonight. Very well. Clean, fast, and no complaints. Good. The others could learn from you. Who knows, maybe, one day, I will speak to the people at the agency and ask them if you can have a trial period working in the bedrooms. You'll like that. People leave things behind – drinks, food, magazines. All kinds of things, and when you bring them to me, I will let you share them. And you will get tips. Yes, sometimes you will even get tips from the rich people. And I will let you keep some of those tips for yourself.'

Nahida nodded respectfully – 'Thank you, sir' – and collected up her cleaning things, stowing them safely in the deep pockets of her overall – knowing that lost materials had to be paid for.

As she walked back out into the night air, arm in arm with Bisa as they enacted their nightly charade of leaving the building, Nahida couldn't wipe the smile off her face. She was earning money, and she was doing so honestly. No man touched her, and no one owned her.

She had a new life and it was all hers.